The night air was cool, much pleasanter than the stuffiness inside. The moon hung just above the rooftops.

'It seems almost near enough to touch and make a wish,' Kate said, gazing up at it.

Simon put his free hand over hers as it lay on his sleeve. 'What would you wish for if you could wish for anything in the world?'

'The same as you, I expect. A world where children can grow up strong and healthy. A world without cruelty.'

'A tall order, but you are right. I wish it too.'

They strolled on in companionable silence until the strains of another waltz drifted out to them from the ballroom. He turned and held his arms out to her, and without speaking she stepped into them. He guided her unerringly into the dance. It was cool and dark and they were alone, with the canopy of a star-filled sky above them and the muted strains of the music guiding their steps. It was magical.

When the music faded they stood still, looking at each other in the semi-darkness, silent, a little breathless, unwilling to break apart. He still had hold of her hands, which he raised one by one to his lips. She felt the warm pressure on her skin and a little shiver passed through her. Was this a man who could break hearts?

AUTHOR NOTE

Although the Hartingdon Home and The Society for the Welfare of Destitute Children are figments of my imagination, they were inspired by the work of Thomas Coram who, appalled by the sight of destitute children living and dying in the slums of London, founded the Hospital for the Maintenance and Education of Exposed and Deserted Young Children, which became known as the Foundling Hospital.

His particular interest was in illegitimate children who had been abandoned, or could not be looked after by their unmarried mothers. He was a persuasive man and appealed to the aristocracy for support. Notable fundraisers were the composer Handel, who gave concerts to raise money, and the painter Hogarth, who displayed his pictures on the walls of the hospital. Other artists followed his example, and the pictures were on show for the public to view, when they were encouraged to donate to the charity.

The charter founding the hospital was signed by George II on 14th August 1739, and the first children were admitted in 1741, seventy-six years before the time of my story, but it was still going strong and was so popular that mothers queued up to leave their children there. A selection procedure became necessary, and it was limited mainly to children of mothers who it was judged could be redeemed from their 'wickedness' to lead useful lives. The children's names were changed and they rarely had contact with their mothers again. At a time when a quarter of children did not live beyond the age of five, when health care and education were almost non-existent and the only help was through the Poor Law, these children were given a home, good food and an elementary education to fit them for work.

The charity later became known as the Thomas Coram Foundation for Children, and is now known as the Coram Family. It still exists, 270 years after its inception, though in a much changed form. Its history, some of its records and the tiny artifacts that arrived with the children are on display, together with priceless pictures, at The Foundling Museum in Russell Square. Well worth a visit.

HONOURABLE DOCTOR, IMPROPER ARRANGEMENT

Mary Nichols

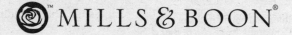

All the characters in this book have no existence outside the imagination of the author, and have no relation whatsoever to anyone bearing the same name or names. They are not even distantly inspired by any individual known or unknown to the author, and all the incidents are pure invention.

First published in Great Britain 2009
Harlequin Mills & Boon Limited,
Eton House, 18-24 Paradise Road, Richmond, Surrey TW9 1SR

© Mary Nichols 2009

ISBN: 978 0 263 86803 6

Set in Times Roman 10½ on 12½ pt
04-1009-77949

Harlequin Mills & Boon policy is to use papers that are natural, renewable and recyclable products and made from wood grown in sustainable forests. The logging and manufacturing process conform to the legal environmental regulations of the country of origin.

Printed and bound in Spain
by Litografia Rosés, S.A., Barcelona

Born in Singapore, **Mary Nichols** came to England when she was three, and has spent most of her life in different parts of East Anglia. She has been a radiographer, school secretary, information officer and industrial editor, as well as a writer. She has three grown-up children, and four grandchildren. Mary loves to hear from her readers, and you can contact her via her website www.marynichols.co.uk

Recent novels by the same author:

TALK OF THE TON
WORKING MAN, SOCIETY BRIDE
A DESIRABLE HUSBAND
RUNAWAY MISS
RAGS-TO-RICHES BRIDE
THE EARL AND THE HOYDEN

Chapter One

1817

Dr Simon Redfern, strolling in Hyde Park, stopped to watch the young lady with the children. They looked healthy and well dressed, and were playing a complicated game of tag, running round and round, shrieking with laughter in which the young lady played a full part. She seemed too young to be the children's mother and he concluded she was perhaps a nursemaid or a governess, but if she was, she was unlike any nursemaid he had ever met, because she was completely uninhibited, holding her pretty muslin skirt up with one hand and displaying a neat turn of ankle. In his experience, nursemaids and governesses were sticklers for correct behaviour.

As he watched, an open carriage drew up and the four children abandoned their game and ran to it, scrambling in beside an elegant lady who was evidently their mother. She had a few words with the young lady and then drove off. The governess, if that was what she was, picked up a parcel from the ground where she had evidently left it while she played, and walked on alone.

Kate had declined Elizabeth's offer to be taken up because she was on her way to Hookham's library and could easily reach it on foot. She was out of breath from running with the children and her cheeks had a rosy glow that her grandmother would deprecate but which made her look very attractive. She tucked strands of her nut-brown hair into the coil on the back of her head from which they had escaped and replaced her bonnet, which had slipped down on its ribbons. She had no idea what she looked like and walked down to the Serpentine to use the water as a mirror.

'Oh, my goodness.' The reflection that looked back at her was unladylike in the extreme. She was flushed, her hair was untidy and the ribbon securing her bonnet was crushed into a sad pretence at a bow. She tried to straighten it and it was then, out of the corner of her eye, she saw the child, sitting on the edge of the lake, with his little legs dangling over the water. He could not have been more than three or four years old and was dressed in filthy rags and had nothing on his feet at all. She looked about for his parents or someone looking after him, but there was no one that she could see. It was up to her to rescue him before he fell in. Not wanting to startle him, she moved slowly and then grabbed him from behind.

He started to squirm and yell and it was all she could

do to hold him. 'Hush,' she said. 'I won't hurt you.' But he screamed the more and pulled the brim of her half-tied bonnet down over her eyes.

'Allow me.' Her burden was taken from her and she swung round to face the gentleman who had spoken, pushing her bonnet back as she did so. He tucked the child under his arm. 'If you do not leave off that noise, you will feel my hand on your rump,' he told him, with a pretence at severity. The child looked up at the man and, deciding he probably meant it, subsided into silence.

The man was, Kate judged, about twenty-seven or -eight, a little above average height, dressed in a plain brown frockcoat and leather breeches tucked into brown boots. His starched muslin cravat was tied in a simple knot. Not one of the *haut monde,* she decided, but definitely not the child's papa. He was holding the lad firmly as if he were used to dealing with recalcitrant children, so perhaps he was a schoolmaster. He was a very handsome schoolmaster, if he was.

'I thought he might fall in,' she said, looking about her, as much to avoid the amused gaze of his grey eyes as to ascertain that no one was claiming the child. 'He seems to be all alone.'

'Do you know who he is?'

'No, do you?'

'No. We had better try to find out.' He fetched the child out from under his arm and stood him on the ground and, without letting go of him, squatted down beside him, so that he was able to talk to him on his own level. 'Now, you imp, can you tell us your name?'

The boy knuckled his eyes, depositing more dirt on an already filthy face. 'Joe.'

'Well, Joe, we should like to know where you live.'

Without speaking, the boy pointed in the general direction of the park gate.

'That is not much help. Can you take me to your home?'

This was answered with a silent look of incomprehension.

'Judging by his clothes, he must come from a very poor area,' Kate said. 'How did he get here?'

'I imagine he walked.' He looked up at Kate, standing hesitantly beside him. The expression of concern on her lovely face did her credit, he decided; not many young ladies would bother about a little urchin and would certainly never think of touching one. 'Do not look so worried, miss, I will take charge of him, if you have other things to do.'

Kate hesitated. How did she know this man was trustworthy? And supposing he could not find the child's parents, what would he do? London was a huge place and the boy's little legs must have carried him quite a long way if he lived in the rookeries of the city, which his ragged clothes indicated he almost certainly did. 'What are you going to do with him?'

'Try to find his parents.'

'How?'

'That is a good question,' he said, noting her wariness. 'I shall take him to the areas where I think he may be known and ask if anyone recognises him.'

'It will be like looking for a needle in a haystack.'

'Probably. Have you a better idea?'

'No. But will you be safe?'

'Oh, I think so,' he said. 'I am a doctor, you see, and sometimes I have to venture into places that respectable young ladies can know nothing of.'

'Of course I know of them,' she said sharply. 'I do not go about with my head in the sand.'

He looked down at the boy, now contentedly sucking his thumb, the only bit of him that was clean, and looking from one to the other, as if wondering which one to cling to. 'You want to go home to your ma and pa, don't you, my lad?'

Joe nodded.

'Are you sure you wish to take responsibility for him?' Kate asked. 'After all, it was I who picked him up.'

The child had tugged at her heartstrings and his welfare was important to her, as was the welfare of all children, whoever they were, rich or poor. She couldn't help it; if she saw a child needing help, she must do what she could. It had got her into trouble with her grandmother on more than one occasion. 'Giving to the poor is one thing,' she had said. 'I applaud that in you, but to touch them is entirely another. You never know what you might pick up. And you will get yourself talked about.' None of which discouraged her.

'What would you do if I left him with you?' he asked.

'The same as you, I expect, try to find his parents.'

'How?'

His question gave her a moment's pause, but she was

not going to admit she was floored. 'Talk to the boy,' she said. 'Gain his trust, ask him to take me to his home, as you have done.'

'You think you can go into the slums knocking on doors?'

'I would if I had to.'

'I do not doubt it, but you would soon be in trouble. No, I think you should leave it to me.'

'Very well, but if you do not mind, I will come with you.'

'I do not think that is a good idea, Miss...' He paused, waiting for her to supply a name.

'I am not a miss. I am Mrs Meredith and I am not a delicate flower, nurtured in a hot house, so you may take that condescending smile from your face.'

'I beg your pardon, ma'am. Doctor Simon Redfern, at your service.' He doffed his hat and swept her an exaggerated bow, which made her laugh. It was a pleasant sound and, in spite of himself, had him smiling in response.

'So, Dr Redfern, let us see where this young man leads us, shall we?'

'I think you will regret it.'

'I will regret it if I leave him.'

'Why? Do I look like an abuser of infants?'

She looked up into his face and felt herself colouring to think that he had so quickly taken her up on what she said. She hadn't meant that, had she? On the other hand, just because a man dressed like a gentleman and had a smile that would melt ice, did not mean he was not capable of wickedness. But she did not want to believe that of him. 'I am sorry,' she said. 'It is only that I feel responsible and I cannot rest until I know he is safely back home.' She looked down at Joe, who was looking bemused rather than afraid. He was thinner than he ought to be, but he was not cowed. Life had already taught him some harsh lessons. Taking his hand, she asked gently, 'Will you show us where you live?'

Simon gave a grunt of a laugh. 'On your head be it.' He could no more abandon her than she could the child.

He fell into step beside her. She was talking cheerfully to the boy, though she received no reply except a pointed finger, which might or might not have been meant to indicate a direction. When she asked him if they were going the right way, he nodded.

'I do not think he knows where he is,' Simon said, as the boy led them from the park and down to the river where the mudlarks paddled, picking up flotsam and jetsam to sell. He called out to the scavengers, asking them if they recognised the child, but they shook their heads. 'It is a long shot, but we could try Covent Garden,' he said. 'Unless you would rather I took him on alone?'

'No. I have come this far, I am not leaving now. His mama must be frantic with worry.'

'If she has even missed him.'

'How cynical you are!'

'With good cause. You cannot know the half of it.'

She wondered what he meant, but decided not to comment. By this time the child's little legs were too tired to carry on, so Simon hoisted him on to his shoulders, apparently unconcerned about the dirt being transferred to his good clothes. Kate walked purposefully beside him, determined to stay with him.

'Supposing we cannot find his parents, what shall we do?' she asked.

'I shall have to take him to a home which looks after destitute children.'

'Do you mean the Foundling Hospital?'

'No, that only takes the children of unmarried mothers and only then if the mother can be enabled to find work and redeem herself. I am thinking of the Hartingdon Home.'

'Hartingdon?' she queried in surprise.

'Yes. Do you know of it?'

'No, but can it have anything to do with Earl Hartingdon?'

'Not the Earl, but his daughter. Lady Eleanor is its main benefactor, through a charitable trust. Why, do you know her?'

'We are distantly related,' she said with a wry smile. She did not know Eleanor well and, on the few family occasions when they met, she had found the lady aloof and distant. She could not imagine her stooping to handle an urchin such as she had just rescued and spoiling her fashionable clothes. 'I did not know she had given her name to an orphanage.'

'It is more than an orphanage. It is the headquarters of The Society for the Welfare of Destitute Children. We also find foster homes for some of the children.'

'We?' she queried.

'I am one of its trustees and, though we take children into the Hartingdon when there is no help for it, I firmly believe that a loving home is far more beneficial to a child's well-being than an institution.'

'A loving home, yes, but how many foster homes are? You hear such dreadful tales about foster mothers beating and starving the children in their care and not only in London. The countryside is as bad, if not worse. I cannot understand why the women do the job if they have no feeling for children.'

'It is a way of earning a few pence,' he said. 'And it can be done in conjunction with looking after their own.'

'But that is half the trouble. If it comes to a choice between feeding their own or feeding the foster child, there is no question who will come first, is there?' She spoke with such feeling, he looked sharply at her and wondered what had brought it about. 'Did you know that less than half the children sent out like that survive?'

'Yes, I did,' he said quietly. 'I deplore the practice of sending little children away from home to be fostered, just as much as you do, Mrs Meredith. The gentry do it in order not to have a troublesome baby on their hands, but they are usually careful to choose a woman who is known to them and whom they can trust. At the other end of the scale there are poverty-stricken mothers, with no husbands, or husbands that cannot be brought to book, who cannot cope with unwanted children and farm them out for a few pence a week. That is where the trouble lies.'

It was coming upon one such foster mother quite by accident that had set Simon on the course he had taken.

The war against Napoleon had ended and he had been making his way to Grove Hall, his uncle's estate, simply because it was the only home he had known; until he set up an establishment of his own, there was nowhere else to go.

He had stopped for refreshment at a wayside inn and was sitting outside in the evening sunshine enjoying a quart of ale while his horse was fed, watered and rested, when he saw three small children being driven along the road by what he could only describe as a hag. The children were in rags and the woman was filthy. She had them tied to each other by a rope, and was hauling them along like cattle. She stopped in the inn yard, tied the children to a rail normally used for tethering horses and went inside.

She was there a long time, while the children, unable to move about, sank to the ground and waited. They were so thin as to be skeletal, eyes sunk deep in their sockets and their arms bruised by fingermarks. They were so listless they did not even try to fight against their bonds. He walked over to them, squatted down and tried to talk to them, but they looked blankly at him. It was more than he could stomach. He went into the parlour where the woman was sitting with a pot of ale and a meat pie in front of her. 'Madam, are you not going to share your pie with your children?' he had asked mildly.

He was answered with invective and a desire that he should mind his own business. 'If you thinks I'm paid well eno' to indulge them with meat pie, you thinks wrong,' she told him. 'They'll get their gruel when I get 'em 'ome.'

He had begun arguing with her, telling her she was a disgrace to womanhood and more besides. He had been so angry he did not notice the rest of the inn's clientele had turned on him until one of them spoke. 'You leave us alone, mister. If it weren't for coves like you, taking your pleasures wherever you fancy, there'd be no need for parish nurses. The brats have been abandoned by their mothers and, if Mother Cody ha'n't taken 'em in, they'd be dead in a ditch long afore now.'

'That is no reason to treat them like animals.' He had refused to be intimidated, although the dreadful woman was threatening him with the knife she had been using to cut up her pie. Had she been a man, he would have had no compunction about disarming her and knocking her to the ground, but he could not do that, repulsive as she was, and he could not beat a room full of men, especially as no law had been broken. Instead he had given her half a guinea, told her to spend it on food for the children, and left, musing about those poor mites. How many more were there like those three? And should women like that not be regulated and their homes inspected periodically?

If he had not been so disappointed by his reception when he arrived at Grove Hall, he might have put the matter from his mind. His aunt, who was never as hard and unbending as his uncle, was pleased to see him, but the presence of Isobel, at one time betrothed to him, but since married to his cousin, stirred up all his old anger and he knew, much as he loved the place, he could not stay there. He needed an outlet for his restless energy, something to make him feel he was doing some good and it was then he remembered those children. It was not enough to say something should be done, he must do it himself, and thus was born The Society for the Welfare of Destitute Children, intended, in some small way, to address the problem, not only of the children, but also his own restless spirit. The first children he had rescued were the three he had seen at the inn, though Mrs Cody demanded an exorbitant sum by way of compensation for the loss of her livelihood.

'Then I am surprised you condone it.' Kate's voice brought him out of his reverie.

'We are very careful where we send the children in our care,' he said stiffly. 'The women are questioned closely and their homes inspected.'

'So they may be,' she said. 'And no doubt the women put on a good show when they are being interviewed. What happens when you turn your back on them?'

'You are very scathing,' he said. 'You ought not to brand them all with the same iron. Some do their best.'

'I am sorry. I am a little too outspoken sometimes.'

'Do not be sorry. It is good to speak one's mind occasionally.'

She laughed. 'I do it a little too often, I think. But the question does not arise here because you cannot take this child anywhere if his parents are looking for him.'

'I shall do my best to reunite them. The Home is full to overflowing as it is; finding more room will be difficult.'

The area around Covent Garden was extremely busy, with stall holders, costermongers, porters and farmers with loaded carts all rushing about as if they did not have a minute to lose, and he wondered why he was persevering. He could just as easily have taken the boy straight to the Hartingdon Home and squeezed him in somewhere, but, like Mrs Meredith, he imagined the boy's mother frantically searching for him. On the other hand, she might not be searching; she might have abandoned him as many another mother had done who could not cope. In which case, the Home it would have to be.

They went from stall to stall, spoke to several of the little urchins who congregated there because there was a chance that they might either be given or filch some food from the stall holders, but no one recognised Joe. 'Now what?' Kate asked. She had been right about the needle in a haystack. London was a very big haystack and perhaps they were looking in the wrong area after all.

'Let us try over there.' He pointed to the steps of a church, surprised that she was still with him. He had expected her to have given up and gone home long before now. He wondered what she would have done about the little urchin if he had not been there. She was evidently very fond of children and not afraid of a little dirt.

Young Joe gave a sudden cry of recognition and wriggled to be put down. Simon set him down and he ran to a woman sitting on the tail of a cart, nursing a mewling infant, surrounded by squashed fruit, cabbage leaves and horse droppings. She looked up from contemplating the baby's head to address the boy. 'Where 'ave yer bin, you little devil?' she said, clipping him round the ear with the flat of her hand. 'I'll tan your hide, that I will. I told you not to run off, didn't I?'

Kate was surprised how young she was. Her hard life made her look older than she was, but she could not have been more than twenty. She must have conceived Joe when she was about sixteen and was probably at that time a pretty little thing, probably could be again if her circumstances were different.

The woman stopped berating the boy to look up at Simon and Kate, her eyes widening at what appeared to be a couple of gentry. 'Did you fetch him back?'

'Yes, he had wandered quite a long way from here,' Simon said.

'Then I am beholden to you.' She paused. 'I reckon I've seen you around 'ere afore.'

'You may have,' he said. 'I am Dr Redfern.'

'I've 'eard of you. I 'eard tell you take children and give them a good 'ome, clothes and food and learnin'.'

'Yes, but only under certain circumstances and if their parents agree.'

'Oh, is that why you brought 'im back, so's you could take him?'

'No, I thought you might be worried about him.'

'So I was, but I can't keep an eye on 'im and do me work at the same time. I have to mind the stall. And there's the babby to look after too.'

'Do you want me to take him?'

'Be better than runnin' wild about 'ere.'

'Will your husband agree to that?' Kate asked, horrified that she could even think of parting with her child.

'You c'n ask 'im if you can find 'im,' she said flatly. 'I ain't seen 'ide nor 'air of 'im these last six months. I'm at my wits' end.'

It was just the sort of family the Society had been set up to help and Simon, having discovered her name was Janet Barber, asked to be shown where they lived.

Mrs Barber led them from the market into the area known as Seven Dials, a notorious slum where seven of the meanest roads in the city converged. Here she took them down Monmouth Street, lined with second-hand clothing shops, pawnbrokers and cheap food shops, and into an alley, where she stopped outside a tenement whose front steps were black with grime and whose door hung drunkenly on one hinge. 'There,' she said, pointing.

Kate, who fully expected the doctor to turn away in disgust, was surprised when he indicated the woman should lead on. They had attracted quite a gathering, but none seemed hostile and she supposed it was because the doctor was well known and respected. They simply stood and stared.

Kate, worrying about the little boy, was even more concerned when she saw the filthy room, which was hardly fit for animals, let alone human beings. There was a bed of sorts, heaped with rags, a table and a couple of chairs, a few pots and pans on a shelf and that was all. Everywhere was covered in a thick layer of grime and the smell was nauseating.

'You goin' to take 'im, then?' Mrs Barber asked, as Kate stood on the threshold, reluctant to venture inside.

'If you are sure, I will take him until you can get on

your feet again. If your circumstances improve, then Joe can come home again.'

She laughed. 'Pigs might fly.'

He gave her half a crown, which she gleefully accepted, then told the boy to say goodbye to his mother and hoisted him once more on his shoulders. It was not a satisfactory state of affairs and he wished he could do more. He wished with all his heart that such poverty did not exist and that all children were as plump and happy as those Mrs Meredith had been playing with earlier in the day.

'I hate separating families,' he told her as they set off for the Hartingdon Home. 'And would not do so, if any other way could be found.'

'Could they not be helped with a little money, so they could stay together?'

'That might be possible, but a decision like that is not mine alone. The Committee have to consider all aspects. If the father is a wastrel or a drunkard, then it would be throwing good money after bad. If there is some hope, then we will do what we can and the boy can return to his parents. That is where we differ from the Foundling Hospital. Once children are taken in there, their names are changed and they rarely see their mothers again. We do our best to restore them to their families.'

The Hartingdon Home was situated in a converted building in Maiden Lane. It was a busy area, being so close to Covent Garden market, but it was certainly a step above Seven Dials. Joe was handed over to the housekeeper who gave him a slice of bread and jam and a glass of milk, which he downed with relish.

Simon waited until he was settled, then took Kate to

the office where he invited her to be seated while he completed the necessary paperwork for Joe's admission. 'Keeping accurate records is an important part of the work,' he explained. 'If it is not done immediately, it might be forgotten. Do you mind?'

'Not at all.' She took a chair on the opposite side of the desk. 'I am very interested in your work.'

'We have to record their names and addresses, the names of their parents and occupations and exactly what action we took and why,' he said, wondering how genuine her interest was. She did not look like the usual wealthy matron who visited and inspected everything before donating. She was young for a start, and though she looked delightful in her simple gown, she was not dressed to impress. 'And when they leave, we write down the circumstances and where we have sent them. In another book we have the details of all the foster mothers we use and how much they are paid. And, of course, there are accounts to be kept up to date.'

'Are you here every day?' she asked him.

'I come most days, but I also visit the foster homes and report on those.'

Kate had lost most of her nervousness and all of her distrust and sat down to watch him at work. His hair, as he bent over the desk, was fair and very thick. One strand fell over his face as he wrote. He had a straight nose and a firm mouth. She noticed his hands, one spread across the ledger, the other holding a pen, strong, capable hands with long fingers and nails neatly manicured. She could easily imagine him comforting the sick and all his female patients falling head over heels in love with him.

He put down his pen and carefully dusted the wet ink before looking up at her and catching her watching him with a slight tilt to the corners of her mouth as if she had found something amusing in what he was doing. He wanted to ask what it was, but decided he did not know her well enough. 'Now that is done, would you like me to show you round?'

'Oh, yes, please, and then I must go home. Everyone will be wondering what has become of me.'

He took her all over the house, showing her the dining room, the dormitories, the schoolroom, the infirmary where he treated the sick and the nursery where the tiny infants were looked after by nursemaids. Some were sleeping, some bawling lustily, others, almost too weak to cry, were whimpering. It touched Kate's soft heart to see them. 'Are they all abandoned?' she asked.

'Most of them. Some are brought in anonymously, others are simply left on the doorstep. Sometimes there is a note attached, telling us the child's name and why they have been left, sometimes a small memento that has some meaning for the parent. Those little items, most often quite valueless, are often the only means we have of identifying the child and they are carefully preserved in case the mother wants to reclaim her offspring. It is the most heartbreaking side to our work.'

'How sad.' She felt the tears pricking her eyes. 'It must be a terrible decision for any mother to be forced to make.'

'Yes.' He led the way back down the stairs to the kitchen and introduced her to some of the other helpers, and even showed her the patch of grass they called a garden and where the smaller children played. 'The older children are all given their allotted tasks about the place,' he told her. 'So we do not have a large staff.'

The children themselves were a mixed bunch. Some were noisy and laughing, others subdued and withdrawn, but all were neatly dressed and well fed. 'It is the quiet ones I worry about,' he said. 'They are the ones who will benefit most from going into a foster home and having a little extra attention.' He indicated a little girl sitting on the floor in the corner of the classroom intent on playing with a rag doll. 'This is Annie Smith,' he said. 'She is nine years old. I was called to her mother when she fell ill. She could not be nursed at home, so I recommended hospital. Annie's father cannot look after her because he has to go to work as a docker and there are no other relatives, so she has come here, but as soon as her mother is well again, she will go home. The family is poor, but she was never neglected. She is bewildered by the other children and has found it difficult to settle.'

Kate went over to the child and squatted beside her. 'Hallo, Annie,' she said. 'I am Kate. What do you call your doll?'

'Dolly.'

'Of course, how silly of me not to know that.'

The child smiled at that, a wan little smile that told Kate she was missing her parents. She talked to her for several minutes, while Simon looked on. So her name was Kate. She was special, was Mrs Kate Meredith, a born mother, able to relate to children in a way that made them feel comfortable. She made him feel comfortable too. He wondered at that; it was a long time since he had felt at ease in the presence of a woman. He did not know a thing about her, except that she was married and had a taste for novels, judging by the books she carried looped to her wrist by the string.

'Poor little things,' she said, as they returned to the front hall. 'I wish I could do something to help.'

'We are always short of money…'

'Oh, I did not mean money, I am afraid I cannot manage more than a small donation. I meant help on a practical level.'

He looked sideways at her. Was that what he had been hoping she would say? She had such a sunny, compassionate nature, she would be an asset to the Society if she became involved. 'We are always glad of help in whatever form: a few hours at the Home, help with the paperwork, raising funds, fostering. But none of it is easy and it takes up time, so you need to think carefully before committing yourself.'

'I understand that, and I will think carefully, I promise.'

'Good. Now, if you have seen all you wish to see, I will escort you home.'

'Oh, do not trouble yourself,' she said. 'I can walk.'

'Not to be thought of,' he said. He had no idea what sort of home she came from, but she was well dressed and well spoken and should not be left to find her own way through the poorer streets of the city, not after sticking to him like a leech all afternoon. He realised, with a jolt, that he had enjoyed every minute of it. 'I have my gig nearby. It is no trouble at all.' He picked up a bell from the table and gave it a sharp shake. It was answered by an urchin of perhaps twelve years old, whom he sent to the stables to have the vehicle brought to the door.

'But you have no idea where I live, have you?' she said with a smile. 'It might be miles away.'

'All the more reason to see you safely home.' He paused. 'Is it miles away?'

She laughed. 'No. Holles Street.'

He was surprised. Holles Street, though not the most affluent address in the capital, was not far below it, and if he had known that was where she came from, he would never have allowed her to accompany him into the slums, nor taken her to the Home. How shocked she must have been! But she had shown no sign of shock. She had held Joe in her arms for all his filth and had squatted down beside Annie and talked to her without a hint of distaste. Perhaps he had been right in his first assessment of her and she was a nursemaid or governess to a wealthy family. It would account for the address. But if that was so, what had happened to her husband? 'Not so far, then,' he said. 'But it makes no difference, I would be less than a gentleman if I allowed you to walk.'

The boy came back to say the gig was outside the door and Simon conducted her out to it and settled her in her seat before jumping up and taking the reins from the ostler who had brought it round for him.

'Now,' he said, 'shall we go to the library first?'

'Library?'

'Was that not where you were going when we met?'

She laughed, holding up her hand with the books dangling from her wrist. 'I had quite forgotten these. It seems an age ago. No, I think it is a little late and I had better go straight home. My father and grandmother will be wondering where I have got to.'

'You live with them?'

'Yes. My father is the Reverend Thomas Morland. I have been living with him since I was widowed four years ago.'

Once again she had surprised him. Not only that she was not a servant, but she did not look old enough to have been married that long ago. She was beginning to confuse him. 'My condolences, ma'am.'

'Thank you. We had only been married six months when my husband went away to war and I never saw him again.' She did not know why she was explaining that to him. It was really nothing to do with him, though he would have to know all about her if she was going to help at the Home, which was an idea that had been growing in her head ever since he had shown her round the place.

'I am sorry,' he said. 'That must have been hard for you.'

'Yes, it was.'

'I assumed you were the children's governess.'

'Children?'

'Those you were playing with in the park. Very happy you all looked too.'

'They are my cousin's children. Jamie is ten, Charlotte, eight, Henry, six, and little Rosemary is four. I love to take them out when their governess has a day off. They are such a delight to be with.'

'You have no children of your own?'

'Sadly, no.'

'One day, perhaps.'

'Perhaps.' She did not want to go into that on so slight an acquaintance. 'I thought at first that you were a schoolmaster.'

'Did you? Why?'

'Because of the competent way you handled little Joe and the strict tone of your voice when you spoke to him.'

'One has to be firm with children.'

'Naturally, but not hard or cruel. Their young minds can be so easily bruised.'

'Oh, indeed. We are at one on that.'

He had first hand experience of bruises, both physical and mental—they had stayed with him all his life. His own governess, Miss Nokes, had been a tyrant who had tried beating his lessons into him. He had soon learned not to complain because his uncle would not believe him and told him, 'Miss Nokes knows what she is doing. If you misbehave, you must be punished.' The fact that his back was lacerated and purple with bruising carried no weight at all. 'It is time you learned to take your punishment like a man. You should be more like Charles. He never complains.' Simon supposed it was only natural that his uncle should favour his own son over his nephew, but he made no effort to hide it and Simon was left feeling like a cuckoo in the nest.

What the beatings had done for Charles, who was three years older, was to make him as cruel as the governess. He could not take his anger out on the real perpetrator and so he vented it on animals, his horse and dogs, and any wild animals he found. Simon had often nursed an injured animal, binding up its wounds and hiding it until it was well again. He had been glad when he was sent away to school, only to find that was even worse for thrashings, which he endured stoically, while vowing that if and when he had children they would never be beaten.

Strangely enough, it was the army that allowed him to be himself, to find an occupation that gave him fulfilment. The army existed to kill, but on the other hand it offered him comradeship and a purpose to his life, especially when he found his doctoring skills could often make the difference between life and death, between a man being crippled and having a whole body. There had been times when he had not succeeded, but no one blamed him—they knew he was doing all he could.

He had been silent so long that Kate wondered what he was thinking. His expression, so easy and relaxed a few moments before, was severe and uncompromising, his jaw set. Had she said something to upset him? 'I suppose being a schoolmaster and being a doctor are not so very different when it comes to children,' she said for want of something to say.

His face relaxed and he smiled, his innate good manners taking over from his grim memories. 'One looks after the body and the other the mind.'

'But mind and body are one when it comes to the whole person.'

He laughed suddenly. 'That is a very profound statement for a summer afternoon, but I suppose having a father who is a Reverend makes you more thoughtful than most.'

'Perhaps. But he has no parish. He gave it up when—' She stopped suddenly as if about to utter an indiscretion. 'When he decided to write a book about comparative religions and needed to be in London close to sources of research and bought the house in Holles Street. My grandmother lives with us. I will introduce you to them....'

'I am hardly fit to go calling,' he said, looking down at his clothes, sadly crumpled after dealing with Joe. 'Perhaps you will allow me to call on you tomorrow afternoon, when I am fit to be presented. And then I can let you know how Joe is settling down,' he added. Why, when he had decided that women were best kept at a distance, did he suddenly want to learn more about her? She was unsettling him.

'Yes, I shall look forward to that.' They were turning into Holles Street. She pointed to one of the houses. 'That one.'

He pulled up, jumped out to hand her down, doffed his hat and watched as she let herself in the door, then climbed back to go to his lodgings in Piccadilly, musing on the events of the day. Was it fate that brought him to that spot in Hyde Park just in time to help rescue the little urchin? Fate or not, he wanted to see Mrs Meredith again, though he told himself it was only because he wanted to enrol her help for the Society.

Chapter Two

Lady Morland was sitting in the drawing room, a cup of tea in her hand and a plate of sugar plums at her elbow when Kate entered the room. 'Good heavens, Kate, whatever has happened to you?' she queried. She was a little plump, due to her partiality for sweetmeats, but was still, at seventy, very active both in mind and body. 'Have you had an accident? Have you been set upon and robbed?'

'No, nothing like that. I am sorry I am late, Grandmama, but I have had such an adventure.'

'You had better tell me at once, for a more bedraggled sight I never did see. It is to be hoped no one of any note saw you or it will be all round town.'

'Oh, Grandmama, of course it will not. I am not one of the *ton*, I do not move in such exalted circles, you know that very well.'

'But you will when the Viscount comes back. He will take you out and about and there must be no hint of gossip. You know how particular he is.'

She did. Viscount Robert Cranford, one-time Colonel of a line regiment and now a diplomat, was very particular indeed, which was why Kate sometimes wondered why he had picked her out for his attention. She had first met him when he called to commiserate with her on Edward's death. He had known and admired her late husband as a valiant fellow officer and felt he owed it to him to visit his widow. He knew and understood the grief felt on losing a loved one, he had told her; his wife had died, leaving him with two daughters to bring up. They were being cared for by his sister, Mrs Withersfield, on his estate near Cookham. 'When Harriet's husband died and left her in rather straitened circumstances,' he had explained, 'I offered her a home. It has worked very well because, being so often away from home myself, I needed someone to run the house and look after the girls.'

Her grandmother had plied him with refreshments and invited him to call again. He had done so several times while he was in England; when he went back to Spain, he and Kate had kept up a regular correspondence. After the war ended, he had left the army to pursue a career in the diplomatic corps and was working at the British Embassy in Paris. He had proposed by letter three months before.

She had adored Edward and there had never been a moment's doubt about her answer when he asked her to marry him, coupling it with a declaration of undying love that had delighted her. Six months after the wedding, he was dead. Did the love die with him? She did not think so, but it changed, became a lovely memory, not something of the present, and should she not grasp a second chance at happiness? She would have a kind husband, two homes, two stepdaughters and, most important of all, the chance to have children of her own.

But she had wondered why the Viscount, who had a tendency to stand on his dignity, should choose her for a wife over others more worthy. She was an easy-going sort of person, not particularly tidy, nor one to make a fuss if something was not exactly where it should be. Nor did she complain if the servants left a speck of dust in a dark corner. She dressed neatly and cleanly without the help of a maid, did not care too much about fashion and the latest fads and, having no children of her own, it was her joy to play with her cousin's children, the more boisterous the better.

Grandmother said she undervalued herself, that she was beautiful, knew how to behave in elite company when she wasn't rushing about after the objects of her charity. She would make a splendid stepmama for his lordship's motherless girls, which was more than could be said for most of the empty-headed débutantes being turned out nowadays. It was four years since Edward had died and it was time she considered marrying again. 'You want to have children of your own, do you not?'

'Of course, it is my dearest wish.' It was more than a wish, it was becoming an obsession. She longed to hold her own baby in her arms, to love it and care for it. She would never consider sending it to a wet nurse, or even having one live in. She distrusted them profoundly. She would look with envy at her friends and relations who had children and could not understand how they could bear to see so little of them. They would

visit them in the nursery, stay a few minutes and then
hand them back to the nursery maid, as if they were
bored by them. Did they never cuddle them, have meals
with them, play with them, listen to their childish problems? If she had children, they would be loved and
considered, but not spoiled. She would instruct them
herself and take them out, show them the countryside,
teach them to appreciate all God's creatures and not be
snobbish. It was a dream she indulged in more often
than was healthy.

'Then you must marry again,' her grandmother had
said. 'Amusing yourself with Lizzie's children and
spending more than you can truthfully afford on the
poor and needy is not the answer.'

Kate loved her cousin's children dearly, but they did
not need her money and others did, so what better cause
could she choose? But she had to admit her grandmother
was right about marrying again. 'So you think I should
accept?'

'Kate, it is your decision, but you must be honest
with yourself. You are twenty-five years old, it is the
only suitable offer you are likely to have and his
lordship will make a splendid husband.'

'Yes, but what sort of wife will I make?' she had
asked. 'I have become so used to living here with you
and Papa, I do not know if I can manage a large country
house or stand at the Viscount's side at diplomatic func-
tions. I might not fit in.'

'Of course you will,' her grandmother had said
briskly. 'You have as much breeding as he has. The Har-
tingdons are a very old and respected family and so are

the Morlands. Viscount Cranford will certainly not be demeaning himself by marrying you.'

Her father was sincere in his Christian beliefs and did not behave like an aristocrat in spite of his connections with Earl Hartingdon and the fact that he was the second son of the late Lord Morland, her grandmother's husband. They were not wealthy, not in the way their illustrious relations were, but they were certainly not poor. After considering the proposal for over a week, she had written to accept, though the engagement had yet to be gazetted. Robert was waiting until he came back to England to do that. 'I want to tell my sister and daughters first,' he had written. Only last week he had said he had applied for leave and was hoping to return home shortly when they would celebrate their engagement and arrange a wedding.

Kate wondered why she was not as elated as she expected to be, but came to the conclusion that it was because it was a second marriage and nothing could recapture that first wonderful sensation of marrying the man you had fallen in love with, especially when both were young and looking forward to a long and blissful life together. She could not expect to feel the same as she did when she married Edward. That did not mean this marriage was not right or that she would not be happy. Her feelings for Robert were strong; he had been her rock and comforter when she was mourning Edward. It was simply that this time it was different, but no less valid.

'Grandmother,' she said now, 'what exactly is my relationship to Lady Eleanor Hartingdon?'

'Let me see,' her ladyship said. 'The third Earl was

my brother, so his son, the present Earl, is your father's cousin. That makes Eleanor his second cousin and your second cousin once removed. Something like that. Why do you ask?'

'Her name was mentioned to me today.'

'By whom and in what context?'

Kate took a deep breath and launched into an explanation of all that had happened in the park and afterwards. 'I never knew Lady Eleanor had a children's home named after her.'

'Neither did I. She never struck me as the maternal sort, but then you do not have to be motherly to have a conscience and support a charitable cause, do you?'

'I suppose not. I wonder how Dr Redfern is getting on with Joe. I can't stop thinking about him.'

'Dr Redfern?'

Kate laughed to cover her embarrassment. 'No, I meant the little boy. He was in the most pitiful rags and so filthy it was difficult to tell what colour his hair was.'

'And you picked him up!' Her ladyship was so shocked she almost recoiled. 'You must strip off those clothes this minute and have a hot bath. You can finish telling me after you have changed.'

Kate went to obey.

She was soon down again, dressed in a blue jaconet gown with little puffed sleeves and a boat-shaped neckline. Her hair was once again brushed and neatly coiled. By then her father had joined her grandmother, ready to go in to dinner, and she went over the afternoon's events again for his benefit.

'What do you know of this Dr Redfern?' her father asked.

'Nothing, Papa. He was simply there and helped me to restrain the child. He seemed a gentleman. He was certainly dressed like one. We took the child to the Hartingdon Home.' She decided to leave out the visit to the rookeries, which would have given her grandmother a fit. 'You will meet him tomorrow. I have said he may call.'

'Was that necessary, Kate?' her grandmother put in. 'A stranger you met in the park without the benefit of an introduction. He could be anybody, a rake, a scapegrace or worse.'

'I am sure he is not, and how else am I to find out how the little boy is faring?'

The old lady sighed. 'I shall be glad when you are safely married and have a family of your own, then perhaps you will not concern yourself with every little urchin you meet.'

'I shall always be concerned about the lives of poor children,' Kate said. 'Being married will not make any difference to that.'

'I think Lord Cranford might have something to say on the matter.'

'Why should he object? Anyone with an ounce of pity would feel the same as I do. He is not a hard man.'

'Hmph,' the old lady said and fell silent.

Kate could not stop thinking about the little boy and thoughts of him were all mixed up with thoughts of Dr Redfern. He did not look a bit like a doctor. Doctors usually dressed in sombre clothes and were often a little shabby, but Dr Redfern was elegantly, if simply, dressed. She had admired the way he dealt with the child, in firm but friendly fashion, and he had not been afraid of dirtying his fine clothes. Such a man must be a wonderful papa. Was he married? Did he have children of his own? Would a married man interest himself in other people's children if he had offspring of his own? But if he was single, surely he should be looking for a wife and setting up a nursery of his own, not concerning himself with slum children?

Kate was sitting in the drawing room with her grandmother the next day when Dr Redfern was announced by their parlour maid, Susan. She put down the book she had been reading and jumped up eagerly, almost too eagerly, to receive him. He was wearing a long-tailed coat of green superfine, yellow-and-white striped waistcoat, skin-tight pantaloons which showed off his muscular thighs and well-polished boots. His shirt was white and his starched cravat was tied neatly between the points of his shirt collar which were high, but not so high he could not turn his head. He had removed his top hat and held it in the crook of his arm. 'Mrs Meredith, your obedient,' he said, bowing.

'Doctor Redfern.' Kate bent her knee slightly and inclined her head, as good manners dictated, then turned to her grandmother. 'Grandmother, may I present Doctor Redfern. Doctor Redfern, the Dowager Lady Morland.'

'My lady.' He managed to contain his surprise and bowed again. How could he have imagined Mrs Meredith was a nursery maid? He felt himself grow hot, remembering how he had treated her with condescension. Why, she came from aristocratic stock! She had said she was related to Lady Eleanor too, and he had simply imagined she was the poor relation. Nothing he could see about him now bore that out. The room was elegantly furnished and the old lady was regal in her bearing. She was looking him up and down through a quizzing glass, taking in every detail of his apparel, and he was glad he had taken trouble with his appearance.

'Redfern,' she said, at last. 'Any relation to the Redferns of Finchingfield?'

'Yes, my lady. Lord Redfern of Grove Hall is my uncle.'

'Ahh,' she said, as if he had answered some conundrum that had been puzzling her. 'Please be seated. You will take tea?'

'Thank you.' He took a seat opposite her and put his hat on the floor at his side.

Kate found another chair close by. 'How is Joe?' she asked him, as her grandmother instructed Susan to bring the tea things. They did not employ a footman. They had a cook, a kitchen maid and a chambermaid besides Susan. Her grandmother had a maid whom Kate shared on special occasions and her father had a valet who also acted as his secretary. Two women came daily to clean and to do the laundry and a man came to see to the garden. Daniels, their coachman, lived in the mews.

'He has settled down well. I am trying to find the family a more wholesome place to live, so that he can be returned to his mother.' He noticed Kate slowly shaking her head and realised she had not told her grandmother the whole of what had happened the previous day and he must tread carefully.

'How did you come to be involved in such work?' her ladyship asked.

'The plight of poor children has always interested me; since the war it seems harder for men to find work and there are so many poor, unwanted children about. I thought something should be done, so I approached as many influential and wealthy people as I could and one of those was Lady Eleanor. Between us we set up an association of like-minded people to raise funds and the result has been The Society for the Welfare of Destitute Children and a home for those we cannot foster out.'

'And why did you choose to be a doctor?' the old lady persisted in her questioning. 'It seems a strange thing for a gentleman to do do.'

He laughed. 'I was always picking up injured birds and animals when I was a boy and looking after them until they either died or were cured, then I would release them back into the wild. And when a choice of career was being considered, I decided on the army. But I would rather preserve life than end it, so I trained to be an army doctor...'

'A far cry from looking after children,' the old lady went on, as Susan returned with the tea things and, having set them out, left Kate to pour it and hand it out.

'There are children with the women who follow the march,' he told her. 'Many were born in camp. I acted midwife on many an occasion, but my main occupation was treating the sick and wounded after the battles.'

Although Kate would not have dreamed of quizzing him as her grandmother was doing, she listened with growing admiration as he talked. If she had been a man, she would have pursued the same calling or something very like it, but such a career was not open to a woman and she had to content herself with visiting the poor and sick and taking them little comforts like food and clothing and helping them in any way she could.

'I collect you were brought up by your uncle, is that not so?' Lady Morland queried, changing tack suddenly.

'Yes, my lady. Both my parents died when I was very young and he became my guardian.'

'But you are not your uncle's heir?'

'I was not, but nine months ago my cousin died in a hunting accident, which has unexpectedly put me in that position.'

'I see.'

Kate looked at him with renewed interest. She could feel for him; her own mother had died when she was seven and she knew the sense of loss never entirely went away. It might account for the bleak look she sometimes saw in his eyes.

Lady Morland was not done with him yet. 'And do you do your work with your uncle's blessing?'

He gave a wry smile. 'Not exactly. He told me to go to the devil in my own way. Fortunately he is in prime kilter and I do not expect to inherit for a long time yet.' It was a mild way of describing his relationship with his uncle, which had been, and still was, a stormy one, especially since the death of his cousin. He was expected to step into Charles's shoes, marry an heiress and give him a brood of grandchildren. 'You should be looking for a wife and setting up your own nursery, not taking on other people's bantlings,' Aunt Matilda told him repeatedly. 'You will catch some dreadful disease, or be set upon and robbed by the very people you are trying to help…' And that was mild compared with what his uncle said.

'I assume from that you have not married.'

'No, I have yet to meet the lady who will put up with my peccadilloes.' It was his stock answer, if not entirely accurate.

'I would not call the wish to help your fellow creatures a peccadillo, Dr Redfern,' Kate put in. 'It is an admirable thing to do.'

'Thank you, ma'am.' He paused and plunged on, unwilling to continue being quizzed on the subject of marriage. 'If you are interested in the work of the Society, there is be a lecture at Somerset House on Friday evening at eight o'clock with the object of raising funds. If you are not otherwise engaged, would you care to attend?'

'Yes, I think I would.'

As Kate spoke, her father came into the room. He was, Simon judged, about fifty, grey-haired and dressed in the dark clothes of a cleric. Kate introduced them.

'Oh, you are the fellow my daughter met yesterday,' the Reverend said, shaking Simon's hand.

'Yes, sir.'

'What happened to the little boy she rescued?'

'He has been taken into the Hartingdon Home. I am hoping something can be done for the family and then he can be returned to them.'

'Kate has told me a little of the work you do,' the Reverend went on. 'It is a thankless task, I think.'

'There are times when I feel despondent, but when things go well and a family thrives, then I am glad that I have done my small part in bringing it about.'

'I think the government should do more,' Kate said. 'Children should not have to rely on charity for the basic things in life, like food, clothes and a home. If I had my way, ex-soldiers would have decent pensions—' She stopped suddenly, realising she was becoming heated. 'I beg your pardon. I am sometimes a little too forthright.'

Simon smiled, admiring her heightened colour, the brightness of her eyes and the passion with which she spoke. How he wished there were more like her! 'I agree with you. The war has ruined so many lives— children left either without fathers or ones so badly disabled they cannot work, and mothers who must work to keep the family from starving and in the process neglecting their children.'

'Papa,' Kate said, 'Dr Redfern has invited me to attend a lecture about the work of The Society for the Welfare of Destitute Children on Friday evening. I have a mind to go. Would you accompany me?'

'That is the charity Lady Eleanor is involved with, is it not?' he asked Simon.

'Yes, sir.'

'Then I see no harm in attending. But if you are looking for a large donation, I am afraid you have come to the wrong person.'

Kate laughed. 'One must not forget the tale of the widow's mite. And perhaps there are other ways to help besides money, even if it is only spending a little time with the children at the Home.'

'Kate, how can you think of anything like that?' Lady Morland remonstrated. 'You don't know where they have come from. You might pick up anything…'

Kate did know where most of them came from, but she was not going to tell her grandmother about her visit to the slums. 'Then I can help raise funds. There is no harm in that, is there?'

Simon, unwilling to witness an altercation between the old lady and her granddaughter, picked up his hat, before standing up and bowing to everyone. 'My lady. Reverend. Mrs Meredith. I thank you for your interest.'

Kate rose to go to the front door with him; it was not their habit to ring for Susan to see callers off the premises. 'I really would like to help you,' she told him. 'I am sure you will be able to find something useful for me to do.'

'But ought you to go against your family's wishes?'

'Oh, take no note of Grandmama, her bark is worse than her bite. I can easily bring her round my thumb and I know my father will let me have my way; he thinks as I do. You have not seen the last of me.'

'Then I wish you good day, Mrs Meredith. I shall look forward to seeing you at the meeting on Friday.' He clamped his hat back on his head and strode down the path to the gate.

Kate returned to her grandmother. Her father had disappeared into his study again. 'What a strange man,' her ladyship said.

'Do you mean Dr Redfern? I do not find him strange.'

'An heir to a baron, grubbing about in the dirt, playing nursemaid to a horde of filthy children is strange, Kate, believe me. But if my memory serves me, there was a scandal there somewhere in the past, a falling out between uncle and nephew. Unless it was his cousin. I cannot be sure. I shall have to make enquiries.'

'Why, Grandmother? Whatever it was has nothing to do with us and if he chooses to spend his time helping the poor, that is commendable, not strange.'

'Nothing to do with us! Of course it is. If he expects to be received, then his character is important. We do not want our friends, and particularly Viscount Cranford, to think we encourage the man if he is not acceptable in polite society. And is a man who spends his time among the riff-raff in the rookeries acceptable?'

'Grandmother, that is unfair. I did not think you were like that.'

'If it were left to me, I would not be so particular, but others might not be so tolerant. We must be careful.'

'Lady Eleanor seems to find him acceptable.'

'As a working colleague, perhaps—that does not mean she is prepared to meet him socially. Your father is going to the meeting with you next week, he can question Eleanor.'

'Grandmother, I think it is reprehensible to go behind

Dr Redfern's back like that. If he finds out, I hope he will not blame me, for I find a great deal to admire in him.'

The old lady looked sideways at her, but did not comment.

The meeting at Somerset House was well attended, which was a testament to Dr Redfern's persuasiveness and also to Lady Eleanor's wealthy connections. The room had been arranged with seats facing a dais on which were a row of chairs and a lectern. Kate and her father found places just as half a dozen dignitaries filed on to the dais and took their seats. All except Lady Eleanor, who stood at the lectern to begin proceedings.

She was regally upright, a handsome woman, if not exactly beautiful, with glossy black hair that was carefully arranged under a bonnet that Kate decided must have cost a small fortune. Her dress was of green silk trimmed with rows of dark green velvet, over which she wore an embroidered cape. Kate wondered idly why she had not married, coming as she did from a very old and wealthy aristocratic family. She could no doubt command an enormous dowry; instead, she chose to be a spinster and spend her money on her various charities.

She introduced the trustees who sat behind her and then invited Simon to take the stand. He was impeccably attired in a black evening coat and pantaloon trousers, a waistcoat in figured brocade and a neat cravat. His fair hair had been carefully arranged. This, Kate knew, was his public persona, that underneath there was a caring, almost boyish figure who loved children and did not care how grubby they made him.

He spoke well, describing how he had met a parish nurse who was ill treating the children in her care and that, on investigation, had discovered the woman was not the only one. The practice was widespread and often resulted in the death of the children, either from physical ill treatment or simply neglect. It was a disgrace to any civilised society. He gave many instances, which appalled Kate and many of his audience, who called out, 'Shame!'

Kate risked a glance at her father, wondering if the doctor's words had brought back bitter memories; he appeared to be listening, but not distressed. Did he never think of his tiny son who had died in the care of a wet nurse? Kate had only seen her brother George briefly the day he had been born, but she could never forget him. Seven years old she had been, left to her own devices in the schoolroom of the rambling old rectory in Hertfordshire with instructions not to leave it until she was sent for. She had known something out of the ordinary was happening and strained her ears for any sound from the room below where she sat, supposedly doing some arithmetic her father had set her.

What she had heard curdled her blood and she longed to go down to her mother, whose cries of pain and distress filled the house. And then she heard the cry of a baby and nothing could keep her in the schoolroom. She had run helter-skelter down the stairs and skittered to a stop outside her mother's bedroom door as their doctor came out of the room, followed by her father.

'Papa…'

'I told you to stay upstairs.'

'I know, but I heard a baby.'

'Yes, you have a little brother.'

She remembered her reaction as one of huge joy. She had been an only child for so long and had always longed to have a brother or sister. Some of the women in the village had very large families; though the children did not appear to have much in the way of clothes and toys, they made their own fun and were company for each other. When she was out with her mother, primly taking a walk in her smart clothes and dainty shoes, she had seen the children romping about and making a great deal of noise. Oh, how she had envied them!

She had once asked her mother why she did not have any brothers and sisters and had been told, 'It is God's will', a statement she had learned to accept, but it did not stop her adding the wish to her prayers in the hope that He might change His mind. Then it seemed He had.

'May I see him? Oh, let me see him, Papa, please.'

'Let her come in.' Her mother's voice, though weak, was clear.

Her father stood to one side. 'A minute, no longer.'

She had darted into the room and run to the bed where her mother lay. She had a shawl-wrapped bundle in her arms. 'Here, Kate, here is your baby brother.' She pulled the shawl away to reveal a tiny pink screwed-up face. 'We are going to call him George.'

Kate had gently touched his face with her finger. He opened bright blue eyes and seemed to be looking straight at her. In that moment something happened to her. Her heart seemed to melt with love. Here was the playmate she had prayed for. 'He is very little,' she said, overawed.

'He has only just come into the world, but he will grow.'

'How did he come into the world?'

'I will tell you one day when you are a little older and able to understand.'

But she never did. Mama died that night and the whole house went into deep mourning. It had been a terrible time. She never saw George or heard his cries again. Her grandmother had moved in to take charge of the running of the house because her father seemed incapable of doing anything, and one day she asked her what had become of the baby. 'He has been sent to a kind lady who is looking after him until he is a little bigger,' she had said. Kate could not understand why he had to be sent away and she was convinced her father, whose grief was terrible, had given him away because he did not want him. He did not seem to want her either. He shut himself up in his study, had his meals sent in to him and took no interest in the parish or his parishioners. Kate had mourned alone.

She had not even had her brother to console her. Whenever she saw someone with a baby, she would run up to them and look at the child, wondering if it was her sibling, until her governess or grandmother dragged her away, tight-lipped and disinclined to tell her what she wanted to know. Where was her brother?

She had been passing through the hall one morning, when she had overheard her grandmother remonstrating with her father. 'If you cannot minister to your flock,' she was saying, 'then give up and do something else. Move away. There are too many unhappy memories here. Brooding will not bring them back.'

Kate, listening outside his study door, waited a long time for his answer and when it came, it shocked her to the core. 'It was my fault. I killed her. Him too.'

She had stuffed her fist into her mouth to stop herself crying out. Why would her father do such a horrible thing? He had loved her mother, everybody did. And what did he mean, 'Him too'? Had Grandmother lied to her when she said George had been sent to a kind lady? She had run and hidden herself in the shrubbery in the garden, half-afraid he would kill her too. It was a long time before she understood what he had meant and it was her grandmother who had enlightened her.

'What is the matter with you, child?' she asked her one day about a year after her mother died. By then her father had come out of his torment enough to make plans to move to London. He was trying his best to be the father he had once been, but Kate was too wary of him to respond. 'You flinch whenever your papa comes anywhere near you.'

She had mumbled something incoherent about not wanting to go to London.

'Why not?'

'We will be leaving Mama behind.'

'No, your mama's spirit will be with us wherever we go. She is watching over you now, just as she always did. She would be ashamed of the way you have been behaving of late.'

'Does she know Papa killed her?'

'What in heaven's name are you talking about?'

It had all spilled out, what she had overheard, her fear. And then to her consternation, her grandmother had laughed. 'Of course he did not kill her,' she said. 'Your papa felt bad because your mama had died and he did not think he had done enough to save her. People often think like that when they are torn with grief, even when there is nothing they could have done. One day you will understand.'

'And the baby?'

'That is another matter altogether.'

'Where is he? Why hasn't he come home?'

'Kate, he was a puny little thing. He did not thrive…'

'You mean he is dead too and Papa did not do enough to save him either.' It was an accusation delivered in an angry voice. She had been looking forward to having her brother home, thinking, in her childish way, that his presence would make everyone happy again.

'No, I mean he was born too weak to live. You see, he was not ready to come into the world and the woman who looked after him did not have enough milk for both him and her own child.'

'We could have given him milk, we always have plenty. There is a whole herd of cows on the farm. And you let him starve to death.' She was furious and stamped her foot. 'That is what Papa meant, isn't it? Oh, how could he? How could you?' And she had burst into tears. 'You lied to me,' she said between sobs. 'You said he was with a kind lady and he wasn't. He wasn't at all.'

Her grandmother had grabbed her and pinned her

arms to her sides because they were flailing about. 'Don't take on so, child. I see I shall have to try to make you understand or you will brood over it for years.' And so Grandmama had taken her on to her lap and, after taking a deep breath, tried to explain about pregnancy and premature births and the need for human milk to make a baby grow strong.

Kate's seven-year-old brain could not take it all in and it had not made her feel any less bitter at the loss of her mother, nor convince her that if her brother had not been sent away, he would have been well and happy and a playmate for her at the rectory where she was often lonely. She did not want to believe he was dead. Dead of neglect, that was the worst part of it.

As time went by and she grew up, she had begun to understand, to accept that both her mother and brother had gone and that her father was not the ogre she imagined him to be, but an unhappy man who had loved his wife, a little too well, for he had been told she should not have more children. That was why he felt so guilty.

She dragged herself back to the lecture, which was coming to a close.

'Children are the future of our country,' the doctor was saying. 'If they are badly treated, they will grow up knowing nothing else but cruelty and indifference and will pass that on to future generations in the way they treat their own offspring. All children should be adequately fed, clothed and educated, even the poorest...'

There was a slight murmur of disagreement at the

mention of education, but he ignored it. 'We call ourselves civilized, yet we allow cruelty to our children
that we would not condone if they were dogs. Foster
parents should be licensed and controlled and their
premises and the children they care for regularly inspected, but until that happy state is realised, we must
do what we can privately. The Foundling Hospital is
doing excellent work and there are orphanages who do
their best for their inmates, while others are less to be
commended. But what of those children who are not
orphans, those who have at least one parent without the
means and often without the will to look after them?

'The Society for the Welfare of Destitute Children has
been set up to remedy some of these ills. We find respectable and responsible foster homes for the children,
until they are able to be returned to their own families, or,
when they are old enough, found suitable occupations. We
have many influential subscribers, but the list of children
needing help in the metropolis alone is growing at an
alarming rate, especially since the war, and we need your
donations, however small. We also need foster parents to
take a child into their homes on a temporary basis. Some
of the women who apply are only doing it for the money
and have been known to neglect and sometimes ill treat
the children. We investigate everyone very carefully
before we put them on our books and we pay them enough
so there is no excuse to neglect the children.'

He sat down amid restrained applause. Kate turned
to look at her father. He was very pale and his hands
were trembling. Perhaps she should not have asked him
to accompany her; some wounds never heal.

Lady Eleanor rose to introduce the treasurer, who outlined the finances of the society and told his audience what was needed to keep a child in a foster home and visit regularly and how much it cost to keep a child in the Hartingdon Home. The meeting was wound up by the Chairman of the Trustees, who said that their members would be on hand to answer any questions his listeners might have.

Although neither Kate nor her father joined in the debate, the question-and-answer session revealed the disparate views of the audience, some decrying what the society was trying to achieve, others praising it, while still more wanted more information about how the finances were managed. When there were no more questions, the evening was brought to an end and Kate and her father found their way to the front where Simon and Lady Eleanor were in conversation.

Simon's eyes lit up at the sight of Kate. He bowed. 'Mrs Meredith, your obedient. Reverend, how do you do?'

Lady Eleanor turned to them. 'Cousin Thomas, I did not know you were acquainted with Dr Redfern.'

'We met earlier in the week and he prevailed upon us to attend this evening.'

'How do you think it went?'

'You have given us all a great deal to think about.'

Simon smiled. 'That is all we can ask—that people think about it and do what they can, however little.'

'I should like to do more,' Kate said. 'Even if it is only helping at the Home or raising funds with soirées and concerts. I am sure there are musicians and singers willing to give their services free for such a worthy cause.'

'We do that already,' Eleanor said. 'There is to be a subscription ball at Hartingdon House next Thursday. Would you like tickets?'

'Yes, please.'

'I will have them sent to you,' Simon said, mentally deciding to deliver them in person.

'How is little Joe?' Kate asked him as Lady Eleanor left them to speak to one of the other trustees.

'He is well, but I think he misses his mother, for all that she was glad enough to hand him over to me. He would perhaps be happier in a foster home, but we are very short of those because, as you heard, we are very particular about those we employ.'

'I am glad to hear that,' Kate said.

The room was emptying; her ladyship and the other trustees had gone. They bade each other goodnight and went their separate ways.

'Kate, I do not see how you can become involved,' her father said as they settled in the family carriage to be driven home. 'The Viscount will be back in England shortly…'

'So? If he comes before the ball at Lady Eleanor's, he can come too. His presence can do nothing but good.'

'Kate, beware you are not assuming too much. You cannot dictate to Viscount Cranford what he should do.'

'I would not dream of dictating, but I do not see why he should not listen to my views and support me in something I feel strongly about.'

'It will not help, you know,' he said quietly. 'Regulating foster homes will not undo the past.'

'No, but it might stop other families grieving as we did.'

'You blame me, don't you?' It was the first time he had ever talked to her about it. 'You think I did not make sure the wet nurse was clean and healthy. If I had had my wits about me at the time, I would have, then…' He paused, swallowed and went on, 'George might have lived.'

'Papa, stop it. Stop torturing yourself. No one was to blame. I wish now I had not asked you to accompany me tonight. It has been too much for you.'

'No, it has made me see that something must be done and I shall support Dr Redfern wholeheartedly. I think I will write a tract about it.'

'Yes, you do that,' she said, reaching out to cover his hand with her own. He could write tracts or whatever made him feel better; she would offer to help at the Home.

Chapter Three

Next day, Simon, busy in the office of the Hartingdon, going over the case notes of some of the inmates, looked up when the door opened and Kate was ushered in by one of the children who had answered the front door bell. He scrambled to his feet. 'Mrs Meredith, what are you doing here?'

'I have come to see how I can be of help,' she said. She was a picture in her striped gingham dress, with her glossy brown hair peeping out of a very fetching bonnet with silk flowers along its rim and a wide ribbon tied in a bow to one side of her determined little chin.

'But how did you get here? This is hardly an area for a lady to venture alone.'

'I assume Lady Eleanor visits, so why not me?'

'Her ladyship arrives in her own coach and is always accompanied by her companion and a male servant.'

'None of which I have.' She said it pleasantly without a hint of envy. 'I came in a cab. The driver was not anxious to wait, so I let him go. Now tell me, how can I be of use?'

'Mrs Meredith, you remember I did advise you to think carefully before committing yourself. The children who are housed here are not like the children you were amusing in the park, you know. They are rough and ready and sometimes their language is appalling. Others are withdrawn and uncommunicative.'

She smiled. 'I am well aware of that, Dr Redfern. There are poor children everywhere. I have always tried to do what I can for them.'

His immediate need was for someone to cook and clean but, mindful of her rank, he could not ask that of her. 'Do you think you could teach some of the younger ones their letters?' he asked. 'Their minds must be fed as well as their bodies.'

'Of course. I shall be delighted. May I start at once?'

'I am afraid there is no remuneration apart from expenses.'

'I do not want wages or expenses; my husband left me adequately provided for and my needs are few. Just being with the children will be payment enough.'

'You will have children of your own one day,' he said, knowing he was probing, but curious to know why she had not married again.

'I hope I may, but that is some way off yet and has no bearing on my wanting to help you.'

He turned to her with a grin. 'Me or the Society?'

She laughed. 'Is it not one and the same?'

It suddenly occurred to him that she might be using the opportunity to banish demons of her own—her childlessness perhaps. Ought he to encourage her? But he could not send her away, could he? They had not been so besieged by people offering to help that he could afford to turn anyone away. And he understood about demons. 'Very well. Let us go and meet the children.'

He took her to the schoolroom, where about twenty children were assembled. The girls were dressed in the uniform of the home: plain grey cotton dresses, white aprons, white mob caps, black stockings and the boys in grey smocks over calf-length trousers. All wore sturdy boots. They were being supervised by a girl of fifteen or so.

'This is Martha,' Simon told Kate. 'She can read a little and it is her task to keep the children occupied when they are not doing their allotted tasks about the house.'

'Is that all the schooling they get?'

'No, I have been teaching them myself, but my time is limited and, as you must have deduced last night, educating the children is not considered the most important of our tasks. If you can take over, it will be a great help.' He clapped his hands to get the children's attention. 'Now, you little monsters,' he said cheerfully, making them grin, 'Mrs Meredith has come to teach you…' He ignored the concerted groan and went on. 'Stand up and say good morning to her.'

They obeyed and Kate returned the greeting with a smile and told them to sit down again. They did so and silently waited. He could almost see their minds ticking over, wondering how far they dare go in tormenting the new teacher. He began to wonder if he had been wise to put her among them; he might have been better giving her some office work to do where she would have minimum contact with them. 'If I hear of any misbehaviour, there will be beatings and no cake for a week,' he said. Turning to Kate, he went on, 'Martha will tell you where the slates and chalks are kept and the books. They have been donated by the church and other improving societies, not designed to grab their attention, I am afraid.'

'Then we must find some that do,' she said. 'But first I must get to know them all.'

'They will take advantage if they can, so do not stand for any nonsense. Send Michael to fetch me, if you need me. That's Michael.' He pointed to a boy of about twelve sitting at the end of the row.

'I am shocked that you would even consider beating them,' she murmured.

'I would not dream of it, but they don't know that.' It was whispered with a mischievous grin.

'Oh, I see. And I am to perpetuate the myth.'

'It helps,' he said laconically. 'Shall I leave you to your fate?'

'Are you doing your best to make me nervous, Doctor?'

He smiled. 'I have a feeling I would not succeed, at least not where children are concerned. When you have had enough, just let me know and I will escort you home.'

He left the room and she turned back to the children. They were staring at her silently, sizing her up, and she knew the next few minutes would be crucial. She had spotted Annie Smith, still clutching her doll, and Joe, whose hair, having been washed, turned out to be the colour of ripe corn. 'Now, children, I need to know what to call you. Stand up, one at a time, and tell me your names; if you know how to spell them, then tell me that too. I know Joe Barber and Annie Smith, and Michael, though I do not know his surname...'

'Sandford,' the boy called out, grinning at her. 'And this 'ere's Sarah Thomsett.' He pointed to the girl sitting next to him.

'Let her tell me herself.'

Simon, standing outside the door listening, smiled to himself. Mrs Kate Meredith was going to be a great asset to the Society—that is, if she did not become discouraged by the children's lack of progress and decided not to continue. As he walked away, he heard her lilting voice singing 'oranges and lemons' and encouraging the children to join in. He could hear them as he returned to his desk and sat down to continue with his work on the records. How happy she sounded!

The time flew by and, before Kate realised it, the morning had gone and Dr Redfern was back to dismiss the children and take her home. He found her sitting on the floor, with Joe on her lap and the others sitting in a circle about her, playing a game that involved remembering a list of everyday articles one after the other in the right order. They seemed genuinely sorry when she stood up and said she must go, carefully removing Joe's hand from her skirt and promising to come back soon.

* * *

'Did you manage to get your work done?' she asked Simon as they set off for Holles Street in his gig.

'Yes, I did, thank you. You were a great help.'

'I did not teach much in the way of reading and writing,' she said.

He laughed. 'They will think that singing and playing games is all there is to education.'

'It is a great part of it. Learning should be fun. Besides, I needed to hold their interest and gain their trust. I would never do that teaching them from those religious tracts I saw.'

'Tut tut, and you a parson's daughter.'

She joined in his laughter. 'I will bring some more suitable books tomorrow.'

'So you intend to come again?' he asked, careful to avoid the worst of the slums and taking a longer route via Pall Mall and Piccadilly, although parts of that were being dug up and houses demolished to make way for the Regent's new road.

'Of course, if you will have me.'

'Have you! My dear Mrs Meredith, you are a godsend. It is not a question of will I have you, but will you want to come.'

'Oh, I do. I have not enjoyed myself so much in years.'

He was not as calm as he looked. He was acutely aware of her sitting beside him, so close her yellow skirt was brushing against his leg. She was a ray of sunshine and colour in those noisy dust-laden surroundings, but it was not only her external appearance that was so charming, but the inner woman, caring, practical and restful. She was looking straight ahead and he could not see her face properly for the flower-laden brim of her bonnet, but her hands were still in her lap. He did not know why he did it, but he took his left hand from the reins and put it over hers. 'Thank you for that.'

She looked down at his strong brown hand with puzzlement as if she could not understand how it got there nor why its warmth was spreading down her fingers, making her shiver in spite of the warmth of the day. She knew she ought to remove her hand from under his, but somehow did not want to. It was, after all, only simply a friendly gesture, a sign perhaps that she had pleased him with her efforts with the children, and it would be churlish to take offence. He seemed suddenly to realise what he had done and put his hand back on the reins without speaking.

She turned to look at him, wondering if he noticed the effect his touch had had on her, but he appeared to be concentrating on his driving, carefully going round the road works and turning up Bond Street. 'I will be glad when they have finished tearing up the streets,' he said to cover his discomfiture. 'And all to please the Regent. It is a pity they cannot spend the money on a more worthy cause.'

'Oh, how I agree with you, though I suppose when the new road is finished, it will be very grand.'

'Everything our future king does is extravagant. I sometimes wish I could take him by the collar and drag him into Seven Dials. He should see how some of his subjects live while he builds roads and palaces and spends money on his mistresses.'

'Oh, dear.' She laughed. 'You do feel strongly, don't you?'

'Yes. It makes my blood boil.'

'What else excites you?'

He was tempted to say, 'You do', but decided that would be a folly. 'Oh, many things. The plight of the soldiers who have fought for their king and country and are now turned out on the streets to make what living they can. The dreadful business of the slave trade. The way the aristocracy will go to any lengths to keep their estates intact.'

'Ah, I collect you are the heir to an estate.'

'Oh, I do not care about that, but when a man is ordered to wed...'

'Have you been ordered to wed?'

'I would not obey if I were. At least, not unless I was in love with the lady in question.' He laughed suddenly to relieve the tension. 'How did we come to be talking about me? Tell me about yourself.'

'I am not very interesting. I cannot say I have travelled or served in the army, or healed the sick.'

'That does not mean you are not an interesting person. Have you always lived in London?'

'No, my father had a living in Hertfordshire when I was small, but when my mother died...'

'I am very sorry to hear that.'

'Thank you. It was a long time ago, when I was seven. She died after giving birth to my brother.'

'You have a brother?'

'No, he died too. He was put out to a wet nurse who—' She stopped. Did she really wish to go over that ground? 'Papa could not get over his grief and Grand-mama suggested he give up the living and move to London. If it had not been for her, I do not know what we would have done. He has since immersed himself in his writing.'

'I am sorry if I have upset you with my questions,' he said, beginning to understand some of what drove her to help poor children and why she became so heated over the question of foster mothers. 'I did not mean to make you sad.'

'You have not made me sad. It was eighteen years ago and I have learned to accept it was God's will. We cannot know what He has in store for us and perhaps good will come of it.'

'Let us hope so.' They turned into Holles Street. 'Here we are,' he said, drawing up outside her door. 'Are you coming to the Hartingdon again tomorrow?'

'Yes, of course.'

'I will fetch you.' He laughed when he saw her mouth open to protest. 'And do not argue, it will not make me change my mind.'

She thanked him and he jumped down to hand her down, then drove back to his rooms, musing on the events of the last few days. The arrival of Mrs Meredith was having a strange effect on his state of mind. It was very disturbing, but in a most pleasurable way. He had been so busy with his work for the charity he had had no time for a social life, except when forced upon him by his aunt or the need to raise funds. Mrs Meredith made him want to change all that. He was beginning to look forward to Lady Eleanor's ball.

* * *

It was some time since Kate had been to a society ball; according to Lady Morland, none of her gowns was at all suitable and she must have a new one made and so they had taken a cab to Madame Lorette's in Bond Street.

The woman called herself Madame Lorette and affected a French accent, but Kate suspected she was as English as she was. On being told Kate's requirements, she fetched out bolt after bolt of silks, satins, nets, lace and velvet in a myriad of colours. Soon every available surface was covered with material and patterns. It made it harder, not easier, to choose. If Kate liked a particular material, Lady Morland did not; if Lady Morland found a pattern that she considered just the thing, Kate dismissed it as too fussy.

'But you cannot wear something plain to go to Hartingdon House,' the old lady said. 'It will undoubtedly be a very select affair considering the price of the tickets. Fifty guineas is a scandalous amount.'

'It is in aid of the charity.'

'Yes, and Eleanor has made sure it will be a very select gathering and there will be no one present who is not of the *ton*. It will be reported in the newspapers and journals, who was there and what they wore, so you must be suitably attired.'

Kate was unconcerned about what the newspapers might report, but she was looking forward to the ball and perhaps standing up with Dr Redfern. He worked so hard, he deserved a little relief and she hoped he would relax enough to ask her to dance.

'Well, which is it to be?' Lady Morland became impatient with her apparent indecision. 'If you do not choose the material today, there won't be time to have it made up before the ball.'

'The aquamarine, I think,' Kate said, running her hand down the delicate silk. 'And this pattern.' She picked up a drawing of a simple round gown with tiny puffed sleeves and a scooped neckline edged with pearls. The high gathered waist was outlined with a ribbon studded with more pearls.

'Madame will require accessories?' the modiste enquired, having agreed to deliver the gown three days hence, the morning of the ball, and do any necessary alterations on the spot.

'Of course,' her ladyship put in quickly before Kate could say that she would make do with whatever she had in her clothes press at home. 'Green shoes and cream gloves and that.' She pointed to a sumptuous silk shawl draped over the back of a stuffed chair. 'And you may send the account to me.'

'Grandmother!' Kate protested; the shawl alone looked very expensive. 'There is no necessity for you to do that. I can afford to buy my own clothes.'

'I know you can, but it pleases me to treat you. Considering your father has given me a home, I have little to spend my money on. Now let us go to Gunter's and have a cup of tea and a slice of cake. I am famished.'

It was only a short step from Bond Street to Berkeley Square and they were soon sitting at a table in the confectioner's, enjoying the refreshments. 'I think the green will make up very well,' the old lady said. 'It is a pity his lordship will not be back to escort you.'

'His lordship?' Kate repeated vaguely.

'Yes, Cranford. Has he written when he will be home?'

So much had happened in the last week, Kate had almost forgotten about the man she had agreed to marry. Being with the children and Dr Redfern, too, had occupied her mind to the exclusion of all else. 'No, only that he hoped it would be this summer. He is at the beck and call of the Foreign Office and if they want him in Paris, then he must stay there.'

'Perhaps you should consider going out to join him.'

'Marry him in Paris, you mean? Oh, no, I could not do that. I want to be married here, with all my family and friends round me. Besides, if he wanted me to do that, he would have suggested it himself.'

'Are you not impatient to see him again?'

Kate had to think about that. Was she? Did she have doubts? Had anything changed? The only thing that had altered was that she had had some firsthand experience of looking after children and that made her longing for one of her own greater than ever. 'Of course I am, but I must be patient. We must both of us be patient.'

The old lady looked closely at her, but decided not to comment. She beckoned to the waiter to pay for the refreshment and asked him to send out for a cab to take them home.

Hartingdon House was in Hanover Square and was a substantial mansion with a wide frontage. On the night of the ball every window was lit and lanterns were strung across the railings. The long line of carriages waiting to go up to the front door contained the cream of London society and people in the street stopped to stare and comment on the guests as they arrived and were admitted.

Kate, with her father and grandmother, took over an hour to travel the short distance from Holles Street. They could have walked it in a quarter of the time, but that would not have been considered the thing and so they sat in their coach and waited, moving up a few yards at a time as each carriage disgorged its load, rattled away and the next one moved up. But at last they were making their way up the steps to the front door. The Reverend's hat was taken from him and they moved towards the ground-floor ballroom, where they were announced by a liveried footman.

The room was brilliantly lit and rather hot and airless. Kate stood and marvelled at the fine decorations, the gilding of the plasterwork, the painted ceiling, the swathes of greenery round every pillar, the huge bowls of flowers on stands in every niche, and the polished floor, already crowded with people dancing to the music of an orchestra sitting on a dais at the far end.

'Come, let us find chairs,' Lady Morland said, as the Reverend disappeared in the direction of the library where he planned to take advantage of the Earl's large collection of books.

They moved into the room just as Lady Eleanor spotted them and came forward to greet them. She was magnificently dressed in amber crepe with a head-dress of curling green feathers, which bobbed as she walked. Kate, whose own hair had been arranged *à la grecque* by Corinne, her grandmother's maid, and threaded with ribbon, was fascinated by them and wondered if they would last the evening without drooping.

'What a squeeze!' Lady Morland said. 'Eleanor, I fear you have overdone the invitations.'

Lady Eleanor laughed. 'But every one of them has paid fifty guineas for the privilege. If it becomes too crowded, we can open up the windows on to the terrace. I believe Dr Redfern has saved seats for you near one of the windows. I hope it will not be too draughty.' She waved a hand in his direction.

He had seen them and was coming towards them. He looked nothing like the man Kate had been working alongside all week. Gone was the brown-and-beige clothes, the untidy hair, the look of harassment, the worried frown. Here was a pink of the *ton* in a blue brocade coat, white pantaloon trousers, dark-blue satin waistcoat, frilled shirt whose cuffs fell over the backs of his hands, and a starched muslin neckcloth that was an art form in itself. He stopped and bowed. 'Ladies, your obedient.'

Kate bobbed a curtsy, almost open-mouthed in admiration, but managed to say, 'Good evening, Doctor.'

'May I escort you to seats? I am afraid it is a dreadful crush. We did not expect so many.'

'But that is good thing, don't you think?' Kate said, putting her hand on the arm he offered, while her grandmother took the other. 'All the more for the Society's coffers. You will be able to do so much more for the children.'

'We certainly hope so. Our aim is to buy land and

build a new home designed for its purpose, but we are a long way short of our target.'

'Then I wish you well of it.'

They reached their seats. Lady Morland sat down immediately and began using her fan vigorously. Simon turned to Kate. 'May I have the honour of a dance?'

Kate handed over her empty card. 'Have as many as you wish. I am not likely to be in demand.'

'There I must disagree,' he said. 'You will have the young men buzzing about you like bees, so I must stake my claim at once.' She was looking exceptionally beautiful and had taken his breath away when he first beheld her. The pale green dress flowed about her slim figure and the silk shawl with its swirls of different shades of blue, green and pink set off her shoulders and creamy neck, about which was fastened a single rope of pearls. Her eyes sparkled and her cheeks were rosy; it was good to see such evident enjoyment and he felt his own spirits lifting.

He wrote his name against two dances, which was all he dare do, given the conventions. Although she was a widow, she was single and presumably available, and it would cause comment if he danced with her more than twice, but he meant to make the most of those. One was a country dance, which was then beginning, and the other a waltz, immediately before supper; he intended to escort her to that if she would allow it. He felt safe with her, safe from predators who had heard about his change in circumstances. They seemed to have forgotten the scandal of a broken engagement in their anxiety to be considered the next Lady Redfern.

'Thank you,' he said, returning the card and offering her his hand. She slipped her shawl from her shoulders and draped it over the back of her chair before taking his hand to be led on to the floor.

'It is a very sumptuous affair,' Kate said as they stepped out together between the ranks of dancers. 'It must surely swell the Society's coffers by a prodigious amount.'

'Yes, and as Lady Eleanor and her friends have paid all the expenses, it is all profit.'

'It is very generous of her. I wonder why she never married. I cannot believe she had no offers.'

'Perhaps her requirements were too exacting.'

'Requirements! How cold and calculating that sounds. I do not think marriage should be like that.'

'But it often is,' he said. 'Especially if great estates are involved. The estate must be protected at all costs, even to sacrificing the happiness of the people involved.'

The tone of his voice, sounding both hurt and bitter, made her look at him sharply. He was looking directly ahead, his expression grim, and she decided it would be unwise to ask him what he meant. As they neared the end of the line they ducked their heads to pass under the clasped hands of the last couple, then separated to walk up the outside to the head of the line before joining hands again. By that time he was smiling again and she supposed she must have imagined that look.

The dance came to an end, the couples bowed, curtsied and dispersed and Simon offered his arm to escort Kate back to her grandmother. The conversation had not gone at all as he had planned it. In his mind they had engaged in light and flirtatious banter, nothing too serious; instead, they had talked about Lady Eleanor and the way great estates were held together, which had momentarily disconcerted him. He wondered if she had noticed. He had never envied his cousin his inheritance except that he could take the woman he loved from him. If he had married Isobel, he would not have gone soldiering or taken up the challenge of helping poor children. Perhaps that was his destiny, to look after society's children and have none of his own.

He shook his thoughts from him as they reached Lady Morland. Kate took her hand from his sleeve and he bowed. 'Please excuse me. I am expected to go round and make sure everyone is enjoying themselves. I will be back.'

'He certainly presents well,' Lady Morland said as she watched him walk away. 'I do not remember his father, but his uncle was a handsome man in his youth.'

'You knew him?'

'Yes, I knew him. Everybody did. A noted horseman, as I recall. Married a Symonds-Taylor. Pretty little woman inclined to tubbiness. He had several mistresses. I heard his son was a chip off the old block.'

'Dr Redfern's cousin?'

'Yes—Charles, his name was.' She stopped suddenly. 'Ah, that was it, that was the scandal. Now I remember.'

Kate did not think they should be discussing it, but she had to admit she was intrigued. 'Well, are you going to tell me?'

'Yes, give me time. As I recall, Charles married the young lady the doctor had been courting. Now what was her name? Annabel? Isobel? Yes, Isobel, daughter of the Earl of Kendal. By all accounts, Lord Redfern was heard to say he was glad of it, she was much too good a catch for his good-for-nothing nephew…'

'You mean Simon?' Kate put in.

The old lady looked sharply at her and she blushed furiously, realising she had used the doctor's given name. 'Yes, Dr Redfern, as he is now.'

'But why did he call him good-for-nothing? That is surely unfair.'

'I have no idea. Though I did hear tell it was his fault, that he was the one to break off the engagement.'

'I wonder why?'

'Cold feet, perhaps. But it was a scandalous thing to do. A betrothal is almost as binding as a marriage and breaking one off is simply not done. Not unless you want to cut yourself off from society.'

Kate found it difficult to equate that story with the Dr Redfern she had come to know. He was a gentleman in every sense and, though he was soft-hearted, was certainly not weak or cruel. She had seen him at work, seen the determination and strength of mind he put into the work he did, the way he argued on behalf of the children. It was as if he were driven. She began to wonder exactly what it was that drove him. Surely not guilt?

'There must be more to it than that. Perhaps the lady was not the right wife for him. It would have taken courage to admit that and do something about it, especially if there was gossip. Gossip can kill a man's reputation stone dead. No wonder he has not married, which is a great pity—he would make a wonderful husband and father...' She stopped in confusion. Whatever had made her say that?

Again the old lady looked at her granddaughter in surprise. 'As Charles has died and the lady is a widow, I wonder if he will renew his suit?'

'I think he would be foolish if he did. Is she here tonight, do you think?'

'No, she must still be in mourning.'

They stopped speaking as a young man Kate had known for years came to ask for a dance. He was followed by several more, bearing out what the doctor had said about her being in demand. She enjoyed dancing with them, but they did not turn her head or make her heart beat any faster. The room was becoming even hotter and she was glad when several liveried footmen came and opened all the long windows on to the terrace and a cooling breeze began to lift the curtains.

Kate had declined the previous dance and was sitting beside her grandmother fanning herself, when the doctor came to claim his waltz.

'My dance, I think,' he said, bowing and holding out his hand. She took it and stepped on to the floor with him.

It was not as crowded as it had been; there were still some people who found the German dance shocking and would not let their daughters stand up for it. In Kate's opinion, it was a great pity because the music and the timing of the waltz lent themselves to dancing. And Simon executed it very well, transporting Kate to another world. She forgot who he was, who she was. She forgot about Robert and her grandmother's gossip in the enjoyment of it.

'Is there no end to your accomplishments?' he queried, with a smile.

'What do you mean?' His hand holding hers, his other hand on her back, disturbed her more than a little, though why it should she was at a loss to know.

'Nursemaid, teacher, singer and now excellent dancer.'

'None of which is exceptional,' she said.

'I disagree. To do all those things, to be practical and intuitive when dealing with children and to remain young at heart, is rare indeed.'

'Flummery!'

'No, honesty. I am so glad we found you, Mrs Meredith.'

'We? Is that a royal we?'

He laughed. 'No, I would not be so presumptuous, I meant to include the children.'

'Ah, the children. They are your first concern.'

'Yours, too, I suspect.'

She smiled. '*Touché*. But that cannot be all your life, can it? You must think about marriage and having children of your own? A man like you cannot remain single all your life.'

'What do you mean, a man like me?'

'You are so good with children and obviously find no difficulty establishing a rapport with them.'

'But children are not all there is to a marriage, Mrs Meredith, one also needs a wife—' He stopped suddenly, realising the conversation was becoming a little too personal for his comfort.

'I am sorry, I should not be quizzing you,' she said, remembering what her grandmother had told her. Was he bitter about that? 'Please forgive me.'

'Nothing to forgive. I, too, have been guilty of asking too many personal questions.'

'How else does one come to know another person, except by talking about who they are and what has formed their characters? You, in particular, must know all about the people you employ, particularly the foster mothers. You would be failing in your duty if you did not.'

'But you are not in my employ, Mrs Meredith. You are a volunteer and can stop coming to the Home at any time you have had enough, though I should be very sorry if you did.'

'Thank you. I shall continue to come so long as I am useful.'

He hoped she would. For the first time in years, he had met a woman he could admire and respect, who felt as passionately as he did about the world's ills, who made no demands. She did not expect costly presents, did not spend a fortune on clothes, did not want to be taken out and about in society, did not turn her pretty nose up when he stooped to help a child or an animal in distress. Nor, he suspected, would she prove fickle and greedy. He had been in the habit of judging all women by Isobel and keeping them at a distance. Yet here he was, holding Mrs Meredith around her waist, closer than the twelve inches the waltz demanded, and enjoying every minute.

The dance came to an end, they rejoined Lady Morland and went in to supper together and the conversation turned to general topics and a little gossip. Her ladyship seemed to know everyone and kept them entertained with comments about the other guests. One young lady had had three Seasons and had still not taken on account of being so fond of horses that she smelled of the stable; another young man had gambled away his fortune and was looking for a rich wife; old Lord Marven had so many mistresses and so many offspring he had lost count and had to have his secretary keep a list of them, and so on.

'Do you know everyone, my lady?' he asked.

She laughed. 'There is not much goes past me, young man, but never fear—I have heard nothing but good of you.'

'Thank goodness for that,' he said, laughingly affecting relief. Kate was glad her grandmother had told that little fib.

They finished their supper and then returned to the ballroom. The orchestra was taking a break and the dancing had not been resumed. Simon suggested a walk on the terrace where it was cooler.

'You go,' Lady Morland said. 'I shall sit here until the music starts again.' She picked up Kate's shawl. 'Better take this, you must not catch a chill.'

Simon took it from her and draped it over Kate's shoulders, then offered his arm to escort her outside.

The night air was cool, much pleasanter than the stuffiness inside. The sky was clear, its velvety darkness pricked by stars. The moon hung just above the roof tops. 'It seems almost near enough to touch and make a wish,' Kate said, gazing up at it.

He put his free hand over hers as it lay on his sleeve. 'What would you wish for if you could wish for anything in the world?'

'The same as you, I expect. An end to poverty and hunger and disease, an end to war and man's inhumanity to man, a world where children can grow up strong and healthy. A world without cruelty.'

'A tall order, but you are right, I wish it too.'

They strolled on in companionable silence until the strains of another waltz drifted out to them from the ballroom. He turned and held his arms out to her and without speaking she stepped into them. He guided her unerringly into the dance. It was cool and dark and they were alone, with the canopy of a star-filled sky above them and the muted strains of the music guiding their steps. It was magical.

When the music faded, they stood still, looking at each other in the semi-darkness, silent, a little breathless, unwilling to break apart. He still had hold of her hands, which he raised one by one to his lips. She felt the warm pressure on her skin and a little shiver passed through her. Was this a man who could break hearts?

The spell was broken by a drum roll sounding from the ballroom.

'I must go,' he said, his voice sounding a little cracked. 'The Earl is about to address the assembly and then Lady Eleanor is planning to call for more funds. I must be at her side.'

They returned to the uncomfortable warmth of the ballroom, back to reality.

Chapter Four

Simon and Kate were in the office of the Hartingdon Home two days later when Lady Eleanor came for one of her periodic inspections. If she was surprised to see Kate there, she made no comment. She examined the accounts, the children and the home and was satisfied with what she saw, except for the overcrowding. 'Dr Redfern, we have always said fifty was the most we could take,' she said. 'You have fifty-seven here.' She tapped the ledger she had been examining. 'And where did Annie Smith and Joseph Barber spring from?'

Simon explained about Annie and how Kate had rescued Joe from falling in the lake and how they had found his mother with a new baby, living in appalling conditions. 'I could not leave him there,' he said.

'There are hundreds like that,' she said. 'We have to be more selective in those we help.'

Kate did not see how anyone could pick and choose.

What criteria were used? How could you turn your back on any child in need? She had been going to the Hartingdon Home every day for the last two weeks and had enjoyed every minute. It gave her a purpose to her life and if, in some small measure, it meant that children would not die as George had, then it was reward enough. She loved the children and had learned to appreciate the single-minded dedication of the doctor. He worked so hard, dashing all over the metropolis on one errand or another on behalf of the children. If it was not negotiating grocery supplies, it was arguing with a haberdasher about materials for the children's uniforms, or persuading a carpenter to knock up a few desks, or subduing his pride and going cap in hand for funds.

'If we could only find more foster mothers, we could let some of the children go,' Simon said. 'But very few of the women who make a living fostering young children reach our high standards, as you know.'

'Naturally, I know that—'

'I could take Joe,' Kate said suddenly. 'We have plenty of room.'

They both turned to look at her in surprise. 'You?' Lady Eleanor said. 'What do you know about looking after children?'

'Enough, I think. I have always helped Cousin Lizzie with her four.'

'They are not street urchins.'

'Children are children, the world over. All they need is love and attention.'

'And food in their bellies, clothes on their backs and strict discipline,' Eleanor added. 'Children, especially those who have been deprived by poverty or neglect, can be difficult to handle.'

'I know that. I have worked with charities before and have been working here for nearly two weeks and have come to know the children.'

'You have? I did not know that.' She looked at Simon, one eyebrow raised in a query.

'Mrs Meredith has been teaching them on a purely voluntary basis,' he said.

'So will you allow me to help you out?' Kate asked. 'I am sure I can manage.'

'Oh, I am sure, you can,' Simon said, less disparaging than Eleanor because in the past two weeks he had come to know and appreciate Kate's qualities. 'But really you ought to discuss it with your father and grandmother before you commit yourself.'

'Yes, Katherine,' Eleanor put in. 'I cannot imagine Great-Aunt agreeing; as for your father, you know he cannot abide small children…'

Kate knew she was referring to events of eighteen years before and thought she was being unfair. 'You are mistaken, Lady Eleanor,' she said firmly. 'Papa is very fond of children. He adores Lizzie's.'

'Yes, when he visits Mount Street and when they come to see you. An hour in their company at the most. That is not the same as having them in the house all the time.'

'The house is big enough for little Joe not to trouble him at all. We have rooms on the top floor that have not been used since I was small and my governess taught me up there. Papa never goes there. He rarely comes out of his study during the day. I shall love having Joe.'

'On your own head be it,' Eleanor said, drawing on her gloves. 'Since you seem to have taken the child's welfare on your own shoulders and we are desperately short of good homes, I will say nothing against it. If your father agrees, that is. But please be warned, Katherine, it does not do to become too fond of one's charges. They are not used to the luxury of fondness and it can spoil them.'

Kate was about to argue that fondness could never spoil a child, but decided against it. She had been right about Lady Eleanor—she was aloof and distant. It was difficult to imagine her having any softer feelings, but surely underneath that stiff exterior there was a warm heart or how could she do the work she did?

'And do not come here to teach again,' Eleanor added. 'We are very particular about what the children are taught and cannot have people coming in just as they please and imbuing the children with their own notions of education. Heaven knows what radical ideas would be put into their heads.'

'My lady,' Simon put in, 'Mrs Meredith is simply teaching them their letters to help me out.'

'If you need assistance, then the Committee will decide whom to employ.' She turned to Kate. 'You will soon learn that looking after a child of the lower orders is as much, if not more, than you can manage. Now I must go.' To Simon, she said. 'And the other surplus children must be found homes, you understand.' And with that she left.

'My goodness, that put me in my place,' Kate remarked as soon as she had gone.

'I am sorry for it, Mrs Meredith, but as she is the main benefactor of the charity and can withdraw her support at any time she chooses, it would be unwise to go against her. I have been glad of your help and will be infinitely sorry to lose you.'

'I understand. I shall be sorry not to come, but having Joe might compensate a little for that.'

'Are you sure your father will agree?'

'I do not see why not. After all, I shall be the one who will be looking after him.'

'I will not try to dissuade you because I am sure Lady Morland and the Reverend will do that,' he said. 'But if they do agree, I want you to promise me that if Joe becomes too much of a handful, you will tell me at once.'

'Oh, I am sure that will not happen.' She would rather die than admit to him she could not look after one small child.

'And another thing. Beware of becoming too attached to him—not for his sake, but your own. Always remember he is not yours and one day he will go back to his mother. Try and stay a little distant.'

'I will try,' she said, though she did not know if she would succeed.

'If you are ready, I will take you home.'

'What are you going to do about the overcrowding?' she asked, as he conducted her out to his gig and they set off along the now-familiar route. If she wondered what people would say about her being seen so frequently in his company, she dismissed it. The drive home was something she looked forward to at the end of each day, when they would go over what had happened, the progress they had made and laugh at some of the antics of the children. She and Dr Redfern dealt so well together, it was as if she had known him all her life. They agreed on so many things and were never short of subjects to talk about. And now Eleanor had put a stop to it. She was angry, but realised there was nothing she could do about it. The Society was Eleanor's baby and she would brook no interference.

'I shall have to find homes for some of them. There is no immediate hurry; Lady Eleanor does not visit very often. I think she only came today to check the accounts and confirm how much money we made from the ball.'

'It was a great success, was it not?'

'Yes. We took nearly seven thousand pounds. We can begin looking for land and an architect. If we get the home we planned, we will be able to take more children.' He went on to explain a little more about his plans and found in her a ready listener. She even made one or two helpful suggestions, which showed she had been paying attention.

'The land and the plans are only the beginning, there is still a long way to go,' he said, as he pulled up outside her house and jumped out to hand her down. 'It all has to be maintained. We cannot rest on our laurels.'

'I would ask you in for refreshment,' she said, letting her hand rest in his for a moment, 'but I think I should talk to Papa alone. Do you mind?'

'Not at all. I shall think no less of you if you find you cannot do it.'

'You think he will say no, don't you?'

'I would hardly blame him.'

'What about a little wager, then? I bet you a five-guinea donation he will agree.'

He laughed. 'Done. It will be worth five guineas to be proved wrong.' He lifted her hand to his lips. 'Good day to you, Mrs Meredith. I shall wait with bated breath for the verdict.'

He watched her until she went indoors, then climbed back in the gig. If Lady Eleanor was right and the Reverend Morland disliked children, he would surely not welcome a street urchin into his home, and as her ladyship had forbidden Kate to teach at the Home, he did not have much hope of seeing her again. And that would be a terrible shame.

He was wrong. Kate was back at the Home the following morning. He was in the office puzzling over his list of foster mothers, wondering if any of them would take an extra child, when she breezed in, all smiles, and held out her hand. 'Five guineas, Dr Redfern.'

He stood up and grinned at her. 'You mean your father agreed?'

'Yes. Do you know what he said—after I had pointed out the terrible fate that awaited the children if they were turned away, that is? He said, "We are put on this earth to do God's work and if that is how you choose to do it, then I cannot condemn it."' She did not tell him the other arguments she had used, that she could not bear to think of any child being ill treated or neglected at the hands of an uncaring foster mother, a not-so-subtle reminder of her baby brother's fate, which was wicked of her. She had also pointed out that he had promised to support the doctor, who was at his wits' end not knowing what to do with all the children that needed help.

'Good for him,' Simon said. 'And what about Lady Morland? What did she have to say?'

Kate laughed and then mimicked her grandmother. 'Goodness knows what pestilence the child will bring with him. Can he speak properly? Is he even house-trained?'

He laughed; her imitation of her grandmother's voice was uncannily accurate. 'What did you say to that?'

'I said Joe is not a dog, he is a little boy who is missing his mother; as for pestilence, Dr Redfern can vouch that he is clean and free of disease.'

He was still smiling. 'Does she want that in writing?'

'No, of course not. I told you before, her bark is worse than her bite. I would not be surprised if she rolled up her sleeves and helped. She was always there to help and comfort me when I was a child.'

He reached into the pocket of his tailcoat and took out a purse, from which he extracted five guineas. 'Put them in the offertory box,' she said. 'Then tell me which children I should take.'

'Children?' he queried in surprise. 'I was only thinking of Joe.'

'He will be lonely on his own. He must have at least one playmate.'

'Are you sure?'

'Of course I am sure.'

It was because he did not want to give Mrs Meredith one of the worst of the children, many of whom did not know what cleanliness was and whose language was sometimes shocking, that he suggested Annie. The child came from a decent household, her father did not drink to excess and her mother had kept their home clean. Annie was unlikely to shock the elderly Lady Morland.

They went to the classroom where the children were waiting for Kate. She looked round at their bright eager faces and felt sad that she would not be teaching them again. Some of them would soon be separated and sent to foster homes. Simon had said they were careful whom they employed, but hadn't her father also been careful? It hadn't stopped George dying. But if she could not come here again, what was to stop her taking them home? She could not take them all, but she could manage four.

'Four!' Simon exclaimed when she told him. 'Four is far too many. Joe and Annie, yes, but I cannot allow you to burden yourself with more.'

'Children are not a burden,' she told him firmly. 'They are a joy. We have two spare bedrooms in the attic, with two beds in each, so I can take two boys and two girls. If I had more room, I would take a dozen.'

He gave in and was even more surprised when she chose Michael and Sarah as well as Annie and Joe. Michael was already an adult in his own eyes, having had to fend for himself since he was half that age, and Sarah, though the same age as Annie, was older by far in the ways of the world. Mrs Meredith had not chosen the easiest. He tried dissuading her, but she could be stubborn when she chose and in the end he agreed. He could always fetch them back if she found them too much of a handful and it would give him a reason for calling on her. That thought brought him up short. What had happened to his resolve to keep all women at a distance?

'Very well, I will bring them to Holles Street in two days' time. That will give you time to reconsider, should you wish to.'

'I will not do that, but the time will be usefully spent preparing the rooms for them.'

'How did you arrive here?' he asked.

'By cab.'

'Then I will take you home.'

Once again Kate found herself beside him in his gig. 'I should buy a conveyance of my own,' she said. 'Then you would not be put to the trouble of escorting me.'

'It is my pleasure and no trouble at all. But if you are worried about what people will say…'

'No, why should anyone interest themselves in me? I am a widow and not under the same constraints as a girl of seventeen up for the Season.'

He still found it difficult to think of her as a widow. She was still so young and so refreshingly lovely. Although neither of them had mentioned the waltz on the terrace, he found himself going back over it again and again. What exactly had happened? Something had, he was sure. Was it that he had suddenly realised that he could put the past behind him and look at another woman without seeing the fickleness of Isobel

and imagining they were all like her? Had he spoken?
Had she? No, he was sure the whole episode had passed
in silence. But it was a silence that spoke volumes. He
found himself wishing he had met Kate before he had
fallen in love with Isobel. Looking back now, he
wondered if he really had been in love at all. Was the
young woman who sat beside him setting him free or
binding him fast?

'Did you have a Season?' he asked.

'Yes, that was how I met Edward. He was the only
one of the young gentleman on the scene that year that
I found I liked and luckily he liked me too.'

'Is liking enough when choosing a partner for life?'

'No, of course not. It is much better to be in love. I
adored Edward and was struck down when he was
killed, but he came from a long line of military men;
soldiering was his life and I had to accept that he would
not have wanted to stay at home when his friends and
comrades were fighting. The time we did have together
was very happy and I can look back with fondness and
not regret, except…' She stopped with a sigh.

'Except?' he prompted.

'I did not have a child. I hoped I might be *enceinte*
before he went away, but it was not to be.'

'I have no doubt you would make an admirable
mama,' he said quietly.

'Thank you.' She turned to look at him. 'And you a
very good papa. I cannot believe you have not thought
about marriage and setting up your own nursery.
Looking after other people's children is no substitute—' She stopped suddenly, remembering the tale

her grandmother had told her about him. Perhaps she should not have spoken. They had established such a good rapport, she felt she knew him well, but of course she did not. Oh, she knew about his views on children and ex-soldiers and the Regent's extravagance, things like that, but not the inner man, not whatever it was that drove him so relentlessly. 'That was unforgivably impertinent of me,' she said.

'Not at all. It is no more than my aunt tells me all the time.'

'But I am not your aunt.'

'No, thank goodness. But I could say the same to you. Have you thought about marrying again?'

'It is not the same for ladies, is it? Men can do something about it, find a young lady and propose, but we poor females must wait to be asked.'

'And have you? Been asked, I mean.'

'I might have.' She could say no more, for Robert had not wanted anyone to know before his sister and daughters and she respected that.

'More than once, I'll wager.'

'That would be telling.' She chuckled. 'Are you quizzing me to see if I will make a suitable foster mother?'

'Not at all,' he said a little stiffly. 'I knew that the minute I saw you grab little Joe to safety and that has been borne out since by the wonderful way you have with the children at the Home.'

'I was only teasing. But surely you inspect the homes of your foster mothers?'

'Of course we do. They are subject to a rigorous examination and are visited frequently to make sure they are not breaching their agreement with us.'

'I do not wish to be treated any differently.'

'Oh, Kate…' he laughed '…I would not presume to inspect your home. My goodness, those four are going to think they are in heaven.'

Hearing him address her as Kate made her look at him sharply, but he appeared not to have realised his slip of the tongue and she was not affronted by it. 'But you will visit us?'

'Indeed, yes. It is part of my duty, and in this case, duty is pleasure.'

He drew up outside her house and escorted her indoors, but it was not until after he had been paid his respects to Lady Morland and the Reverend and left again that, Kate told them she had offered to take four children.

'Four!' Lady Morland's exclamation echoed Simon's. 'Have you taken leave of your senses? I thought you were only going to have one.'

'I know, but they all looked so appealing and I could not choose one over the other, so I said I would take four.'

'Kate, this is madness. Thomas, tell your foolish daughter she must retract the offer. We cannot have four little urchins running round the place. We shan't have a minute's peace.'

Her son simply smiled. 'Kate, are you sure of what you are doing?' he asked.

'Yes, Papa. They are only coming for a week or two. Two of them expect to be reunited with their families very soon, and the others will be found more permanent homes.'

'Then, my dear, I shall not speak against it. But...' and he wagged a finger at her '...you are not to over-burden Susan. She has enough to do as it is.'

'You are as bad as Kate,' Lady Morland told him. 'And what about the Viscount?'

'What about him?' Kate asked. 'He is in Paris. I am not having the children permanently, they will probably be gone by the time he comes back to England; if they are not, it will not matter. He will not live here, but at his own home, so I cannot see how the children can dis-commode him. He will not even see them.'

'Kate, are you being deliberately obtuse? He will want to take you out and about and invite you to his home. You have yet to meet his sister and his daughters. How are you going to do all that and look after four children? They are not like Lizzie's four, are they? You cannot hand them back to a fond mama when you tire of them.'

'I shall manage. And I am not going to do nothing waiting for Viscount Cranford to appear.'

'Kate!' her grandmother exclaimed in shock. 'How can you dismiss the Viscount in that way, as if he were of no importance? He is your future husband, or had you forgotten?'

'No, I had not forgotten.'

The trouble was she had. And that made her feel guilty. Of course she was looking forward to seeing him again, but that was laced with a certain amount of trepi-dation. They knew each other well through their letters, but that was not the same as meeting face to face, talking to each other. Supposing her memory of him had played her false? Supposing she did not like him after all? Or he found he did not like her? In a way she wanted him back, but in another way she was half-afraid, though exactly what she was afraid of, she could not put into words. Dare not.

Doctor Redfern brought the children in an old-fashioned town chariot with the name of the home painted on its side. Kate welcomed them literally with open arms and hugged them all, though Michael, considering himself too old for such things, pulled a face and hitched himself out of her way. 'Come upstairs,' she said, after introducing the children to her grandmother and father. 'I have had my old schoolroom made ready for you and two bedrooms made up, one for the boys and one for the girls. Shall you come and see?'

In the face of her enthusiastic welcome, they relaxed a little and followed her up the stairs, with Simon bringing up the rear. In the schoolroom, which would also do duty as their dining room and sitting room, there was a jug of lemonade and half a dozen glasses on a table and a plate of little cakes Kate had made that morning. The children fell upon them eagerly, until Simon reminded them to mind their manners.

Kate invited him to sit down and he lowered himself on to a battered old sofa and sat watching her as she poured lemonade for the children, talking softly to them, her voice a gentle background to his thoughts. Already he felt he knew her, knew what she thought, knew how she would react to any situation, and with the knowledge came admiration. She was definitely getting under his defences, weakening him, and he was not sure he liked it. Ever since he had stormed out of Grove Hall, the day after Charles had told him he had offered for Isobel and been accepted, he had kept himself firmly under control. It had held him in good stead on the battlefields of the Peninsula and afterwards, going round the rookeries of London, doctoring the poor and trying to save the little children; it had been the only way he could keep his self-respect because he had, as a gentleman, been obliged to allow Isobel to be the innocent. To the rest of the world, he was the jilt, the one at fault.

'You will come again, won't you?' Kate asked him, as he was leaving. 'The children will like that.'

'Of course. I have to make sure they are behaving for you.'

He was being a fool, he chided himself as he rode back in the old coach, and dangerous for his hard-won peace of mind. But delightful too.

When he had gone, Kate took the children into the garden to run around and expend some of their energy before taking them up the back stairs to the nursery suite where they were given their evening meal, said their prayers—something they had only learned to do since being taken into the Hartingdon—and were tucked up in bed.

Michael protested loudly that he was older than the others and never went to sleep before midnight. Kate compromised by giving him a book to look at; though he could only read an odd word here and there, there were pictures in it and he reluctantly took it to bed with him.

'He is so determined not to go to sleep, he might end up learning to read some of it,' she told her grandmother. But when she went to look at him an hour later, he was fast asleep and the book lay open on his chest.

Joe wet the bed that first night and then howled because he was expecting a beating for it, but Kate simply scooped him up, pulled off the offending sheet and changed his night attire for his day clothes. Her cousin's boys had been dressed in petticoats at Joe's age, but he was clad in cut-down pantaloons and a loose smock. Remembering her father's admonition not to overburden Susan, Kate washed the sheet and soiled garments herself.

While she was doing that, Michael disappeared and could not be found. 'The little devil is hiding,' Kate told her grandmother. A search of the house and garden and then the surrounding area was made with the help of the servants, but the boy seemed to have disappeared into thin air. Kate was in a panic. She imagined him lying injured or—Heaven forbid!—dead in a ditch, being run over, drowned, carried off. Whatever would Dr Redfern think of her, losing one of her charges the day after he arrived? But he had to be informed and the sooner the better. She was sitting down to write a letter to him when the boy came back on his own.

'Michael, where on earth have you been?' she demanded, grabbing his arm so that he could not disappear again. 'We have been searching everywhere for you.'

He shrugged her off. 'Don' like bein' shut indoors. Went for a walk by the river. Brought this for you.' He pulled a wriggling eel from his pocket.

She recoiled. 'What am I supposed to do with that?'

'Make a pie. Very tasty is eel pie.'

'Then take it to Cook at once. And don't go off again without telling anyone. I am responsible for your safety.'

'Weren't in no danger.'

'All the same, I want you to promise you will not go near the river,' she said. 'It is dangerous. If you were to tumble in and drown, I should be very upset and in dire trouble with Dr Redfern.'

The jobation washed off him like water off a duck's back and he went off to the kitchen to present his trophy to Cook. Kate knew she ought to tell Dr Redfern what had happened, but did not want him to think she was incompetent, so decided to say nothing.

'Better send him back where he came from,' her grandmother said.

'No, I am not going back to Dr Redfern and admit I failed.'

'Stubborn as a mule. You will wear yourself out.'

Kate conceded her grandmother had a point. 'Do you think Susan's young sister, Joan, would come and help with the children, until Dr Redfern makes more permanent arrangements for them? I can afford to pay her a little.'

'Then I suggest you ask her.'

Joan was installed in the nursery suite. She was only fifteen, but she was one of a large family of whom

Susan was the eldest, and she had been helping her mother with her siblings. A younger sister was now able to take over that role, freeing Joan to follow Susan into service. She did the children's washing, swept, dusted and tidied their rooms and fetched their meals from the kitchen, glad to have a comfortable home and a wage. But it was Kate who ministered to their emotional needs, talking to them, cuddling the younger ones, giving the older ones some schooling, scolding them when necessary.

Joe was still little more than a baby and he was no trouble as far as discipline was concerned, and surprisingly Michael seemed to enjoy looking after him, though Kate had to watch what he was teaching him. Sarah was always hungry and ate everything put in front of her at such speed, Kate wondered how often she had gone without food in the past. Annie was the quiet one. She clung to Kate as if to a lifeline and followed her everywhere.

'Do not let her become too dependent on you,' Simon warned when he visited two days later.

'She is lonely and afraid. When she realises there is nothing to be afraid of, she will join in the games with the others.'

'Shall we take them to Hyde Park for a little outing?' Keeping an eye on children he had fostered out was part of his duty, although that did not include taking them out and amusing them, but he found himself wanting to prolong the visit. For once he was not thinking of the past; it was slowly beginning to lose its importance.

Kate agreed it would be a good idea. 'Papa is in his study, endeavouring to work on his book, and he will appreciate a little peace and quiet.'

As soon as they arrived, the children tore off across the grass, running and jumping and tumbling head over heels, shrieking in voices that were far from genteel. Kate and Simon followed, smiling indulgently. Neither seemed aware, or perhaps did not care, that they were the subject of gossip among the park's other visitors. There were matronly ladies out with their daughters taking the air in open carriages, young men driving phaetons and others riding handsome horses, not to mention the strollers, intent on sharing the latest *on dit*. The contrast between the well-dressed adults and the noisy plainly clad children was worth a comment. And there were some who knew who they were. The scandalous heir to Lord Redfern and the daughter of the noted scholar, Reverend Morland. What a pairing! And who were the children? Redfern's by-blows?

'It is good to see them happy,' Simon said. 'Even Annie seems to be coming out of her shell.'

'How is her mother?'

'She is not yet ready to be discharged from hospital. You are not anxious to be rid of her, are you?'

'Not at all. I am pleased to be able to help her.'

'Bless you.' He went chasing after Joe, who was wandering down to the water again, and grabbed him up before he could reach it. 'No you don't, young fellow-me-lad. You stay close to the others. Here, Annie, take his hand.' He relinquished the child to the

girl and turned to find Kate chasing Sarah with a but-
tercup in her hand. The girl was laughing as she tried
to escape. And then Michael joined in. Simon stood and
watched and was filled with wonder that in a few short
days Kate had managed to work a near miracle. He felt
a lump come to his throat and swallowed hard.

All too soon it was time to go and the children were
marshalled together to return to Holles Street. 'We have
all enjoyed ourselves today,' Kate told Simon, prompt-
ing the children to add their thanks to hers. 'You will
come again, won't you?'

'Wild horses would not keep me away.'

Doctor Redfern had been right when he said it would
not be easy; Kate found looking after four children and
coping with their tantrums and tears took all her time,
even with Joan's help. But she did not regret taking them
in and not for a moment would she have considered
sending them back to the Hartingdon. And the doctor
was a great help with his frequent visits and advice.

He arrived one afternoon, just as she was going to
take the children out for a walk. 'The weather is too nice
to be indoors,' she told him.

'Splendid idea,' he said. 'I will come too.' He knew
he ought not to spend so much time with this particular group when there were dozens of other children on
his list, but Kate was so delightfully refreshing and he
was curious to know how she managed them so easily
when other foster mothers constantly complained of the
children and their behaviour, and the small amount the
charity paid for looking after them. Kate had refused

that allowance, saying she could manage without it. She was a marvel and he blessed the day he had met her. He would not admit, even to himself, that it was not only the charity that was benefiting, that some of the tension had gone out of him too.

They went to Hyde Park as before, where they left the paths and wandered across the grass, bright with buttercups and daisies and scarlet poppies. Kate kept hold of Joe's hand, but when his little legs tired Simon hoisted him on his shoulders. The girls picked the wild flowers and Michael tried chasing a rabbit that had been so foolish as to put its head above ground. It soon disappeared down another hole and he put his arm down it, hoping to reach the animal.

'Why do you want to catch it?' Kate asked. 'It is a wild animal, you cannot tame it.'

'Don' want to, but it'd make a shilling in the market, if'n I was to get it out and kill it.'

'You would do that, kill a living creature?' she queried.

'Course. Bash it on the head with a rock.'

'Then I hope you do not catch it.'

'It's only meat,' he said, removing his arm from the hole and standing up. 'You eat meat, don't you?'

Simon laughed. 'He's got you there, Mrs Meredith.' To the boy he said, 'Taking rabbits off someone else's land is poaching, Michael, and this is Crown land. You can go to prison for it.'

'Got to catch me first,' he said complacently.

Kate looked at Simon, wondering if he was as concerned as she felt. Did the boy have no respect for the law? What had his parents taught him? Then she remembered that he had been orphaned very early in his young life and had spent most of it on the streets, until Dr Redfern found him.

They continued their walk and he was soon boasting of his prowess swimming in the Thames and diving for pieces of coal that had fallen from the barges. Kate wondered if he was going to tell the doctor about catching the eel and nudged him, shaking her head slightly. He grinned, understanding.

They returned to Holles Street in time for tea in the schoolroom, which Simon shared with them. He watched Kate dispensing cordial and bread and butter and correcting the children's manners and marvelled. She had everything he looked for in a woman: gentleness combined with practicality, a certain willfulness, which was engaging, a sympathy with other people's problems, an intolerance of bigotry, a love of children and an ability to reach out to them at any level and an indifference to gossip, which was something he had learned to ignore over the years, all combined with a serenely beautiful face and a trim figure.

He imagined her at Grove Hall, enhancing the lovely old place with her presence, surrounded by children, not foster children, but her own. And his. He shook himself suddenly. Had he run mad? Since his own engagement ended he had vowed he would not marry, and, remembering his own miserable childhood, had promised to devote his life to the welfare of deprived children. Until he had met Kate he had been content with that, but she had shown him something was

missing, that, inside the core of him, was an emptiness
that needed filling.

'Shall we take the children to the fair on Hampstead
Heath on Saturday?' he suggested, as he was leaving.
'Would you care for that? I can bring the coach and we
could have a picnic.'

'Say yes, Mrs Kate,' Michael begged her. 'I ain't
never been to the country afore.'

Kate laughed at the new name the boy had found for
her. 'Yes, Doctor, I am sure we will all enjoy it.'

Lady Morland was becoming increasingly concerned
about the time Kate was spending with Dr Redfern. 'You
will get yourself talked about,' she said, when told of the
proposed outing. 'What will the Viscount say when he
returns to England and hears about it? I really think you
should discourage the doctor from coming so often.'

'He comes to see the children. It is part of his duty.'

Her grandmother looked closely at her. 'Are you
sure that is all? Have you told him about Robert?'

'What is there to tell?' She was feeling defensive.
'Robert does not want anyone to know about our engagement until he has told his sister and his daughters.'

'Then you should find some other way of discourag-
ing Dr Redfern.'

Kate realised she did not want to do that. How could
she tell him not to call? It was part of the work he did
for the children and he might take them away from her
if she objected to his calls. Besides, she enjoyed his
visits. She felt as if she had known him for years and
years and could hardly believe it was only a matter of

weeks. They were so at one with each other in their determination to better the lives of poor children. She loved his cheerfulness, his way of taking every setback in his stride, his easy way with everyone, not only children, but adults too. She would miss him dreadfully if he did not come again, miss his broad smile, the easy way he had with everyone, not a bit stiff or formal. And he cared about destitute children, enough to try to do something for them when he could have had an easy life at home.

He arrived on Saturday in the old coach belonging to the Society to take them to Hampstead Heath and Kate pretended to be caught up in the children's excitement, laughing and joking with them and pulling Joe on to her lap as they all crowded into the coach, the girls on either side of her and Michael sitting beside Simon on the opposite seat. Simon seemed to sense something was on her mind and let her run on, smiling now and again, but refraining from comment.

Once there and they had seen the horses safely tethered, they set off to walk round the stalls with Joe on Simon's shoulders and the others dancing round them. There was everything there: clothing, furniture, tinware, chinaware, pictures and ornaments. Fire-eaters and jugglers vied for attention with boxing booths, purveyors of quack medicine and pamphlet sellers with an axe to grind. There was food and drink in abundance and the children were soon scoffing cakes and drinking lemonade. An arena had been set up by horse traders, who were busy taking wagers on a race to be held later in the day to prove their steeds were the best there was to be had. It was a wonderful day out for the children, especially as Simon gave them each a sixpence to spend on anything they fancied.

Then he turned to offer Kate his arm and they strolled round together, watching the children's bright eyes and smiling faces. Did it have to end? Must she discourage him as her grandmother had suggested?

'You are quiet, Kate,' he said. 'Are you not enjoying yourself?'

'Oh, yes,' she said. 'I was thinking…'

'About what?'

'Oh, nothing, this and that. What a lovely day it is, hardly a cloud in the sky and how happy the children are.'

'That is down to you.' The more he saw of Kate, the more Simon realised that the past was losing its significance and his hurt over Isobel was fading into nothingness.

'Not just me. It is you who took them from their sad lives and gave them hope, I simply love them.'

'And you have a great capacity for love, my dear.' He stopped himself. It was too soon to tell if the scars of the past had healed and he was reluctant to plunge headlong into another disaster. It might be that her love for children did not extend to adults. How did he know she was not still mourning the husband she had lost and if he could live up to that ideal? He had learned caution over the years and it was caution that governed him now. One great disappointment in a lifetime was enough.

She turned took at him. His expression seemed sad

and she wondered what had made it so. 'Love is a funny thing,' she said slowly. 'The more of it you give, the more it comes back to you.'

'Do you think so? Have you not heard of unrequited love, or treachery?'

'Yes, but I was not thinking about it in that context,' she said, wondering what had occasioned that remark. Could it be the woman he was supposed to have jilted? She believed him to be an honourable man and could not imagine him doing anything like that. 'Perhaps the loved one was not the right one after all.'

'Perhaps.' He paused before adding in a brighter tone. 'Come, let us catch up with the children before we lose them in the crowd.'

He sped after Michael, who was leaning over the ropes where the horses were being paraded before the race. The moment was gone and Kate could not bring herself to tell him not to visit her again. He might be hurt and that was the last thing she wanted, the very last thing.

Chapter Five

Kate was so busy with the children, she hardly gave a thought to Viscount Cranford and when he might be returning to England. Her omission was brought home to her a week later, when a letter arrived from him, telling her he was already in England and proposed calling on her that afternoon.

The news put Kate in a dreadful panic. She had always known he would come back to claim her one day and now that day had arrived. Why was she dismayed rather than joyful? Why had he not given her advance warning instead of springing it on to her like this? What should she do about the children? She could hardly send them back where they came from; they had only been with her a few weeks and had settled down so well, it would be cruel to uproot them again. What should she tell Dr Redfern? Perhaps she had been remiss not to tell him about Robert.

'I knew it was a bad idea to have those children,' her

grandmother said when she was told the contents of the letter as they sat over breakfast. 'Now, what are you going to do about them?'

'Nothing. They are settled and happy.'

'But the Viscount will want to take you out and about.'

'I will manage with Joan's help. After all, most of our engagements will be in the evening and the children will be in bed by then.'

After spending the morning with the children, she left them to Joan and went to change ready to greet her fiancé. She tried to still the trembling of her hands as she dressed carefully in a rose-coloured jaconet gown trimmed with cream lace and had Corinne arrange her hair. She was just putting the finishing touches when she heard the door knocker. 'My, goodness, he is early,' she said and rushed to slip on her shoes.

But when she reached the drawing room, she discovered it was not Robert, but Dr Redfern who was waiting for her. She stopped in confusion. 'Oh, Dr Redfern, I was not expecting you today.'

'I was in the area and thought I would take the opportunity to call.' She was looking particularly fetching, he decided, and a little flushed and breathless. He did not flatter himself that he was the cause of it. His arrival had been inopportune. 'If it is inconvenient, I will go away again.'

'No, of course not. You are always welcome. Do you want to see the children?'

The children were always used as a reason for his frequent visits, even though he knew, and he suspected she did too, that he did not need to come so often. 'No,' he said. 'I assume they are well?'

'Oh, yes, perfectly well.'

'Then I will see them another time.'

They both turned as Susan burst into the room and then stopped. 'Viscount Cranford, Mrs Meredith.'

The man who entered behind the maid was tall, lean and classically handsome. He wore a slate-grey frock coat, and dove-grey kerseymere pantaloon trousers. His waistcoat was white, as was his meticulously tied cravat. He bowed. 'Katherine.'

'My lord.' She bobbed a curtsy, trying to still the swift beating of her heart. 'May I present Dr Simon Redfern. Doctor Redfern, Viscount Cranford.'

He was a darkly handsome man, Simon was obliged to admit, as he bowed in response to the other's stiff acknowledgement.

'I sincerely hope no one is ill,' Robert said.

'No, we are all well,' Kate put in. 'The Doctor is here on behalf of the Hartingdon Home.' She turned to Susan, who stood uncertainly by the door. 'Susan, bring in the tea things, please.'

'I was about to leave,' Simon said. 'Mrs Meredith, your obedient. Viscount.' He bowed to them both and followed Susan from the room, though he would have given almost anything to have heard what was going on behind him.

'What is the Hartingdon Home?' Robert asked as soon as the door had closed.

'It is part of Cousin Eleanor's charitable society, set

up to look after the children of the poor. The Home is overcrowded and I am fostering some of the children for a short time.'

'Fostering?' he queried. 'Good heavens, you surely do not mean you are housing urchins from the slums?'

'Children are children wherever they come from.' She was a little annoyed by his evident abhorrence. 'And they are as good as gold.' She hoped they would not do something in the next few minutes to prove her wrong.

'And Redfern is involved?'

'Yes. He told me he sees so much deprivation in the course of his work, he felt he had to do something to alleviate it, so *The Society for the Welfare of Destitute Children* was set up with Lady Eleanor Hartingdon and other benefactors, to house the children, either in the Home or with foster mothers.'

'But how did you become involved?'

She told him about finding Joe as succinctly as she could, but even without the visit to Seven Dials she could see he was appalled by the tale. 'Doctor Redfern asked Papa and me to a meeting and we met Lady Eleanor there. The Society home was overcrowded and so I offered to take some of the children.'

'But is he a gentleman?'

She laughed. 'Indeed, yes, a very gentlemanly gentleman.'

'I was not referring to his conduct.'

'If you are talking about breeding, he is the heir of Lord Redfern of Grove Hall, Finchingfield.'

'Unmarried?'

'I believe so.'

'Gentleman or not, you should not be receiving him alone.'

'My lord, he comes to see the children. It is part of the work he is required to do for the charity. Would you have me turn him away?' She had not expected to be quarrelling with him the minute he returned. It was not a good beginning.

'No, of course not. But where are Lady Morland and The Reverend?'

'Papa is in his study working on his book. Grandmama is about somewhere. I think she meant to be discreet and allow us our reunion in private.'

'Yes, of course.' His severe expression suddenly changed to a smile and he stepped forward to take both her hands in his and lift them to his lips, one by one. 'I have been looking forward to it for so long.'

'I, too.' He had been a great comfort to her after Edward's death and had brought her out of her grief and given her strength to go on. His letters had been the mainstay of her existence for months, until she felt able to face the world again. She must remember that and then this awkwardness would go away. She smiled and led him to a sofa where they sat side by side. 'When did you arrive in England?'

'Yesterday. You received my letter?'

'Yes, thank you. Are you home to stay?'

'I do not think so. I have finished my time in Paris, but expect to receive advancement and be posted elsewhere in due course. I hope it might be Austria, but I have yet to hear from the Foreign Office. In the meantime I have received an invitation to a ball at the

Austrian Embassy on the twentieth of June. I shall be delighted if you will accompany me.'

'But that is only a week away.'

'Yes, I am sorry it is short notice, but it is very important that I attend.' He stopped to correct himself. 'That we both attend. You see, the Foreign Office likes its diplomats to be married...'

'They are looking me over too.' She was horrified.

'In a way I suppose they are,' he admitted. 'But you have nothing to worry about. I am sure you will not let me down.'

Kate was not so sure. Supposing she inadvertently said or did something that was unacceptable in those exalted circles and they rejected him on her account—whatever would she do? She had been nervous before; now she was shaking with the enormity of what lay before her. He turned to smile at her. 'Do not look so stricken, Katherine, you will come through with flying colours, I am sure.'

Susan returned with the tea tray, closely followed by Lady Morland who had decided they had been alone together long enough. The old lady greeted him fulsomely, and while tea was dispensed she asked him about Paris and if the city was much changed since the war, and about the social life and the fashions, all of which he answered knowledgeably. It left Kate to muse on what he had told her. She felt as if the breath had been sucked out of her. It had all happened so suddenly.

She pulled herself back to pay attention and realised Robert was explaining about the Embassy ball and how important it was to him, and her grandmother was nodding and smiling. 'I thought of announcing our betrothal at the ball,' he was saying. 'But I decided it would not be appropriate at a function like that. Perhaps later at some other function.'

The prospect of being on show at the ball was enough to have her in a quake without the added apprehension of a public announcement. 'If we need a celebration at all, I would rather it was a private one,' she said.

'As you wish.' He rose to take his leave. 'I am going home to Cranford Hall tomorrow to acquaint my sister of our betrothal and will not be back until the morning of the ball, so I will not see you again before then. I shall call for you at eight o'clock.'

'I am looking forward to it,' she said, not altogether truthfully, as he put his lips to the back of her hand and took his leave.

'I told you he would want to take you out and about,' Lady Morland said, as the door closed on him. 'We must pay another visit to Madame Lorette as soon as possible.'

Kate was about to suggest that she wore the gown she had worn to Hartingdon House, but decided it would not do. It would forever remind her of Dr Redfern and that waltz on the terrace. Neither had spoken of it since, but she knew it had marked a turning point in their relationship. It could no longer be called a purely business one. And yet she did not know what to call it. Friendship was the nearest she could think of, but that wasn't quite right either. Whatever it was, she would be very sad if it were severed.

Next morning, she left the children with Joan and set off with her grandmother for Bond Street. Lady

Morland was a very good customer, but even so, Madame Lorette was dubious about making a gown in the time available, even if she took her girls off every other order. 'I shall have to wear the gown I wore to Hartingdon House,' Kate said, a statement that made her ladyship throw up her hands in horror.

'You cannot have the *haut monde* think you are so impoverished you cannot afford a new gown for the most important ball of your life,' her grandmother said. 'Perhaps we should go elsewhere.'

Madame Lorette certainly did not want that to happen. 'I have a half-finished order that has been cancelled,' she said. 'It is about madam's size. We could easily alter it to fit.'

It was brought out from its muslin wrapping for Kate to see. It was made of the finest gossamer, in a blue the colour of a summer sky, intended to be worn over a white satin slip. It had puff sleeves and a round neck and the bodice was caught under the bosom with a cluster of white flowers from which a wide blue ribbon floated down to the hem. It was far more costly that Kate would ever have agreed to, but as it was a cancelled order, Madame Lorette offered them a substantial discount. Kate put it on and stood on a chair for one of the seamstresses to mark where alterations were needed and to pin up the hem, after which it was back to Holles Street and the children.

'Joan told us you are goin' to a ball,' Annie said, when she went up to join them. 'What's a ball?'

'It is a very grand occasion when everyone dresses

in their very best clothes and goes to a ballroom to dance to the music of an orchestra.' She paused. 'Shall you like to learn to dance?'

'I can,' said Michael and began cavorting all over the place, making Kate smile.

'A ball is a little less boisterous than that,' she said, and proceeded to teach the girls some of the steps, humming a tune as she did so. She did not notice Simon creep into the room and sit down at the piano, until he began to play for them. She stopped, overcome by embarrassment. 'Oh, Dr Redfern, I did not hear you come in.'

'Susan was busy and told me to find my own way up. Go on dancing with Annie. I will play for you.'

She handed Annie over to Michael so that she could give Sarah a turn, while little Joe sat on the floor at Simon's feet, sucking his thumb. It was a cosy domestic scene, not lost on Kate. He was made to be a husband and father and she wondered why he had not married. Surely that broken engagement was not still haunting him? She would not be put off by it, because she knew him well enough to know there was more to it than the gossips would have. If only…

He stopped playing and his hands fell to his lap. The children became still as if they realised something was in the air, something they could not be expected to understand when Simon and Kate did not understand it themselves. He moved over to her. 'Come, Mrs Meredith, let us show them how to waltz.' He grasped her hands and pulled her to her feet, then began to hum, dancing her round and round, much to the delight of the four children.

'Do you remember?' he murmured. 'The music and the moonlight and our steps fitting so well together?'

'Yes, I remember.' How could she forget? She had only to shut her eyes and she was back on the terrace in the moonlight, the distant music setting a time and rhythm to their beating hearts. She could feel again the pressure of his hand on her back, the warmth of his breath upon her cheek. Those few minutes had been very special. And it came to her in a sudden flash of insight that he was important to her, more important than Robert.

'I did not want it to end,' he said, unaware of her tumbling thoughts. 'It was like a dream from which one is forced to wake to find reality is nothing like the fantasy.'

His words served to bring her back to the present and she became aware of the children watching and listening. She stopped and broke away, her cheeks flaming.

'Mrs Kate is going to a ball,' Annie said in the silence that followed.

Simon looked at Kate, one eyebrow raised. Now would be the time to explain about Robert, but she could not do that in front of the children. 'At the Austrian Embassy,' she said.

'Escorted by Viscount Cranford?'

'Yes.'

'Will you be going to the ball, Dr Redfern?' Sarah asked.

'Me? Oh, no, it will be much too grand for me.'

'Doctor Redfern is teasing,' Kate told them, forcing herself to sound normal. 'Of course it is not too grand for him. It is simply that he has not been invited.'

'Do you have to be invited?' Michael asked. 'Can't you just turn up?'

Simon laughed. 'No, young man, you cannot just turn up. There are very strict rules.'

'Oh, rules!' Michael said. 'Who cares about rules?'

This precipitated a lecture from Simon about why rules were important and what would happen to the world if there were none, which silenced the boy for a few minutes, but he was soon his old self again. 'Then if I was you,' he said, 'I'd make sure I had an invitation.'

Kate risked a look at Simon, who turned away to look at the doll Annie was playing with, and she quickly changed the subject. After he had gone, Kate read them a story until it was time to prepare for bed, though her mind was most definitely not on what she was reading. Doubts about her future were beginning to surface with unsettling frequency and growing larger with every day that passed. Nerves, she told herself firmly.

On the evening of the ball, Lady Morland came to her room to watch her put on the dress. It was finished off with a silk shawl, blue shoes, matching blue gloves and a bead reticule.

'Lovely,' her grandmother said, watching Corinne arrange her hair in thick coils about her ears and fasten them with pretty combs. 'You will be the belle of the ball.'

Kate laughed, though it sounded hollow to her ears. 'I am a little too old for that, and in any case I am not sure I want to be the centre of attention.'

'You had better become used to it, Kate. When you are Viscountess Cranford you will be in the public eye. What you wear and what you do is bound to be the subject of discourse.'

'Oh, no, I hope not. I am sure to make some dreadful *faux pas*.'

'Do not be so silly, child. You are a Hartingdon and a Morland, your breeding cannot be questioned. Just remember that and hold your head up. It would not hurt to be a little more disdainful.'

And with this meaningless comment, the old lady dismissed Kate's concerns and went off with Corinne to be dressed herself. That Kate was a widow and not a green girl mattered not to the old lady, who was determined she should be properly chaperoned on this most important of occasions.

Her granddaughter returned to the children. She had established a routine with the children of washing and changing into night attire and had fixed a time for them to go to bed, depending on their age, which she was determined to stick to, but she had promised them they should see her in her gown before she left.

Robert arrived exactly on time to find Kate coming down the stairs at the top of which four eager young faces watched her progress. He gave them a glance of disapproval, then turned his attention to Kate, bowing over her hand and saying, 'You look very beautiful tonight, Katherine.'

'Thank you.' The blue dress flowed about her slim figure and the silk shawl set off her shoulders and creamy neck on which was fastened a necklace of sapphires set in silver filigree, one of the few pieces she had inherited from her mother. Corinne had arranged her hair becomingly in ringlets that fell from a coronet of hair, and added a little discreet colour to her cheeks. 'You are far too pale,' she had said.

Robert was resplendent in dress uniform, the gold of the braid, epaulettes and buttons of the coat gleaming against the red material and the decorations he had won hanging from his neck. By contrast his white breeches and stockings were pristine. His hair had been carefully cut. She knew he had taken every bit as much care over his appearance as she had, which did nothing to make her feel any better.

He produced a narrow box, which he handed to Kate. 'A betrothal present.'

She took it and opened it. Inside, nestling on black velvet, was a diamond necklace, which flashed in the lamplight. 'Oh, my lord,' she gasped. 'This is too much…'

'Not at all. When we are married you shall have the pick of all the Cranford jewels; this piece does not belong to the family collection. I want you to have it as a token of my earnest desire to make you happy.'

She wondered briefly why he imagined expensive jewels were the way to her heart, but thrust the thought from her as unworthy. 'Thank you.'

'Shall I help you put it on?' he added, when she stood with it draped over her hand as if she did not quite know what to do with it.

'Oh, yes, of course.'

The blue stones came off and the heavy necklace went on where it lay against her throat, the stones sparkly like pieces of ice. His fingers felt cold against her skin as they fastened the clasp. She sped up to her room to put the sapphires back in her drawer, shooing the children away from the landing as she did so.

Returning downstairs, she found Lady Morland, dressed in mauve taffeta, waiting to accompany them. After going to the study to say goodbye to her father and show him the gift, she took a deep breath and proclaimed herself ready. Aware of the children still giggling and whispering on the landing, she dared not look back at them as Robert escorted her and her grandmother to his carriage, which was waiting at the gate.

The ball was a dazzling affair. The guests consisted of diplomats and their wives from many countries and every one of them sparkled with jewels, even the men with their decorations, rings, cravat pins and ornamented quizzing glasses. The colourful dresses of the ladies were easily matched by the bright hues of the uniforms of most of the men. The Prince Regent was there, dressed in the blue Hussar uniform he had devised for his own regiment.

Robert led her forward and presented her to his Highness and then the Foreign Secretary, the Austrian Ambassador, and several other dignitaries whose names she forgot almost as soon as she had heard them, so bemused she felt. 'You must always try to remember people's names,' Robert whispered to er. 'It flatters them.'

Later he left her with Captain Feltwell, a friend from his army days, while he went off to have a private conversation with the Ambassador. Captain Feltwell was young and cheerful and something of a dandy. He asked her to dance, during which they did not say much, the steps of the dance making conversation difficult, but afterwards, while they promenaded the ballroom, he kept up a lively conversation with tales of his adventures in the war in which Robert featured largely, then, having exhausted that topic, asked her about herself, which she did not mind at all. 'Cranford tells me you have been married before,' he said.

'Yes. My husband was killed at Vittoria.'

'My condolences. I am surprised it was so long ago.'

'Why?'

'You seem so young. You could not have been more than a schoolgirl when you married.'

'Captain, that is nothing but flummery.'

'You have children?'

'No, we were not married very long.'

'Oh. I saw you with some children in Hyde Park the other day with a…their papa perhaps? You appeared to be enjoying each other's company. Frolicking, quite uninhibited.'

Unless he was singularly unintelligent, he must know she was not old enough to have mothered Michael, Annie or Sarah and was fishing for information, but could see no reason for secrecy. 'I expect the children you saw were—'

She got no further before Robert's voice interrupted. 'Feltwell, I must take Mrs Meredith away for the moment. We will see you again later.' And with that he took a firm grip on her elbow and led her away.

'My lord, were you not a little abrupt with your friend?' she admonished, as they walked back to where her grandmother sat, enjoying a gossip with a friend she had found among the guests.

'No, I do not think so. You were about to tell him about those dreadful children, weren't you?'

'They are not dreadful. They have simply lacked the advantages of a stable and loving home life. I am trying to remedy the deficiency in some measure.'

'I am appalled that you took them to Hyde Park where you could be observed.'

'Why not? Fresh air and exercise is good for them and it is better than letting them wreck the garden.'

'I hope they are gone when I next call on you.'

'I cannot promise that, my lord. Doctor Redfern has to find permanent homes for them. At least for all but Annie—she will go back to her own home as soon as her mother leaves hospital.'

'He is a queer fish.'

'Who is?'

'Redfern. It is almost as if he is denying his birthright, hob-nobbing with the ne'er-do-wells.'

'Oh, how can you say that?' She rose immediately to the doctor's defence. 'Doctor Redfern is a philanthropist…'

'I hope I may be called a philanthropist, but that does not mean lowering my standards. I give generously to charity, as is my duty, but I would never think of entertaining the object of that charity in my own home.' He moved away from the seats where Lady Morland sat and led her from the ballroom into an anteroom, where groups of people stood about talking. 'I have something to say to you,' he said, guiding her to a corner where there were two empty chairs. 'Please sit down.'

She sat down, wondering what was coming. He sat beside her and leaned forward. 'It has yet to be formally announced, but I have been offered the post I wanted at the embassy in Austria. I am to take it up on the first day of August. I want you to accompany me as my wife.'

'But that is only six weeks away!' She could not hide her dismay. Why hadn't she realised what his ambition would mean to her?

'You sound reluctant.'

'It such a big step. I shall have to leave Papa and Grandmother and my home And I really would have liked a little longer to settle my affairs…' She was stumbling over her reasons, none of which sounded very convincing in her ears.

'I have told the Foreign Secretary I shall be married by the time I take up the appointment. It is important, Katherine.'

What could she say? That she had changed her mind about marrying him? The consequences of that would be disastrous. It would ruin his career, and as for her— no one of any consequence would marry a jilt. She would be condemned to a life of widowhood. And there was her father and grandmother to consider, too; they did not deserve the ignominy such a step would mean.

'Very well,' she said with quiet resignation. Others had made a success of a marriage in which love was not the dominant factor and she must too. 'I will be ready.'

'Good. I will put an announcement in the *Gazette*.'

She found herself wondering if he had delayed doing that until after she had been presented to the Foreign Secretary and the Austrian Ambassador and passed their critical appraisal. 'Have you a particular date in mind?'

'I leave that to you as long as we are married before I take up my appointment, that is all I ask.'

'I will talk to my father and grandmother. I am sure Grandmama will want as long as possible to make the arrangements. She likes to do things properly, you know.' She said it with a smile, but already she was trembling at the enormity of what she was undertaking.

'Of course, that is as it should be.' He paused. 'And you will get rid of those children?'

'I shall have to, shan't I? I cannot leave them to Papa and Grandmama. It is a pity, since they have settled down so well.'

'Perhaps you should have thought of that before taking them on.'

'I know I should, but I felt so sorry for them and I wanted to help and I had no idea you would want the wedding to take place so quickly or that we should be leaving the country immediately afterwards. I thought when you said you were coming home, you meant to stay. It will be a disappointment to Dr Redfern, having to begin all over again finding somewhere for them.'

'To hell with Redfern,' he muttered under his breath,

but then he smiled and stood up, holding out his hand to her. 'Come, let us go and enjoy the dancing. We can talk about it tomorrow.'

They returned to the ballroom and the rest of the evening passed in a blur of colour and music and muddled thoughts.

At two in the morning carriages were called for and Robert escorted her and Lady Morland home. He did not come in when they arrived, but saw them to the door and promised to call the next afternoon to discuss the arrangements for the wedding.

The Reverend had retired and Lady Morland was very fatigued, so they said goodnight to each other and climbed the stairs to their beds. Before she went to her room, Kate visited the nursery suite where Joan sat knitting. 'Have they been good?'

'Yes, though Joe cried a bit. He thought you were not coming back, but I told him you would be here when he woke up.'

'Thank you, Joan. You go off to your own bed now and you do not need to hurry in the morning. I can manage the children's breakfast.'

The maid disappeared and Kate crept along the landing to their bedrooms. The boys were asleep and she stood looking down at Joe's golden curls and was overwhelmed with a need to cuddle him. But she desisted. Dr Redfern had warned her against becoming too attached to him and she must heed the warning, because she was going to have to part with him and the others sooner than she had expected. On the other hand, she might, before another year passed, be mother to her own little boy. She left the boys and moved on to the girls. Sarah was snoring, but Annie was wide awake. 'Not asleep, Annie? It is very late, you know.'

'I wanted to wait for you to come back. Joan said you were going to marry that man and then you would go away.'

'So I am. But not for a little while yet.'

'I didn't like him.' It was said flatly.

'Now, Annie, how can you know that? You have never spoken to him. He is a very nice gentleman.'

'He made you take off your lovely blue necklace.'

'He did not make me take it off,' Kate said, fingering the diamonds at her throat. 'He bought me this and it is only polite to wear something if it is given to you as a gift.'

'I like the blue one best.'

'They are both very fine. Now you must go to sleep. It will be morning before you know it.'

Annie sighed and snuggled down into a bed a hundred times more comfortable than anything she had known before, and looked up at Kate. 'Goodnight, Mrs Kate.'

Kate smiled at the mode of address. 'Goodnight, Annie. Sleep well.'

She was just moving away when she heard the child say, 'I like Dr Redfern best. You could marry him.'

Later, in her own bed, she lay awake. Annie's words had unsettled her, making her realise that once she married Robert, she would not see Dr Redfern again. Simon. Was he the hub of her disquiet? She put her hand to her face and was surprised to find her cheeks were wet. She rubbed at them with the back of her hand and tried to sleep, but when it came at last she was beset by bad dreams, none of which made sense.

Next morning, she set the older children some arith-metic to do and bade Annie look after Joe while Joan was busy with her daily chores, then she joined her father and grandmother to discuss the arrangements for the wedding, which would have to be on Saturday the twenty-sixth of July at the very latest.

'I hate to be rushed,' the old lady said. 'Why can he not give you a decent time to arrange it? There will be whispers.'

Kate managed a laugh. 'About Viscount Cranford? Oh, Grandmama, that is absurd. No one could ever accuse him of impropriety. As for me, what have they to whisper about? I am not interesting enough to be tattled over.' Even as she spoke, she remembered Captain Feltwell. How many other people had seen her with Dr Redfern and commented on it?

'It is still too quick. We shall have to send the invi-tations out this week to give people time to reply. And you must have a whole new wardrobe. There will be re-ceptions and balls, entertaining and being entertained when you arrive in Austria. You will be Viscountess Cranford and in the thick of high society.'

Kate had hardly given the matter any thought, had been thinking of the wedding as the end of everything, when it was really only a beginning, the beginning of the rest of her life, and her heart sank. She had come to the conclusion there was nothing for it but to agree; the alternative was too terrible to contemplate, not only for her and Robert, but for her father and grandmother. 'I wish we could go somewhere and marry quietly without all this fuss,' she said. 'Just you and Papa for witnesses. After all, it is a second marriage for both of us.'

'Not to be thought of,' the dowager said. 'Think of the Viscount's position.'

She did think about it, all the time. Her life was going to change beyond anything she had dreamed of and sooner than she expected. If only she could have had more time, she might have been able to find a way out of her dilemma.

The old lady turned to her son. 'I assume you are going to marry your daughter, Thomas?'

'I can hardly marry her *and* give her away. I'll see if the bishop will conduct the ceremony.'

'And the wedding breakfast,' her grandmother went on, her head buzzing with the excitement of it all. 'We must think about that too.'

'Why not have it at Morland House?' her father suggested. 'It has some elegant reception rooms. I am sure James and Lizzie will agree.'

'Capital idea!' the old lady said. 'It will impress the Viscount and his guests no end. Let us go this afternoon and put it to them.'

'Thank you, Grandmama,' Kate said. 'Are you sure it is not all too much for you?'

'Fustian! I am not in my dotage yet. And I shall enjoy it. And we must pay a visit to Madame Lorette tomorrow. If she is going to create your wedding gown, she must have as much time as you can give her.'

Everything was going to plan, at least her grand-mother's plan. Kate herself was beginning to feel breathless and more and more afraid. This wedding was not going to be anything like the quiet ceremony she and Edward had enjoyed, but then he had been a Captain of a cavalry regiment and not a Viscount, and his regiment had been expecting to be sent abroad at any time. And they had been so much in love it did not matter.

'And that's another thing,' her ladyship went on. 'The children. You cannot look after them and get ready for your wedding at the same time. You will be worn out.'

'I cannot turn them out, can I? I shall have to speak to Dr Redfern and give him a little notice.' Even speaking his name made her falter. 'The poor things have been pushed about enough in their young lives. I want to be sure they are well and happy wherever they go.'

Robert, when informed of the discussion later that afternoon, heartily approved of the idea of using Morland House, but he had little patience with her pre-varicating over the children and said she must simply tell Dr Redfern to take them elsewhere, which she refused to do. It made the atmosphere between them strained for a time, but as each was anxious to please the other, it was soon mended and, over cups of tea and Cook's honey cakes, they set about arranging a wedding. He agreed a date and a time for the nuptials and promised to give Kate a list of people he would like invited. She asked him whether his daughters—Roberta, who was ten, and Caroline, who was eight—would like to be her attendants, but he said he was not sure. 'I shall have to ask my sister what she thinks. I do not want them upset.'

'You think they will be upset?' she queried, taken aback.

'They might.'

'Why? I am becoming part of the family, not taking you from them. I shall be their stepmama as well as your wife.'

'That is true and I will make arrangements for you to meet them. Now it is time I was off.' He rose to take his leave and bowed to Lady Morland and the Reverend.

Kate rose to accompany him to the front the front door. 'You will let me know when to expect your girls,' she said. 'I am sure we shall deal well together. It will be an adventure for all of us, learning about a new country.'

'They are not coming to Austria with us, Katherine.'

'Why not?' She was shocked.

'They are happy and settled with my sister and have their lessons with their cousins and taking them to a strange country will certainly unsettle them, especially as we shall be busy entertaining and being entertained. It is a large part of the job.'

'I see.' But she did not see. 'Later, perhaps.'

'Yes, later they can come for a visit. And of course I shall have home leave in due course and probably in a year or two another posting, and we cannot drag them all over the world with us.'

Kate was about to say, 'What about our own children,' but decided against it. When it happened, there was no way she would part with them. She watched him go down the path to his phaeton and then turned back indoors, pondering on what he had said about his daughters and the way he seemed to have shifted their welfare on to his sister. Did he not like children? Not even his own? All her doubts resurfaced and overwhelmed her.

She returned to the drawing room where her grand-mother had already begun on a list of things to do. 'You will have to speak to Dr Redfern about the children now, Kate,' she said.

'I know.'

'Would you like me to do it?'

'No, I must.'

'The sooner the better.'

'Yes.' If she had any thought of confiding her doubts to her grandmother, she found she could not. She must do what was expected of her.

Chapter Six

Simon called the following afternoon, suggesting an outing to Richmond Park. 'We could combine it with nature study,' he said, smiling and tearing at Kate's heart.

While the older ones got themselves ready, she helped Joe into his boots, worrying all the time about breaking the news of her impending marriage and telling him the children would have to be moved again. She felt guilty about it and realised it had perhaps been unkind to take them in the first place, but, oh, how they had wrenched her soft heart and she wanted to make them happy. The wrench would be even greater now she had come to know them and love them. Doctor Redfern had warned her about that but she had thought herself strong enough to resist it. She was not strong at all or she would have had the courage to reject Robert. But how could she? If it were only her own happiness she had to consider, she would have braved the condemnation and followed her heart, but every reason she had for going on with the wedding was as valid now as it ever had been. And Dr Redfern, this gentle, caring man, would have to be told.

Once they had left the coach in a convenient spot, the children ran off to pick wild flowers; Kate had said she would help them name them afterwards. Watching them, she was glad it was not the sort of day out that the *haut monde* habitually enjoyed and they were unlikely to be seen by anyone who knew her, like Captain Feltwell, who had not confined himself to baiting her, if what her cousin James had told her was true.

She and her grandmother had gone to Morland House to tell her cousins about the betrothal and ask if they would allow their home to be used for the wedding breakfast and if their eldest daughter Charlotte could be one of her bridal attendants, to which Lizzie had agreed whole-heartedly. 'I have no doubt it will be the wedding of the year,' she said. She was a tall slim woman, not known for her beauty, but she had a pleasant, open countenance and was adored by her husband and four children.

'Don't tell her that,' her grandmother had put in with a chuckle. 'She is already in a ferment over it. Wants a quiet wedding, would you believe?'

'Not possible,' Lizzie had said. 'Given the standing of the groom in Society.'

'So I told her.'

While they were chatting, James had arrived back

from Tattersalls where he had been looking over some horses. After being told the news, offering his felicitations and endorsing his wife's agreement over the wedding breakfast, he had added, 'What's this I hear about Kate and a mob of slum children invading the Holles Street?'

'Where did you hear that?' Kate wanted to know.

'At Tattersalls. I met Feltwell there. He said he'd seen you cavorting in the park with them. Man with you too.'

'That was Dr Redfern.' Kate had gone on to explain about the doctor and the charity and how she had taken in four of the children.

'That's all very well,' James had said. 'I admire your kind heart, but it won't do to be talked about, you know. Doctor Redfern is already known as an eccentric and there is that business over his broken engagement. Did his reputation no good at all and mud sticks, you know.'

'If people cannot find anything else to gossip about, then they must lead very impoverished lives,' she retorted.

'Does the Viscount know of the children?'

'Of course. In any case, they are only with us for a week or two, just until Dr Redfern can find permanent homes for them.'

'I say no more, then, but I must warn you, Kate, Feltwell is a notorious gabblegrinder, so please watch your step.'

She was wondering for the hundredth time what Captain Feltwell could possibly have against her, when Simon's voice broke her reverie. 'You are quiet, Kate,' he murmured. 'Are you not enjoying yourself?'

'Oh, yes,' she said. 'I was thinking…'

'About what?'

'Oh, nothing, this and that.'

When they arrived home she sent the children up to the nursery to play with some of the toys she had had as a child, while she spoke to Simon over cups of tea in the drawing room. Lady Morland, knowing what they would be talking about, had found an excuse to leave them.

'Out with it,' he said with a smile, after they had been sitting in silence for a whole minute.

'Out with what?'

'Whatever is on your mind. You have been in a brown study the whole afternoon. Is there something wrong?'

'Not wrong exactly.' She paused and then burst out, 'Oh, I can't bear it. I have done more harm than good having the children here.'

'How can you say so? That is nonsense.'

'No. You see, I am to be married sooner than I expected and will be leaving here, so I am afraid I must ask you to make other arrangements for the children. You do not know how sorry I am, not only to lose the children, but to lose your good opinion of me.' It all came out in a breathless rush.

'Married?' He was so startled he only just managed to save his tea from spilling. 'I did not know you were even contemplating it.'

'The Viscount wanted to delay the announcement until he returned from Paris and could tell his daughters first.'

'Viscount Cranford?' He felt angry, betrayed, as if she had deliberately deceived him. Why had it never come out in the course of conversation that she was engaged to be married, unless she had been deliberately withholding the information from him? Why could she not have told him when they were dancing with the children and talking about the ball? Or when they talked about her having children of her own?

He would never have let her have the children if he had known. He certainly would not have taken them to Hyde Park, or to Hampstead Heath, or Richmond Park. Why had he not obeyed his own rules to hold himself aloof? Why had he not stuck to his vow to hold back from all women? He had allowed her to pierce his defences, to make him think she was different enough to make him forget Isobel and wonder if there might be a future for them together. He should have known, the minute he set eyes on Cranford, what was in the wind. But he hadn't. What a blind fool he had been! It was a monumental effort of will to speak calmly. 'May I offer my felicitations.'

'Thank you.' She sensed his anger, though not the reason for it, assuming it was only the fate of the children that concerned him. 'But you do not have to take the children away immediately. I can keep them until you find somewhere else for them. In truth, I would like to have them for a little longer.'

'But surely you will be busy? I believe a wedding takes a prodigious amount of organising.' He said it lightly to relieve the tension, but inside he was in turmoil. He wanted to yell at her, take her by the shoulders and shake her, tell her that Cranford was not the man for her. Make her see. But that would only compound his idiocy.

'Not too busy that I cannot look after them as I have been doing for a little longer,' she said. 'And I do not want to uproot them again before I need to. They have settled in so well.'

He cooled his anger. He had no right to be angry with her; she did not know what had been in his mind, and he thanked God for that. If he had spoken, what an idiot he would have made of himself. A second humiliation was more than he could have tolerated. 'When is the wedding to be?' he asked, once more in control of himself.

'The last Saturday in July, the twenty-sixth. I hope you will be able to attend.'

'Thank you,' he said, though he told himself he would find some pressing engagement not to go; he could not bear to see her married to Viscount Cranford. He was convinced the man was wrong for her. What he could not understand is why she could not see it for herself. 'How did you meet the Viscount?'

'He was my late husband's senior officer and was with him when he died at the Battle of Vittoria. He was slightly injured himself and came home to recuperate and came to see me to offer his condolences. He was a great help and comfort to me and after he returned to the Peninsula we kept up a correspondence.'

'And you fell in love with him.'

'I do not think it was as sudden as that. We are a widow and widower and you would not expect the giddiness of youth. We developed a fondness for each other.'

That was all it was, she admitted to herself, and even that was fading as she became more and more disillusioned.

He was not sure if it was the answer he expected or wanted. It did not make him feel any more sure that this was a match made in heaven. And she was far from old; he put her at twenty-five, no more, young enough to display a little giddiness, especially as she was obviously a demonstrative woman who did not hide her feelings. And that was another thing; she had never hinted she did not welcome his attention. There was that dance on the terrace at Lady Eleanor's ball; something had happened between them then, momentous enough for him to dwell on it again and again. And there had been other occasions when they had been close, when he had allowed himself to hope.

'I wish you happy,' he said. 'And do not worry about the children. I will take them off your hands in good time.'

'There is no rush. I can manage a little longer. Joan is a great help and my grandmother has taken over most of the arrangements for the wedding. She is as excited as a child over it.'

'But you are not?'

'Of course I am,' she said quickly.

He stood up. 'I will let you know what arrangements I have made.' His voice was cool, his tone abrupt. 'Are you going to tell the children, or shall I?'

'I will tell them. If it were not for moving to the British Embassy in Austria immediately after the wedding, I would ask my husband if we could keep them.'

He knew that was out of the question; the stiff-necked Viscount Cranford would never countenance such a thing and she must know that.

After he had left, Kate made an especially nice tea for her charges and sat with them while they ate it. All but Annie had been half-starved when they came to her and were beginning to fill out. Had she condemned them to going back where they came from, to hunger and poverty, dirt and rags? It was breaking her heart to think she had. And Dr Redfern was hurt and angry. She could hardly blame him, but she was hurting too and the reason for it was not hard to find.

Michael and Sarah accepted the news with a shrug of their shoulders. They had been shunted about between the Home and foster families for years and had learned to take the good along with the bad. She worried about what sort of adults they would make with a background like that. Joe, of course, did not understand and only Annie cried at the thought of going back to the Hartingdon Home. Kate hoped the child's mother would be fit enough for her to go to her own home before that became necessary.

After the others had run off to prepare for bed, Kate took Annie on to her lap to console her. 'Your mama will soon be better and then you can go home again. Think of your stay with me as a little holiday.'

'I don't want you to go away.'

'But I must. You understood when I explained about going on a ship and living abroad, didn't you?'

'Yes, but must you?'

Kate pondered this. 'Yes,' she said. 'But what do you say to being one of the attendants at my wedding?'

'What's that?'

By the time Kate had explained, the child was much more cheerful, but Kate wondered what the Viscount would say. She had made the suggestion on the spur of the moment, without thinking, and she could not and would not retract. And surely she could have whom she pleased to attend her on her wedding day?

She had gone downstairs for dinner and afterwards helped her grandmother to write out invitations, wishing the list was not quite so long and wondering how many would accept, given the short notice.

It was while they were doing this she told Lady Morland about her promise to Annie, which appalled the old lady. 'Oh, Kate, you foolish, foolish child,' she said. 'Whatever made you do it?'

'She was upset at having to go back to the Home and I felt I had let her down. It was meant to be a sort of recompense…'

'She is highly unsuitable, you must know that. Do you want to quarrel with your husband before you even get him to the altar?'

'The choice of attendants is mine, Grandmother, and Annie is a sweet girl and knows how to behave. She is thrilled at the prospect and I will not go back on my word.'

'Oh, dear, I can see squalls ahead. Kate, you have been having your own way for far too long.'

'Grandmama, I am a mature widow. I am not a newly

come-out innocent who knows nothing of anything except to obey her father until she is married and then obey her husband. I have had a measure of independence and I value it.'

'It is not too late, you know.'

'What for?'

'To cancel the wedding. It will cause a dreadful scandal, but we should live it down eventually, but it would mean you would never have another offer.' She paused. 'It comes down to whether you can accommodate yourself to the Viscount's ways or say goodbye to ever having a family of your own.'

'Of course I am not going to cancel it. Whoever heard of such a thing, especially over something as trivial as who should be my bridal attendants? Now, please say no more about it.' She spoke sharply because her grandmother had only put into words the doubts and worries she already had. Would there be squalls or would she learn to subjugate herself to Robert's will? She shook herself. 'I must go and see to the children's tea.'

She went up to the schoolroom, where Michael was teasing Annie and she put the Viscount and her wedding from her mind to deal with them.

The drawing room at Cranford House in Upper Brook Street was crammed to suffocation. It seemed to Kate that half the *haut monde* was there, all talking at once, all with raised voices, trying to make themselves heard. This was not how she expected to meet Robert's daughters and she began to wonder if she had made a mistake in the day or the hour. But the invitation, sent by Mrs Withersfield, had definitely said Tuesday the twenty-fourth of June at two o'clock of the afternoon.

She had dressed with care, not wishing to seem dowdy, or outrageously modish. The impression she wanted to create was a naturalness that the children could understand, neither top-lofty nor girlish. She did not want them to be shy of her, or disdainful either. The weather was warm and a yellow muslin seemed to fit the bill. Joan, who was learning fast from Corinne, had put up her hair upon which she had tied a straw bonnet trimmed with silk daisies. A pair of white cotton gloves and a neat little reticule completed the outfit. Now, in this gathering, she felt decidedly under-dressed.

As they were spotted, the hubbub of conversation died and everyone turned towards the newcomers. 'They have been gossiping about us,' she whispered to her grandmother.

'Let them.' Lady Morland put her chin in the air and made her way towards a tall, regal lady in mauve silk and a dancing feather head-dress, who was so like Robert in looks, the same dark hair and arched brows, that Kate did not doubt she was his sister.

'Lady Morland, so good of you to come to my little gathering,' she said, though there was little warmth in her voice. 'And this must be Mrs Meredith.' It was said almost as an afterthought, as she looked Kate up and down, her lip curling disdainfully at her simple dress.

'Mrs Withersfield,' Lady Morland said. 'May I present my granddaughter, Mrs Meredith.'

'Mrs Withersfield.' Kate refused to be cowed by her haughty look. 'How do you do?'

'Very well, thank you. Do take a seat. Tea will be served directly. Robert is about somewhere. I will go and see if I can find him.'

'She is going to have to come down off her high horse when you are the Viscountess,' her ladyship whispered to Kate, as she left them. 'I do not think she will like it, not after having the ordering of his household for so long. I hope Cranford has made her position clear to her.'

'I do not think it will make much difference,' Kate said. 'Robert intends to leave her at Cranford Manor with the children while we are in Austria.'

'Hmph.'

Robert was approaching them and they stood up to be greeted by him. He enquired how they were and if they had been offered refreshments, all very polite, all said with a smile, but Kate could not help feeling that he would have treated every other lady in the room with equal courtesy and she was no different. Her doubts were assuming gigantic proportions and it took an effort of will to keep them down.

'My lord, I thought I was to meet your daughters today,' she said.

'So you shall. My sister will fetch them down directly.'

'Here, in this crowd?'

'Yes, I thought it best. You will be able to speak to them and see how well behaved they are in company, and they will think nothing of it.'

'You haven't told them, have you?' It was an accusation. 'You have not told them you are to marry again, nor that I am to be your wife and their stepmother.'

'I will do so this evening, after everyone has gone.'

'And am I to be present?'

'I think not. Not on this occasion. Later, when they are used to the idea.'

As he finished speaking Mrs Withersfield re-entered the room with a little girl on either side of her. They were dressed exactly alike in pink dimity dresses with wide ribbon sashes and pink ribbons in their dark curls. They were paraded round the room and stopped to curtsy to each guest and say 'good afternoon' before moving on. Kate and her grandmother were treated in exactly the same way.

Kate was having none of it. She smiled at them and held out her hands to take one of each of theirs. 'Now let me see,' she said, leaning back a little and looking from one to the other, as if trying to decide. 'You must be Roberta and you are Caroline.'

The youngest of the two giggled, but it was quickly stifled by a look from her aunt. 'No, I am Caroline. That is Roberta.'

'Oh, dear, how can I have got it wrong? I do beg your pardon. I am...' She paused. Mrs Meredith sounded so formal. 'I am Mrs Kate. I hope we shall be friends.'

They curtsied again. 'Thank you, ma'am.'

Mrs Withersfield moved them on and very soon they left the room to go back to their own quarters. Kate watched them go, feeling sad. It was not how she had imagined the meeting would be. She had hoped for informality, for questions and answers, to ask them about themselves, to tell them a little about herself, perhaps give them a little hug.

'Mrs Kate,' Robert murmured beside her. 'Where did that come from?'

'One of my foster children. It seemed less formal than Mrs Meredith, and I could not ask them to call me Mama, could I? Not yet.'

'No.' He paused. 'How are the wedding arrangements coming along?'

'Very well. The invitations have been sent, the caterers booked and the food and drink decided upon. My gown is being made. The only thing yet to be determined is what my bridesmaids will wear. Have you decided whether Roberta and Caroline will attend me?'

'I think not. My sister thinks it will be too disruptive for their routine and seeing me married again might upset them.'

'But won't they enjoy dressing up and being with their relations? And they must surely be curious about me after our meeting.'

'Their curiosity will be satisfied when we spend two days at Cranford Manor before leaving for Austria.' He paused. 'Do you need attendants? Have you no friends or relatives to be bridesmaids?'

She wondered why he allowed his sister to make such decisions. 'Yes, of course,' she said. 'I have promised Annie and there is Charlotte, my cousin Elizabeth's eldest.' She did not explain who Annie was and was glad he did not ask.

'Good. Now, let us take a stroll about the room and I will introduce you to some of our friends. Many of the names you will recognise, for they are on the guest list…'

And so the visit drew to a close and Kate returned home, feeling confused and disturbed and wondering if she would ever fit into Robert's life the way he expected her to. She could not help thinking that if it had been Simon's children she was being introduced to, they would have been chattering away in no time, and ready to be hugged. He was that kind of man; he would ignore the convention that said a gentleman must hold himself aloof from his children, that bringing them up was the domain of women: wet nurses, governesses, school teachers, and sometimes their mothers. He would be down on the floor with them, making them laugh, making her smile too.

He did not visit her again and she missed him dreadfully, but perhaps he was wise to stay away; his presence was too disturbing. The Viscount was busy himself, but on the few occasions he called, he enquired if the children had gone, to which she replied, 'Not yet, but there is plenty of time.' But time seemed to be hurtling towards the day when she became Viscountess Cranford. If it had been Simon she was marrying, she would have been as excited as her grandmother, but it wasn't Simon, it was Robert. Why, in the middle of all the preparations for her wedding, was she having thoughts like that? She must stop it at once.

Simon was sitting in the office at the Hartingdon, wondering what Lady Eleanor would say when he told her the children were coming back to the Home. He should never have allowed Mrs Meredith to take a child into her home, and certainly should never have agreed when she enthusiastically offered to take four. Now he had four children for whom he had to find homes or squeeze them into the Hartingdon, which was already bursting at the seams. He supposed he would manage something; after all, he had been doing the job successfully for the past three years.

In the beginning the work was part of his determination to put Isobel from his mind. Having decided never to marry, he had made the children of the Home his family. As he settled into the role, it became all-engrossing and gave him a great deal of satisfaction. He told himself he did not need women. Meeting Kate had changed all that. He cursed Viscount Cranford for taking her away, not only from the children, but from him and making him vulnerable again. It was a feeling he did not like and he rejected it with the same determination he used for everything else and set to work, writing letters. He wanted to place Michael where he could make something of himself and Sarah needed to go into service with a kind family who would not treat her as a drudge.

He posted the letters on his way back to his lodgings and his lonely dinner, only to find his Aunt Matilda ensconced in one of his armchairs waiting for him. 'Aunt, what are you doing here?'

'I have come to see what you are up to. Have you done anything at all about finding a wife?'

'I have had no time.'

'You mean that charity is still taking up all your time?'

'Most of it.'

'Then find someone else to do the work. I should not have to remind you of your duty. Your uncle was saying only two days ago that he wished he could see his next heir before he cast up his accounts.'

'Is he ill? I thought he was in the best of health.'

'He is perfectly well, but I still think you should make a push to find someone to marry. If you do not, then offer for Isobel. It is your uncle's wish.'

'It was his wish she should marry Charles, in spite of the understanding we had. If he had not interfered…'

'You cannot blame him entirely. Charles and Isobel wanted it and her father was all in favour. After all, Charles was the heir.'

'And now Charles is dead, I am to step into his shoes and his bed. No, thank you, Aunt.'

'Then find someone else. There must be any number of young ladies come up for the Season from which to choose.'

'They are not lining up to marry me, Aunt,' he said wryly, thinking of Kate.

'Then do something about it. Go to Almack's, that's the place to meet them. I can get vouchers.'

'I do not doubt you can, but—'

'I will entertain no buts. We will go next Wednesday.'

'Is my uncle with you?'

'No, you know he abhors the capital, especially in the Season.'

He was relieved to hear it. 'Where are you staying?'

'Not here, you can be sure. I never saw such poky rooms. Could you not have found something better?'

'These are bachelor rooms and they suit me perfectly well.'

'I shall stay with my cousin Emmeline. You will call for me at eight o'clock on Wednesday dressed in evening clothes and that means breeches and stockings.'

He sighed. 'Very well, Aunt. Just to please you.'

The first person Simon saw on entering Almack's ballroom that Wednesday evening was Kate, dressed elegantly in cerise silk decorated with rosebuds. Naturally she was accompanied by the Viscount. He knew he should have bowed to her and passed on, but when he tried to do so, she smiled at him and wished him good evening as if genuinely pleased to see him and that meant he had to present her and her escort to his aunt.

He knew he was compounding his folly, but his pride was at stake and so, after the courtesies had been completed, he asked her for a dance.

'Yes, of course,' she said with a smile, handing him her card on which the Viscount's name was inscribed twice, along with two or three others. He scribbled his name against a waltz and handed it back. 'I shall look forward to it,' he said, bowing before walking away beside his aunt.

'Who is she?' she asked him.

He told her how he had met Kate and about her involvement with the children and her engagement to the Viscount, to be answered with the withering comment, 'Then you are wasting your time there, young man.'

The evening proceeded as evenings at Almack's

always did, with a strict eye being kept on etiquette by the ladies who ran the events which took place every Wednesday with the sole purpose, so it seemed to Simon, of introducing naive young ladies to eligible bachelors. The refreshments were scanty and the drinks provided non-alcoholic; he decided one would have to be desperate to resort to looking for a wife under such circumstances. But he was not looking for a wife, he was looking at Kate, saw how she and Cranford leaned towards each other to murmur comments and the intimate way they smiled at each other, and concluded she was truly looking forward to being the Viscount's wife. He danced with several young ladies, daughters of his mother's friends, and then the time came to claim his waltz with her.

As always they danced well together, but he would have enjoyed it more if he had not been so aware of Viscount Cranford watching them.

Kate stopped her chatter when he appeared unresponsive and looked up into his face. He had a faraway look in his eyes, as if he were struggling with a dilemma. 'I am sorry,' she said.

'Sorry? Whatever for?'

'Giving you more problems to solve.'

The only problem he had at that moment was reconciling himself to the fact that he was in love with her and that endangered all his hard-won immunity from women, however attractive. And she was certainly that. And already spoken for. 'Solving problems is my forte,' he said lightly.

'I am glad you were able to take time from them to

enjoy an evening's leisure,' she said. 'You cannot be at work all the time.'

He gave her a wry smile. 'The work I do is my pleasure, Mrs Meredith. I derive a great deal of satisfaction from seeing poor children happy.'

'Oh, so do I.' It was said with the genuine warmth he had come to expect of her. 'If I were not going to Austria, I would become more involved, but as it is, I have put you in the suds.'

'Not at all.'

'Then why the long face?'

Only Kate could speak so personally without risking a put down. 'Do I have a long face? Rest assured, I am not sad, not when I am with you. I enjoy dancing with you, but I was thinking that this is very different from waltzing under the stars.'

'Yes,' she said thoughtfully, remembering the terrace of Hartingdon House. 'And from dancing to a pianoforte in the schoolroom, and Michael trying to learn the steps with Annie and treading on her toes.'

'They will miss you,' he said, meaning *I will miss you.*

'And I them. But I shall think of them often. Will you write to me from time to time, tell me how they are faring?'

'Not a good idea, Mrs Meredith,' he said laconically. It was not so much that he did not think it was a good idea for her to cling to her relationship with the children, but what correspondence with her would do to him. Knowing she was making a new life with a new husband would only prolong the agony in both instances.

'I see,' she said. He evidently did not want to keep in contact with her and that disappointed her because she thought they had established a good rapport that went beyond the business of the charity. At least, they had until she told him she was going to be married and he must find other homes for the children. Since then he had become distinctly frosty. She did not really blame him. 'You are probably right. You did warn me not to become too attached to them.'

'Yes, I did, didn't I? You must harden your heart, as I have had to do.'

'You! Hard-hearted? I do not believe it. You could not do the work you do if that were true.'

'Neither could I do it if I fell to pieces every time I saw a child in rags, begging in the street. We have to stand back from it and get on with doing what we can to alleviate their condition.'

'Have you always been able to do that?'

'No, I have had to learn it. It is the same for many things we are faced with in this life. We have to override our feelings, in order to function. Bear that in mind, Mrs Meredith, won't you?'

She was not sure what he was trying to tell her. That she should be more like him and not mind when the children were hurt? Or was there something else behind his words? Had he guessed how he affected her, made her yearn for something she could not quite explain, even to herself? She was mortified to think he might have.

The dance ended and Simon returned Kate to the Viscount and strolled back to his aunt to find her talking to Isobel. She was a little plumper than he remembered, but still a very beautiful woman. 'Good evening, Cousin,' he said, recovering quickly from the shock of seeing her. He knew his aunt had engineered the meeting and was annoyed that she had said nothing to him. 'I did not know you were here.'

'I arrived a little late.'

'No, I meant in town.'

'Oh, that was Papa's idea. He said it would cheer me up.'

'And has it?'

'Seeing you again has.' She looked about her as Kate and the Viscount passed them on their way into the dining room. 'Are you going to take me in to supper?'

Out of courtesy, he offered her his arm and they followed Kate and the Viscount. Finding themselves moving towards the same table, he was left with no choice but to introduce them. 'Mrs Meredith, may I present Lady Isobel Redfern. Isobel, this is Viscount Cranford and Mrs Meredith. Mrs Meredith has been helping me with my charity work.'

Robert bowed and the ladies bobbed to each other. Kate became aware that the other woman was eyeing her up and down, making her feel uncomfortable. 'What brings you to London?' she asked, as they sat down together, more to make conversation than because she wanted to know.

'Why, this dear man,' Isobel said. 'I have come to take him back where he belongs. Charitable work is all very well, I applaud those who can do it, but it should not take over one's life, should it?'

'We are at one there,' Robert said, a ghost of a smile flitting across his features.

Kate and Simon remained silent as the other two conversed cheerfully about the weather and the ball and Paris. Kate realised her grandmother had been right; the doctor was renewing his suit with his one-time love and it left her feeling unaccountably sad, while Simon was wishing Isobel anywhere but where she was.

Then they returned to the ballroom, where the musicians were tuning up again. They bowed to each other and the Viscount took Kate off to dance with her, leaving Simon with Isobel, who hung on to his sleeve and insisted on perambulating around the room with him, chattering about nothing at all.

It was two o'clock in the morning when the Viscount took Kate home. He helped her alight from his carriage and accompanied her to the door. She had told everyone not to wait up for her and she expected the house to be quiet. He paused on the step to say goodnight to her and it was then they heard the sound of screaming coming from the nursery suite.

Kate bounded up the stairs without even bidding Robert goodbye and dashed along to the boys' room. Joe was standing upright on his bed, yelling at the top of his lungs while Joan tried vainly to quieten him and grab the bedclothes, which were heavily stained and smelled dreadful. He was fighting her off with surprising strength for one so young. 'He won't let me see to him,' Joan said, seeing Kate come into the room. 'And he's messed the bed.'

As soon as Joe saw her he stopped crying and held out his arms to her. Joan just had time to snatch up a clean towel and wrap it about him before he was picked up and crushed against the beautiful silk rosebuds on Kate's evening gown. 'There, there,' she said, soothing him. 'I'm home now. Let's get you cleaned up and back into bed, shall we?'

Joan suddenly caught sight of the gentleman right behind her mistress and her mouth fell open. 'Oh…'

Alerted by her cry, Kate swung round to face Robert, who stood in the doorway. His face was a picture of disgust. 'Put the boy down, Katherine,' he said. 'Leave him to the servants.'

'I cannot do that, he is upset. Please go downstairs and I will join you in the drawing room in a minute when I have cleaned him up.'

He looked as though he was about to argue, but became aware of the servant staring at them and the lad in the other bed, his brown eyes peeping over the bedclothes and taking everything in; one did not quarrel openly in front of children and servants, who liked nothing better than to gossip. He turned on his heel and left the scene.

Kate put Joe down on a chair and helped Joan strip the bed and remake it, then while Joan fetched a bowl of warm water to wash him, she stripped him off. By the time he was clean and been put into a clean nightshirt, he was almost asleep again. She put him back to bed and stayed a few minutes, singing softly to him until his eyes closed. Joan took the soiled linen away and Kate went down to the drawing room.

Robert was sitting in an armchair reading the *Gazette*. He put it down and stood up when she came in. 'He's gone back to sleep, the poor little mite,' she said.

'Katherine, I am appalled. I did not know that having those children in the house meant that you were reduced to the condition of nursemaid. Whatever were you thinking of, picking him up in that disgusting state...'

'He woke up and I could not be found. Next to his mother, I am the only stable person he knows and in his eyes I had failed him. I had to reassure him and giving him a cuddle is the only way.'

'Ugh! That is why we have nursemaids. I cannot remember my first wife behaving in that way towards my daughters and they are none the worse for it.'

'Perhaps she did it when you did not see her. I cannot imagine any mother not wanting to hold her children.' She paused, wondering what he expected of her. Not a biddable and malleable just-out-of-the-schoolroom débutante, she hoped. Her children would be cuddled and listened to and not banished to their own part of the house. On that she was determined. 'May I offer you some refreshment before you go?'

'No, thank you, it is very late.' His nose curled in distaste. 'You need to take that gown off and throw it away.'

'Throw it away? What a monstrous waste that would be. Susan is very good at cleaning. She will have it looking like new in no time.'

'Katherine, as my wife, you will never have to make economies like that. If you do not want to throw it out, then give it away.'

'Very well.' It was not worth arguing about, she decided. He was only concerned that looking after the children would prevent her being ready for the wedding and the changes to her life that were bound to occur after that. And the children would soon be gone and then everything would go back on an even keel. But it wouldn't, would it? Her life would never be as smooth or as happy as it had been in the last few weeks. She would have to do as Simon suggested: harden her heart in order to function. But was that fair on Robert? He did not deserve that.

She opened her mouth to say something, then shut it again because he was taking his leave. He bowed and made his way to the door, making no attempt to touch her or kiss her hand, his face still registering distaste. After he had gone she sank into a chair and burst out laughing. She laughed until the tears ran down her cheeks and then suddenly she was crying and tears of another sort streamed down her face.

She could not go through with the wedding, she really could not. Robert was not the man she had hitherto believed him to be. In her heart of hearts, she knew she could never be happy with him. He did not think the same way she did; what was important to her he dismissed as of little moment, and his top-lofty attitude to those beneath him she found repugnant. Simon was different. Simon understood…

Chapter Seven

Unexpectedly it was little Joe that left Kate first. 'His baby sister has died,' Simon told Kate when he called two days later. By dint of always appearing to have something else to do, he had avoided Isobel, who was staying at her father's home in Park Lane, but he was unsure how long he could keep it up, especially with his aunt still in town. 'His father has returned home and they have moved into more salubrious accommodation and they want their son back.'

Her heart leapt at the sight of him; she wanted to throw herself into his arms and sob out her problems. But he was part of the problem. She took a deep breath and forced herself to sound as businesslike as he did. 'Will he be looked after properly?'

'It is to be hoped so. In any case, we cannot legally keep him from his parents. Nor would I wish to, but I will visit them from time to time.' He was sticking strictly to the business of the children, trying to be once more the self-contained man he had been before he met Kate, hard though it was. He remembered his warning to Kate to harden her heart, and he must do that too. 'I have arranged to take him home tomorrow, if that is convenient.'

'May I come with you?'

He should not have been surprised; it was typical of her. 'Why? I am persuaded you would find it disturbing.'

'Doctor Redfern, you forget I saw that other awful place in Seven Dials and nothing could be worse than that. I should still like to see Joe safely home.'

'Your concern does you credit, but there is little you can do if you do not approve.'

'I know.' It was said with a sigh. 'But I should still like to come.'

'Very well,' he said, calling himself all kinds of a fool even as he agreed. 'I will call for you and the boy at ten tomorrow morning.'

'We will be ready.'

When he arrived promptly the following morning she was ready in a plain grey cotton dress and straw cottager hat, with Joe, face washed, hair brushed, new shoes polished, beside her. She carried a small bag of spare clothes and toys she had made up for him.

Simon, who was himself dressed very simply in a brown frock coat and plain brown pantaloon trousers, helped them into the gig and climbed up beside them. As they travelled Kate talked to the child, repeating what she had told him the evening before, that he was going back to his mama, who was waiting anxiously to have him home again. He was to be a good boy and not to run away again and much else in like vein, all designed to prepare and reassure him.

'Do not be tempted to promise to visit him,' Simon murmured under his breath. 'You will not be able to keep it.'

'I know that,' she said sharply.

They left the prosperous streets behind them and ventured along Maiden Lane. At first Kate thought they were going to the Hartingdon, but Simon drew up at a tenement a hundred yards short of it. Mrs Barber, who had evidently been on the look out for them, hurtled from the door.

'Joey! Joey! You are come home!' She ran up to the gig and took Joe from Kate's lap. 'My, aren't you the little gentleman, eh?' She plucked at his new clothes and then hugged him so tight, the breath was almost squeezed from his body. He looked about to burst into tears until Kate said, 'He has been looking forward to coming home, Mrs Barber. Haven't you, Joe?'

He nodded, but did not speak because his thumb was in his mouth again.

Simon had jumped down from the gig and given an urchin a penny to mind it, and now he helped Kate down and said, 'Shall we go inside?'

The accommodation was still only one room, still sparsely furnished with a table, two chairs and a cupboard on one side and a large bed and a cot on the other, but Mrs Barber had made an attempt to keep it clean. There was a fire in the grate and a blackened kettle sang on the hob. There were cups and saucers put out on the table; none matched, but they were clean. 'You will take tea?' she queried. 'Alf would have been here to meet you, but he's got 'isself a job down at the docks and won't be 'ome 'til evening.'

Kate did not fancy the tea, which she knew could only be the dust left after the good leaves had been sold, but would not for the world have hurt the young woman by refusing and Simon, in his heartiest voice, said it would go down a treat. And so all three sat at the table and drank the tasteless beverage, while Joe played on the floor with the toy lamb he had brought with him. Kate was glad that he seemed content and made no fuss when she and Simon left.

'One down, three to go,' Simon said, making light of it as they drove away.

She smiled a little wanly. It had hurt to leave the child, even though she had prepared for it. And the doctor had changed too and that was something for which she had not been prepared. Their previous intimacy had disappeared and he was being cold and unbending. She supposed it was because she had disappointed him over the children. 'I think of the four, he might be the hardest to part with,' she said, maintaining the myth that it was only the welfare of the children that mattered. 'He is so little. I do hope he will be loved and cared for.'

'I will see that he is,' he said. 'It is a good sign that Barber has found work, though if it is on the docks, I suspect it is only casual labour.'

'Mrs Barber seems very young to have a child of four.'

'They married when she was sixteen and he barely twenty.'

'Too young to be parents.'

'Perhaps, but in their world youngsters have to grow up quickly to survive; they are older than their years.'

'What are you going to do about Michael and Sarah and Annie?'

'I can put Michael into an apprenticeship or, if he likes, he can sign on as a ship's boy if he fancies a naval career. Sarah can go into the Hartingdon until she is old enough to be put into service and Annie's mother is on the mend, so you can go to your wedding with a clear conscience.'

She had been so concerned about the children she had not thought about her wedding for days. 'I have told Annie she can be one of my attendants,' she told Simon. 'Would you ask her parents if they will consent?'

'Good Lord!' he exclaimed. 'Has Cranford agreed?'

'I have mentioned Annie is to be an attendant, I cannot see why he should object,' she said, on the defensive. 'She is a pretty child and well behaved and it is up to me to say whom I would like to attend me.'

He could just imagine the furore it would cause. There would be an unholy clash of wills and he wondered who would win. It might, he told himself almost gleefully, result in the wedding being called off. But he soon sobered. Would someone so keen on the proper observance of the proprieties, as his lordship undoubtedly was, back out of an engagement once entered into? No, of course he would not, he answered himself; it would cause no end of scandal, and for someone who aspired to be of importance on the diplomatic scene, not to be thought of. Cranford must go through with it, or, if he was not prepared to do that, then the gentlemanly thing to do would be to allow Mrs Meredith to find some compelling reason for breaking off the engagement herself, but even that would cause tattle, as he had discovered for himself. He pulled himself up sharply. Whatever was he thinking of to wish unhappiness and gossip on someone who most certainly did not deserve it?

'I will speak to Mr and Mrs Smith,' he said. 'I cannot think they will be other than pleased.'

He turned to concentrate on driving the gig. The traffic was very thick on Piccadilly, carriages, carts and cabs filled the road, while pedestrians hurried along the pavement. He drew to a stop as a little crossing sweeper with an overlarge broom stepped into the road to clear the way for a gentleman waiting to cross. And that man was Captain Feltwell. He looked up and saw them; there was a smile of malicious glee on his face as he stopped to doff his hat before crossing the road in front of them.

Kate did not like the man and felt sure he would delight in telling Viscount Cranford he had seen her and, considering the jobation Robert had given her before about being seen about with the doctor without a chaperon, that would undoubtedly cause more dissent. She turned to look at Simon, but he appeared not to have noticed the man's mockery and was staring straight ahead.

They drew up outside the house in Holles Street to

find the Viscount's phaeton standing outside. Simon declined to go in for refreshment; he had no wish for a meeting with the Lord Cranford, knowing he would find it difficult to conceal his dislike of him. And the only reason for that, he told himself as he drove away, was his concern for Kate and her future happiness.

He returned two days later to take Michael and Sarah back to the Hartingdon Home. Kate had prepared them for it and they had accepted it philosophically. It was this stoical acceptance of everything that happened to them that made Kate feel sad. 'I hate the idea of never seeing them again,' she told Simon. 'And as you do not think we should correspond—though heaven knows why—do you think you could tell Papa from time to time how they go on? He can include news of them in his letters to me.'

'I will if I can, but once Michael goes to sea, I doubt I shall hear anything of him again. And Sarah might go too far away for me to keep in touch with her. To be honest, Lady Eleanor does not encourage her helpers to maintain contact. Her view is that once the children have left the care of the Society, they are no longer our concern and keeping in touch with them prevents us concentrating on the ones we are still responsible for. And I must say I agree with her.'

'But I've still got Annie. If I can keep her until her mother is home again, I should like to do so.'

She watched him drive the children away and went back to Annie. The child was a little tearful, knowing she would be the next to go. 'But you will be glad to go back to your mama and papa, won't you?' Kate said. 'Shall you like to go shopping with me tomorrow?'

'Oh, yes.' The child brightened at once.

Even though she had made up her mind not to go through with the wedding, which would mean going back on her promise to Annie, she could not deprive the child of the promised dress. They chose a pale blue muslin, decorated about the waist and puffed sleeves with narrow white lace. Kate also bought her a lace-trimmed petticoat, a fetching straw bonnet, some white stockings and tan leather shoes. They were on the way back from their expedition when Simon drew up beside them in his gig.

'On the way home?' he queried, noting how charming Kate looked in pale pink with a darker pink straw bonnet.

'Yes, we have been shopping.'

'So I see. Allow me to take you home.'

'We would not wish to take you out of your way.'

'You won't do that.'

'Then thank you.' They climbed up beside him. Annie was so excited she could not stop chattering and would have pulled all the shopping out if its wrappers to show Simon if Kate had not stopped her. 'Not now, Annie,' she said. 'Wait until we are home again.'

Simon smiled. 'You seem to have had a rewarding expedition.'

'Yes. It was fun, wasn't it, Annie?'

'Oh, yes. And Mrs Kate let me choose what I wanted.'

He accompanied her indoors to pay his respects to Lady Morland and to be shown Kate's purchases by an eager Annie. 'I'm going to leave them here when I go home,' she told him. 'Ma will bring me on the wedding morning to dress here. But Mrs Kate says I can keep them after that.'

He smiled at the child's excitement. The clothes were far finer than anything she had ever owned before and he wondered if the temptation to sell them might be too much for her poor parents to resist, but he was careful not to say it aloud. 'I have arranged to take you home tomorrow, Annie.' He looked up at Kate and swallowed hard, trying to keep his voice level. 'Mrs Smith is home from hospital and anxious to have her daughter back and the sooner the better, don't you think? You need time…'

'Yes,' she said flatly, but it was not time she needed, but the courage to tell Robert she could not marry him.

'I will come at eleven o'clock, if that is convenient.'

'Perfectly.'

He left them and carried on to visit his aunt at her cousin Emmeline's in Duke Street. The two ladies were entertaining. The widowed Lady Woodham was the same age as Lady Redfern, both in their fifties, both a little plump, both lovers of gossip.

'What have you been doing with yourself?' Lady Redfern enquired of him, after they had greeted him effusively.

'Oh, this and that,' he said evasively, glad that Isobel was not present.

'Looking after your bantlings.' Lady Woodham,

being his aunt's confidante, had heard of the way in which he spent much of his time.

'Good God! They are your children, then.'

Simon swung round to face Captain Feltwell, the man who had so disconcerted Kate when they crossed his path the other day. She had not commented on the man's mocking action, but he had seen it. 'I beg your pardon?'

'Saw you with them in Hyde Park. With Mrs Meredith. Thought she was the children's governess until I met her at the Embassy ball. Introduced to me by Viscount Cranford.'

'I have met the gentleman.'

'Then you will know she is engaged to marry him.'

'Yes, I do. I wish them happy.'

'Not the done thing, you know.' The Captain had the bit between his teeth and was not about to let it go. 'Taking another man's intended into the park to play with your children, and being seen out and about with her, driving her in your gig. Don't look good, don't you know. Don't look good at all.'

'It might not look good to someone who thrives on gossip, adding two and two and making five, but then not everyone is so petty-minded, I am glad to say.'

It was a fierce put down and the young man retreated with a red face, but Simon knew he and Kate were courting trouble to be seen out so often in each other's company and he ought to be the strong one and put a stop to it. She, who would never believe ill of anyone if she could help it, would not expect others to believe ill of her, but life was not like that and with people like

Captain Feltwell about, it only took a word here and there to ruin her for ever. He did not care for himself, but it might hurt her. After he had fetched Annie, he would have no reason to visit Kate and perhaps that would be for the best.

Saying goodbye did not get any easier, Kate thought, as she turned from watching Simon driving Annie away in his gig and went back indoors. The house seemed empty and quiet and she felt very flat. She would miss the children, their happy laughter, even their tantrums and quarrels, and she would miss Dr Redfern more than she could put into words. He had become a presence in her life, someone to whom she could turn whenever she had a problem, and it was not only about the children. He was there in her head, in her heart, like a comforting cloak. That set her thinking about Robert and her future life with him and she knew she could not face it.

She went to find her grandmother, who was sitting in the drawing room, reading one of Jane Austen's books, her spectacles perched on the end of her nose. She looked over them at her granddaughter. 'Have they gone?'

'Yes.' She took a deep breath and sat on a stool at her feet. 'Grandmama, what would happen if I told the Viscount I could not marry him?'

The old lady dropped her book with a clatter and snatched her spectacles from her nose. 'Are you contemplating that?'

'Yes. I do not love him and I do not think he loves me.'

'Kate, that is romantic nonsense. Love is not all there is to a marriage. It is perfectly possible to be content without it.'

'Not for me.'

'You know what the consequences of calling off will be, don't you?'

'Yes, I will be branded a jilt, but I can put up with that. It is not me I worry about but how it would affect you and Papa and James and Lizzie.'

'My dear child, we would weather the storm far better than you would, but his lordship will be furious.'

Kate managed a smile. 'Furious, yes, disappointed, perhaps, but not heartbroken.'

'Kate, have you thought about this carefully?'

'I have thought about nothing else since the Viscount came back from France. Everything about him is wrong for me. He is top-lofty and arrogant and he does not like children. I wish I had known that before I agreed to marry him, but he never showed that side of his character when he first came to call, or in his letters.'

'Then you must tell him.'

'I intend to do that. I just wanted to know I have your support. What do you think Papa will say?'

'Much the same as I did, I expect.'

That proved to be true. If anything, her father was more supportive than her grandmother. 'There can be nothing worse than a loveless marriage,' he said. 'I always did think the man was wrong for you.'

She had flung herself into his arms and hugged him. 'Oh, thank you, Papa, thank you.'

Now all that was left was to tell Robert and she was

dreading it, but the sooner it was done, the better. She sent a note round to his house by the gardener's boy.

Robert arrived later that afternoon. She received him in the drawing room, standing alone in the middle of the room. He bowed, she curtsied.

'Katherine, what is this about?' he asked. 'Your note said it was urgent. I had to leave an important meeting.'

'My lord,' she said and swallowed hard. 'There is something I must say to you.'

'Go on.'

'I am afraid I cannot marry you.'

He stared at her for several seconds before finding his voice. 'Not marry me?'

'No, I find that, after all, we should not suit each other.'

'Oh, this is mere nerves,' he said. 'You will get over that. I am persuaded it happens all the time.'

'So it may, my lord, to giddy young débutantes, but I am a mature woman and I have been married before. I do not think you can dismiss what I say as mere nerves. I have thought about it very carefully. In truth, I have thought of little else for the past three weeks. I…' She gulped. 'I do not love you and, if you are honest, you will admit you do not love me.'

He still did not want to believe her. 'Who has put this idea into your head? It was Redfern, I'll wager.'

'No, it was not,' she protested, but her cheeks flamed at the very mention of Simon's name.

'I will sue,' he said. 'He will rue the day he ever interfered in my life.'

'Sue, my lord?' she asked, puzzled.

'Yes, for enticing you away from me, to whom you have been affianced for some months. It is a binding contract and I am entitled to satisfaction.'

'You would never challenge him to a duel?' She was horrified by his reaction. She had expected him to be disappointed, a little angry perhaps, but not vindictive.

'I could, but there are other ways to make him pay without shedding blood. I will take him through the courts. His name will be blackened beyond repair.'

'Oh, no,' she exclaimed. 'He has done nothing, nothing at all. Believe me, my lord, he has nothing to do with my decision.'

'Give me leave to doubt it.' He paused, looking at her thoughtfully, making her feel uncomfortably transparent. 'If you insist on this foolish course, then I will have no choice, but, my dear, on sober reflection I am sure you will realise that, for everyone's sake, it would be better to forget that we have had this conversation and go on as before. Marriage to me will not be so very bad. I am not an ogre. I can give you everything you can possibly want, a home, children, jewels and clothes. I am prepared to be generous.'

'But why do you want to marry me? You do not love me, do you?'

'Love! That is sentimental nonsense. I need to marry and you have all the right requirements. Your antecedents are impeccable and, as you have been married before, you know what is expected of you—you are young enough to give me a healthy heir.'

'How cynical you are. Have you never been in love?'

'I once thought so, but I soon learned not to trust it.

Now we will not speak of it again. You will marry me and we shall deal comfortably with each other.'

'Supposing I say I will not.'

'Then, my dear, you know the consequences.'

She stared at him. Never in her wildest dreams had she expected him to blackmail her into submission. She wanted to defy him, to tell him to do his worst, but who would suffer most from that? Not her, but her father and grandmother and Simon, who was good and true and had never even hinted he had feelings for her. He might have lived down that broken engagement, but it would not take much for the story to be resurrected and he would lose his good name and everything he had worked so hard for. She could not subject him to that. And Robert knew it!

She turned and fled to her room, where she sat on her bed, too angry to cry. She railed against it, punched her pillow and opened her mouth to scream, but no sound emerged. She heard voices in the hall as Susan showed him out of the front door and then the girl came up and knocked on her door.

'His lordship says he hopes you will soon recover from your megrim and he will call for you to go to Lady Podmore's ball as arranged,' she said.

Pretending to be looking forward to the wedding and going ahead with all the preparations was dreadfully difficult. She had not told her father and grandmother about the blackmail, but simply said Robert had persuaded her to change her mind. She went about in a dream, which everyone put down to anticipation of her coming nuptials and the move to Austria. She told everyone she was looking forward to living in Vienna; she had heard it was a beautiful city in beautiful surroundings; she would write and tell them all about it and she hoped they would write back and keep her in touch with everything that was happening at home.

After the children had gone she had not had the heart to send Joan away and had offered to keep her on as her personal maid. That Joan had no idea of the work of a lady's maid was, in Kate's opinion, of no importance at all. Before they left for Austria, she would learn a little from Corinne, her grandmother's maid, and pick the rest up as she went along. She had no doubt that they would both make many mistakes along the way, but that would all be part of the big adventure. It was play acting, all of it play acting. The reality was very different.

She missed the children and found herself wandering about their empty rooms, wishing they were still there. She wondered how they were faring. Were Mr and Mrs Barber dealing well together now and treating Joe lovingly? Was Annie's mother well enough to look after her? Was Michael keeping out of mischief and Sarah content to wait to see what Simon had arranged for her? And Simon? What was he doing? Did he ever think of her? He had no reason to call on her now, nor she to go to him, and the emptiness in her home and in her heart was not only caused by the absence of the children. She missed Simon. It was like a great aching lump that would not go away.

She would go to the schoolroom and stand looking

out of the window, remembering the way they danced together; the feel of his warm hand over hers; the way he sat on the sofa with one of his long legs flung casually over its arm; the sound of him playing the pianoforte, which had not been used for years and was sadly out of tune; the way he hoisted Joe on his shoulders without giving a thought to the damage the child's boots were doing to his smart clothes. His chuckle. He would not be easily forgotten, could not be forgotten at all.

The evening of Lady Podmore's ball arrived. She had not seen the Viscount since their confrontation and was dreading it, but, for Simon's sake, she must not falter.

She had chosen to wear a pale blue crepe gown with an open front, over an embroidered satin slip. It had puff sleeves and a bodice caught under the bosom with a cluster of silk flowers in several shades of pink, from which floated long blue satin ribbons. The neckline was low and dipped down to the posy of flowers. She would have preferred to wear her sapphire necklace, but decided Robert would expect her to wear the diamonds. She reached into the drawer of her dressing table for the box, but could not find it.

She turned the drawer out. Her pearls were there, so was the sapphire necklace, together with a brooch of garnets set in silver. There were some pearl eardrops, her mother's wedding ring and a silver crucifix her father had given her to mark her confirmation. All her valuables were there except the diamond necklace.

'Joan, have you seen my diamonds?' she asked the

girl who was standing behind her, hairbrush in hand, mouth agape at what seemed to her to be untold treasures.

'No, ma'am. What do they look like?'

'White stones set in gold, graded by size with the largest set in a drop from the middle.'

'Oh, that one. No, ma'am, I ain't seen it, not since you wore it to go to the ball. When did you have it last?'

Kate tried to think back. Had she seen it since the Embassy ball? She did not think so. 'I must have put it somewhere else for safety, or perhaps it was accidentally wrapped up in my ball gown.' Beginning to panic, she pulled everything out of her clothes press, her drawers and cupboards. It was not to be found.

'Hev someone took it, do you think?' Joan asked timidly.

'No, I have simply mislaid it.' She did not want even to begin to think it had been stolen. She hurried to her grandmother's room, where the old lady was dressed in purple silk and having her coiffure arranged by Corinne.

'I shall not be long,' she told Kate, looking this way and that in her dressing mirror. 'If this creation manages to hold together. Are you ready?'

'No, Grandmama, I have lost Robert's diamond necklace.'

'Lost it!' Her ladyship swivelled round, pulling her white tresses from Corinne's grasp and making the maid mutter under her breath.

'I cannot find it anywhere. You have no idea where it can be, have you?'

'No, why should I know? Where have you looked?'

'Everywhere. It will soon be time to leave and if I have not found it by then, what am I to say to the Viscount?'

'We had better search your room.'

'I have done that.'

'Then do it again. And if you still do not find it, we will get everyone searching the house. It cannot be lost.'

But it was. A thorough search revealed nothing. The servants were questioned closely, although Kate refused to believe that any of them had taken it. Apart from Joan, they had all been in the Vicar's employ for years and years and there had never been a hint of wrongdoing. There was Joan, of course, but she was Susan's sister and was looking forward to her job as Kate's maid. She would not be so foolish as to put that in jeopardy.

She burst into tears on being questioned by the Reverend, who was in his evening clothes and ready to go, and had been impatiently pacing the drawing room, waiting for the ladies to appear. 'What would I want with somethin' like that?' she demanded between sobs. 'I'm a good girl. I never stole so much as a farthin' in me whole life.'

'Kate, I hate to say this,' her father said. 'but it is my belief it was one of the charity children, probably Michael.'

'Oh, no, surely not. And why would he or anyone else take a single item and leave all the rest behind?'

'One item might not be missed as quickly as if everything had been taken. It was a sly thing to do and you have to admit, Michael is very wily. We had better call in the Watch.'

'No, don't do that,' Kate said. She did not want to believe it was Michael, but could anyone have come in from outside and gone to her room without being seen, taken the necklace and disappeared, leaving behind everything else that was of value? It did not make sense. It had to be someone who knew what it was and where to find it. 'I could not bear it. Can we not leave it to Dr Redfern? I am sure he could find out the truth.'

'And what will you tell the Viscount? I doubt he would be prepared to leave it to the doctor.'

'I shan't tell him. Not tonight anyway. I will wear my sapphires; if he asks, I shall tell him they match my gown better than the diamonds.'

'On your head be it,' her grandmother said. 'Telling untruths to your fiancé is hardly a good beginning to a betrothal.'

'It isn't an untruth. The sapphires are more suitable.'

'Very well. Go and put them on and we must be off. We are prodigiously late already.'

Kate went back to her own room to put on the necklace and have her coiffure completed.

Half an hour later they were all three in the carriage and making their way to Podmore House. Kate was worried. Supposing the diamonds were never found? Robert would be furious. He would say his dislike of the charity children had been vindicated and find a way to blame Simon. It would revive all his animosity towards the doctor and she did not want his name brought up again between them. Nor did she want to believe the children had anything to do with it. But what other explanation was there? She made herself put her worries to the back of her mind as they arrived and she put on a smiling face.

Robert was standing beside Lady Podmore, a plump lady of advanced years, who was noted for her lavish entertainments. Robert was elegantly dressed in a black evening coat, blue waistcoat and narrow trousers caught under the instep of his dancing pumps with straps. His shirt was immaculately frilled and his cravat a credit to his valet. For all that he was looking decidedly ill at ease and it occurred to Kate he might have been wondering if she would turn up.

She curtsied to her ladyship. 'Good evening, my lady. I am sorry we are late.' And then to Robert. 'Good evening, my lord.'

'Good evening Katherine. Lady Morland. Reverend.' Robert spoke to each in turn. 'Now we are all here, let us join the others.' He offered Kate his arm and they proceeded into the ballroom. It was crowded. Besides friends and acquaintances, Kate spotted Mrs Withersfield and Captain Feltwell talking together and, standing alone, Simon in a forest green velvet coat and black pantaloon trousers. How glad she was to see him!

The carpet had been taken up, a dais raised at one end for the musicians and gilded chairs arranged around the circumference for sitting out and the whole room was lavishly decorated with fresh flowers and swathes of wide ribbon. Lady Morland made her way to a seat.

'Off you go,' she said to Kate and Robert, as the Reverend disappeared in the direction of the library, where the older gentlemen were enjoying a game of cards. 'Enjoy your dance. I shall have a comfortable coze with Lady Stanton and Mrs Collingford.'

Robert led Kate into the dance, already under way. 'What happened to make you so late?' he asked.

'I tore the hem of my gown and Susan had to mend it.' The lie slipped out more easily than she expected.

'And why are you not wearing the diamonds?'

This was more difficult. She took a deep breath. 'I thought the sapphires went better with the blue of my gown.'

'Diamonds go with anything,' he said. 'I would not like it to be thought I was miserly towards my bride.'

She did not like him referring to the sapphires as if they were worthless. They had been among her mother's most prized possessions. 'Oh, I am sure no one thinks that, my lord. I will wear the diamonds on our wedding day.' She prayed they would have been restored to her by then.

She took the opportunity of a change in the direction of the dance to look about her for Simon. The sooner he was told about the loss of the necklace the better. She spied him standing beside the large windows that looked out onto the garden. He was in conversation with Captain Feltwell and, judging by his expression, he was not pleased.

Robert claimed her attention until the dance finished and then he tucked her hand into his arm and they promenaded the circumference of the room. When they reached Simon, Robert would have carried on past him without acknowledging him, but Kate, reluctant to move on, hesitated. 'Doctor Redfern, I am so pleased you found time from your work to enjoy a little recreation,' she said, trying with her eyes to convey her need to speak to him.

If he noticed it he did not react, except to bow to her. 'Mrs Meredith.'

She could say no more as Robert tugged on her arm to continue their perambulation. Simon watched them go, wondering what that message had meant, for message it undoubtedly was. He had not meant to come, had intended to plead a previous engagement, but Lady Podmore was one of his aunt's bosom bows and she would not consider allowing him to refuse the invitation. He had not known Kate would be among the guests, but he should not have been surprised. Cranford was determined to take her out and about.

Seeing her had lifted his spirits. He did not know what he hoped for. A miracle, perhaps. And when the Viscount arrived without her he had hoped… But here she was, on the arm of her future husband. He had almost made up his mind to make an excuse to leave when Kate addressed him. Her eyes had looked troubled and her body, usually so vibrant, seemed to have shrivelled, though her mouth smiled. There was something very wrong with her and he had to find some way of speaking to her alone.

He watched her dancing with other partners and then approached her directly. 'Mrs Meredith, might I claim a dance?'

She glanced about her. Robert was on the other side of the room, talking to his sister. 'Of course,' she said.

It was not until they were on the floor she realised it was a waltz. It brought back so many memories. How easy they had been with each other, enjoying their time with the children, dancing at Lady Eleanor's ball, as they were dancing now. No, she must not think of that. 'Simon,' she began and then realised what she had said and stopped in confusion. 'Oh, I am sorry. How discourteous of me. I should not—'

'Yes, you should. If you think of me as Simon, then I am pleased and flattered.' He paused and looked down at her. 'I think of you as Mrs Kate.'

'Do you?'

'Yes, but I could make it plain Kate. No, no, I did not mean that. You are far from plain, you are very beautiful and Cranford is a lucky man. But he calls you Katherine, does he not?'

'Yes.'

'Then to me you are Kate. Now, what can I do for you?'

'Do for me?' She was flustered beyond anything. The conversation was not at all what she had expected and, though his flattery was pleasing, it also troubled her. They seemed to be moving towards an intimacy that was highly improper and they were on view for all to see, including the Viscount. She was afraid of giving herself away.

'Yes. You are troubled. I can always tell, you know, your eyes betray you. If there is anything I can do for you, you have only to ask.'

'Something terrible has happened and I need your help.' She looked about her. Robert was still talking to his sister, but facing towards her, watching her. 'I cannot speak of it here. Do you think you can call on me tomorrow afternoon?'

'Of course,' he said. If she needed him, whatever he had arranged for that time would be cancelled. 'It will be my pleasure. But can you not tell me something of it? Is it something I have done or not done? Or the Viscount?'

'Neither. Please do not ask me any more. The Viscount is coming towards us.'

And with that he had to be content, but his imagination was running riot. Whatever it was, she did not want the Viscount to know of it. Or had she heard the rumours being circulated? He felt guilty about that for taking her about in his gig so often, but he had become so used to people pointing the finger at him for his eccentricities, he took no note of it, but he should not have allowed her to suffer it. He had warned Feltwell against spreading gossip, but he doubted the man would be able to resist a juicy bit of scandal. He released Kate into the Viscount's care, ignoring the look of pure venom that gentleman gave him, and then wandered over to Lady Morland to see if she might enlighten him, but though they spent several minutes in meaningless conversation, he learned nothing more. As soon as he decently could he took his leave.

Kate saw him go and felt an almost irresistible urge to run after him. He had been smiling, but there had been a bleakness in his eyes that she wanted to banish. She supposed she had worried him by telling him something dreadful had happened and not enlarging upon it. Oh, how she wished the diamonds could be found and no one to blame but her own carelessness!

Everyone went in to supper, a lavish affair in which the Podmore caterers excelled. There were roast fowls, glazed hams, lobster and crab pâtés, spinach, water-cress, salsify and fried potatoes, jellies, cake and sweet soufflés filled with fruit, all accompanied by champagne, wine and ratafia. Kate could not eat any of it.

Lady Morland put it down to the heat in the ballroom, but Kate knew it was nothing of the sort. It was seeing Simon disappear and knowing he was lost to her—that was a far greater catastrophe than the loss of the necklace. So far nothing had been said to Robert, but she wondered how long it could be kept from him and what he would say and do when he found out. He would not roar and pace about, it was not his way, but she dreaded his cold anger. She was putting all her faith in Simon. If it was Michael who was the culprit, then perhaps Simon could retrieve the necklace and no harm done. But supposing the boy had disposed of it already? And why was she worrying about a damned necklace when her love had just walked out of her life?

'Why no smiles?' Captain Feltwell asked her. 'Are you not happy with your situation?'

Supper had finished and she was dancing with him, executing the steps like an automaton, while her mind whirled. His voice brought her back to the present with a jerk and she managed a smile. 'Naturally I am happy. Who would not be in my place?'

'Once you are Viscountess Cranford there will be no

more frolics in the park with a certain gentleman and his bantlings, nor trotting about town in his gig unaccompanied. My friend Cranford is a stickler for the proprieties.'

'Captain, give me leave to know my future husband's mind better than you do. I know he would be excessively annoyed if he were to hear that you have been spreading unwarranted tattle about me and about a good man who has nothing but the welfare of poor children at heart.'

He laughed. 'His words almost exactly.'

'The Viscount's?' she queried in surprise.

'No, Redfern's. He spoke of your virtues in glowing terms. You have a staunch admirer there, Mrs Meredith.'

His words were innocuous enough, but the implication behind them was not. 'I think you have said enough, Captain,' she told him and stopped dancing so suddenly the couple behind them almost collided with them. 'I wish to return to my grandmother.' She gave him the briefest of polite nods and marched across the floor to where the old lady sat watching proceedings.

'That man is the outside of enough,' she told her. 'He dares to criticise me for taking the children to the park. I cannot understand why Robert is so friendly with him.'

'I believe they fought together in the war,' the old lady said. 'I suppose friendships like that are more firmly rooted than most. Take no notice of him.'

'But he is spreading malicious gossip. What have I ever done to harm him?'

'Nothing, child. I saw you speaking to Dr Redfern. Did you tell him about you know what?' This was said in an undertone.

'No, I could not with so many people around, we might have been overheard. I asked him to call at Holles Street tomorrow. Thank goodness the Viscount is going to Austria tomorrow to meet the people he will be working with and to make arrangements for our accommodation. It will give us a little time.'

They said no more because Robert was coming to claim her and she spent the rest of the evening in his company, pretending to be happy, pretending for all she was worth, in order to protect the man she loved.

Chapter Eight

Simon arrived promptly the following afternoon and was shown into the drawing room by Susan. 'I will go and tell Mrs Meredith and the Reverend you are here,' she said.

He went and stood by the window and looked out on the garden. It was just as it had been the last time he visited, except for the silence. There was no childish laughter and, though the sun still shone and the flowers still bloomed, it seemed bleak and empty. He turned as Kate came into the room, dressed in a simple muslin gown and with her nut-brown hair tied back with a ribbon. His heart lurched as it always did when he looked at her, but he gave no sign of it as he executed a polite bow, to which she responded with a quick bob of her knee and then hurried over to him.

'Doctor Redfern, I am so glad you have come.'

'Doctor Redfern?' he queried. 'What happened to Simon?'

'That was a slip of the tongue and most remiss of me. Please sit down. Papa will be here directly.'

He sat on the chair she indicated, tucking his long pantaloon-clad legs under it. 'You said you needed my help.'

'Yes. We are all in turmoil. A diamond necklace given to me by Viscount Cranford is missing. We fear it might have been stolen.'

If he was surprised at the nature of her problem he did not show it. 'Are you sure you have not simply mislaid it?'

'No, we have turned the house upside down and it is nowhere to be found. That was why we were late to the ball last night.'

'That was the reason, was it? There were whispers that you might have changed your mind about the wedding.'

He must not know the truth. She was quite sure he would not allow her to sacrifice herself for him and she did not want him to suffer for her sake. 'No, nothing like that,' she said. 'And if you hear such rumours, I would be grateful if you would put a stop to them. I believe you have already spoken to Captain Feltwell.'

'Yes. Odious man. Now, to come back to the matter of the necklace. I assume the Viscount does not know of its loss.'

'No, I told him I had had some trouble with my dress.'

'Tut, tut.' He forced a laugh. 'Telling fibs to your intended.'

'Very remiss of me, I know, but I was, and am,

hoping we will recover the necklace before he returns from Austria, and for that I need your help.'

'Anything I can do, I will.'

'We—that is, Papa and Grandmother and me—were hoping you might be able to retrieve it. You see…oh, this is so difficult and I do not want to believe it, but we think it might have been taken by Michael.'

He looked startled. 'Why Michael?'

'There is no one else. We have questioned all the servants. They have been with us for ages and I am convinced they are all innocent.'

'I am loath to believe any of my charges would steal, but given their backgrounds, it is not impossible, I suppose.'

'It breaks my heart to believe ill of the child, and I hope and pray he is innocent.'

'So do I, not only for his own sake, but for the reputation of the charity. Lady Eleanor is very particular. Michael must be questioned. He is to leave the Hartingdon Home to join a ship in two or three days' time and then it will be almost impossible to catch up with him.'

'Then let us go at once.'

'You wish to be present?'

'Oh, yes, please.'

The Reverend came in at that point and Kate acquainted him with what she and Simon had decided. 'Do you need to go yourself, Kate?' he queried. 'Can Dr Redfern not question the boy without you?'

'I have no doubt he could, Papa, but I want to be there. If Michael did steal my necklace, then I want to understand why and try to make him see how wrong it was and get him to promise not to do anything like it again. He must know that if he goes to prison, he will not be able to join his ship and will be for ever branded a criminal. I am anxious to avoid that. If my property comes back to me, then no one outside this house need know it was ever lost.'

Simon realised from that little speech that Kate was anxious to keep the loss from the Viscount. He would undoubtedly hand the boy over to the law whether he were innocent or guilty.

Kate went to put on a bonnet and throw a shawl about her shoulders and they set off in the gig. It was only then she remembered Captain Feltwell's comments about her riding with Simon and supposed if he were to see her now he would have more fuel to add to his gossip. She truly did not care.

'It is unfair to assume Michael is guilty without evidence,' Simon said, as he drove them towards Hyde Park, intending to drive through there rather than take the road, made all more chaotic than usual by the roadworks. 'And we should not condemn the boy without it.'

'No, I would not do that, but perhaps others might.'

He knew whom she meant. 'I collect the Viscount knows nothing of this.'

'No. I would rather he did not. Luckily for me, I have a little respite. He has gone to Vienna on business and will not be back until a few days before the wedding.'

'If Michael did not take the necklace, then we are at an impasse and his lordship will have to be told, surely?'

'Of course. I am dreading it. I have no idea how much the necklace is worth, but am persuaded it is a prodigious amount. Oh, how I wish he had never given it to me.'

'No doubt it was a token of his love for you.'

She gave a cracked laugh, which told him more than she wanted him to know. Why on earth was she marrying the man, when it was making her so unhappy? Had he some hold over her? 'I do not need costly presents for that,' she said. 'On the one hand I want Michael to be innocent, on the other, I want to retrieve the necklace without a fuss.'

'I will do all I can, you know that, Kate.'

'Yes, and I thank you for it.'

'Then let us see what young Michael has to say for himself, shall we?'

He pulled up outside the Home and took her hand to help her to alight. The touch of his hand was warm and comforting. Afraid of her own reaction, of betraying feelings she knew she should not have, she moved away and preceded him into the building, where he conducted her to the office where she had found him the day she came to tell him she would take a child which, in the end, turned out to be four. What an age ago that seemed.

Michael, on being sent for, grinned his pleasure at seeing Mrs Kate again. He was not, nor ever had been, a demonstrative child, but he raced forward and clasped both her hands. 'You have come to see me before I go to sea. I have made something for you—'

'Michael,' Simon interrupted him. 'We have some serious questions to ask you and you must answer truthfully.'

The boy turned from Kate towards Simon, his face clouding. The ominous tone of the doctor's voice bode ill for him. 'What questions? I ain't done nothin' wrong.'

'I sincerely hope you have not. Now sit down on that chair and listen to me.' And when the boy obeyed, went on, 'Do you remember when Mrs Kate went to a ball and you children were permitted to see her in her gown before she left?'

'What of it?'

'Do you remember what she was wearing?'

'Nah. I don' trouble m'sself with ladies' rigs. I remember she looked real top o' the trees.'

'She was wearing a necklace.'

'Was she?'

'Yes. Michael, that necklace is missing.'

The boy was not slow, he knew what Simon meant. Hadn't he been accused hundreds of times before, sometimes with reason, but as often as not simply because of who he was, a street urchin with no one to defend him? He was up in arms straight away. 'I never took it, if that's what you mean.'

'Michael,' Kate put in. 'I do not want to get you into trouble. All I want is to have my necklace back. You see, it was a gift to me…'

''Ow can I give it you back if'n I never 'ad it?' he stormed. 'I ain't stole nothin' from you, Mrs Kate. I wouldn't. You bin kind to me…' And big as he was and independent as he was, he burst into tears.

Kate rushed to put her arms round him to comfort him. 'If you say you did not take it, then I believe you.

I am sorry I ever doubted you.' She handed him her pretty lace-trimmed handkerchief. 'Now dry your eyes and we will say no more about it.' He sniffed and blew his nose and handed it back. 'No, you keep it. To remind you of me and the good times we had together.'

His tears turned to smiles and he carefully folded the handkerchief and put it into his pocket. 'Thank you, Mrs Kate. I 'opes you find your necklace soon.'

Kate sighed. 'So do I, Michael, so do I. Now tell me about going to sea. What ship is it?'

'A warship. I'm to be a cabin boy, not a powder monkey. Doctor Redfern found the place for me. If I study hard and do exac'ly as I'm told, I could be a real seaman one day and wear the king's uniform.'

'Then I wish you well, Michael.' She held out her hand and, after a little hesitation, he took it. 'If you feel up to writing to me, I shall be pleased to have a letter. Now, run along back to whatever you were doing.'

As soon as he had disappeared, Kate sank into the chair the boy had just vacated and put her face into her hands, trying to stop the tears that squeezed themselves through her fingers.

'Kate.' Simon's voice was anguished. 'Please do not upset yourself.'

She looked up at him standing uncertainly above her, but her vision was blurred and she could not see his expression. 'That was a dreadful thing to do, to accuse the boy like that without a shred of evidence. Poor, poor Michael, and now I have lost his good opinion of me.' She was searching in her pocket for her handkerchief, but she had given it to Michael.

'No, you have not.' He handed her his own larger piece of linen. 'You told him you believed him and he was content with that.'

'I did believe him. Didn't you?'

'Yes, he was too upset to be guilty.'

'Oh, Simon, where is this all going to end?' She searched his face. 'I seem to have got myself in a dreadful coil. I am sorry I involved you…'

'Whether you like it or not, I am involved. I have been involved ever since the day we found Joe, you know that.' He bent down and drew her to her feet. 'Come, we are not beaten yet. Do you feel calm enough to leave?'

'Yes. Thank you.' She returned his handkerchief, hoisted her shawl back on her shoulders and straightened her bonnet. 'Let us go and tell Papa the necklace has not been found.'

He escorted her out to the gig and they were about to set off when Michael came running out to them, bearing a piece of driftwood he had fashioned into a boat with a knife. It was crudely carved and the sails were made of muslin. 'For you, Mrs Kate,' he said.

She accepted it and would have burst into tears again if Simon had not put his hand over hers. 'Thank you,' she told the boy in a choked voice. 'I shall keep this in memory of you. One day you will be an admiral and I shall be able to boast that Admiral Sandford gave it to me when he was a boy.'

He stood to attention and gave her a naval salute, as Simon set the horse on its way. They were silent for some minutes, each with their own thoughts. She was wondering how they were ever going to solve the mystery of the necklace and how she would break the news to Robert; he was wishing with all his heart that the Viscount did not exist, that she was free to accept another love. His love. He realised he had probably been in love with her ever since that first day by the Serpentine. All his promises to himself not to fall in love again had drifted away on the wind. And he, like Kate, was wondering where it would all end. He could not see a happy outcome for him, but while she needed him, he would be there.

'Could it possibly have been taken from your neck at Hartingdon House? It was a severe squeeze as I recall and there were some odd characters that would not have attended had it not been for charity. Were you still wearing it when you arrived home?'

Kate had to think a little. She could not imagine anyone taking such a heavy item from her neck without her feeling it go. It was then she remembered. 'Yes, I was. I remember going along to the children's room when I arrived home to see if they were asleep, but Annie was awake. She mentioned it then.'

'What did she say?'

'Something about liking my blue necklace best. And I remember putting my hand up to touch it.' She remembered something else Annie said too, about wishing she would marry Dr Redfern and not the Viscount, but she was certainly not going to tell him that.

'Not done at the ball, then.'

'No. When I get home, I am going to turn the house out all over again. It must be there.'

'And if it is not?'

'I do not know,' she said miserably. 'Would it do any good calling in the Watch?'

'Without evidence, I doubt it. I think we need a little help from the underworld.'

'Underworld?'

'Yes, the world of the criminal. If the necklace has been stolen by a professional thief, he will want to dispose of it as quickly as possible. If we can track down the receiver, what the fraternity call a fencing cully, it might come to light.'

She was ready to grasp at any straw, though she was unconvinced. 'Do whatever you have to, Simon, but please do not put yourself in any danger. I should hate you to be hurt; no jewel, however valuable, is worth that.'

He was considerably heartened and turned to look at her, and though his hands were on the reins, his heart seemed to have jumped out of his body and deposited itself beside hers, where he was convinced it would stay for ever. If only he could tell her so!

He took his left hand from the reins to put it over hers. She felt its strength and warmth and tried very hard not to weep again.

Kate found it difficult to sleep that night. Everything went round and round in her head, Simon's comforting words, Michael's touching gift, the loss of the necklace. She dreaded having to tell Robert it was missing. What would he do? What would he say? Was she asking too much of Simon who had enough to do without worrying about her problems? Supposing he went into the rookeries of the city and was set upon by thieves? If anything bad happened to him, she would want to die.

Her eyes closed eventually but she had hardly been asleep five minutes, or so it seemed to her, when she was woken by the front door-knocker. Not wanting her father or grandmother to be disturbed, she hurried into a dressing gown and went downstairs and opened the door herself.

Simon, his hair dishevelled, his cravat awry as if he had tied it in a great hurry, stood on the step with the whimpering Joe in his arms. The boy was clutching his toy lamb in one arm. The other was heavily bandaged. 'I couldn't think of anyone else,' Simon said, as she opened the door wide and stood aside to admit him.

'What happened?' she whispered, unwilling to wake the household.

'He got in the way when Mr and Mrs Barber had a violent row.' This was also in a whisper. 'Alf was drunk and started throwing things about and hitting his wife. She screamed back at him and he yelled at her and by then the whole tenement was wide awake. A neighbour, who knew I had been visiting them, came and fetched me. The poor little mite is black and blue and he has a nasty cut on his arm. I've bound it up, but I couldn't leave him there, not until things have calmed down. May I leave him with you?'

'Of course you can.' She took the boy from his arms. 'Oh, you poor darling. You can sleep in your old bed. It will take only a minute to make up. And Dr Redfern will make your poor arm better.' She looked at Simon over the child's trembling body. He looked exhausted. 'You will come and see how he is tomorrow?'

'Yes. I am sorry to inconvenience you.'

'What is a little inconvenience compared to the welfare of a child? I am happy to do what I can.'

'Bless you. You are an angel.'

'Fustian!' She could not detain him, not in the middle of the night, not with her in her night attire, which he seemed not to have noticed. 'Now, go back to your own bed and leave him with me.'

'Very well. Until tomorrow.' He smiled suddenly. 'I mean later today, considering it is two o'clock in the morning.'

He let himself out of the front door and shut it softly behind him. Kate heard his gig drive away as she carried Joe upstairs. The boy had stopped crying, but every now and again let out a little sob. She wanted to hold him tight, but was afraid to do so for fear of hurting him.

On the landing she met her grandmother in a dressing gown, long white hair in braids under her nightcap. 'Did I hear the door? What have you got there?'

'Little Joe. He's been in an accident…'

'But you can't have him back, Kate. Whatever will the Viscount say?'

Kate didn't want to think of that. She hoped that Simon would succeed in sorting something out before Robert returned and then he need never know. It struck her then as reprehensible that she was even contemplating keeping secrets from her future husband. First the missing necklace and now this. She took Joe to the room he had slept in before, sat him in a chair while she made up the bed again, then tucked him in and sat with him until he went to sleep.

Joe's sleep did not last long; he woke because he was in pain. He could not understand why he had to submit to the bandage and did his best to rid himself of it, making the pain worse. Kate had to fight him to make him keep it on. It was a battle of wills that exhausted her and him too. At dawn, he fell asleep, giving her a brief respite, though it was too late to go back to bed.

She was enjoying a cup of chocolate with her grandmother when Simon arrived. He bowed to both ladies, accepted the offer of chocolate and her ladyship's invitation to be seated. 'How has Joe been?' he asked Kate. He had to keep everything on a business level, or he would make a complete fool of himself.

'A little difficult.'

'That is putting it mildly,' Lady Morland said.

'He cannot understand the need for the bandage,' Kate said in mitigation. 'He thinks it is that which is causing the pain and so he keeps trying to take it off.'

'I had better have a look at it.'

'He has only just gone to sleep.'

'I will try not to wake him.'

Kate led the way to the boy's bedroom. He was clutching his toy lamb in his good arm, the other was flung out, half the bandaging undone.

Simon sat on the edge of the bed and gently replaced it without waking him, though he gave one or two sobs in his sleep. Then he looked up at Kate, to find her watching him. Their glances met and held for a second, perhaps more, and there was more in that look than concern for an injured child. This was beyond the work they did, it was personal: two people speaking to each other without words, conveying something of their inner selves, feelings that could not be expressed, must never be expressed. Simon was not even sure she was aware of it herself, but her confusion was plain and she looked away and concentrated her attention on Joe.

'Poor little boy,' she murmured.

'Yes. But he will mend.'

'And then what?' It was said sharply, more sharply than she intended. 'More of the same?'

'I hope not.'

'How did it happen in the first place? What were his parents quarrelling about?'

'Alf Barber called in at the tavern on the way home from the docks, had several drinks and got into a card game so that the money he had earned disappeared. When he did arrive home, Mrs Barber became angry and he even angrier that she had dared to question him, and it went on from there, throwing things, pulling hair, punching. Joe's cot was overturned and he was spilled out and that was when I arrived. Alf Barber stormed out past me and I got the story from Mrs Barber and the neighbours who had heard most of it.'

'So, what are we to do?'

He was heartened by the use of the word 'we', but

how could it mean anything when the Viscount would certainly put a stop to any 'we'?

'I will have a talk to Lady Eleanor. She might have some ideas. Can you keep him for a day or two until I make other arrangements?'

'Of course. You do not have to ask.'

He stood up and they returned to the drawing room where he said his goodbyes to Lady Morland and the Reverend who had joined her, and Kate saw him to the door.

'Well?' her grandmother said, as soon as she returned to them.

'Joe is to stay here for a day or two. You do not mind, do you, Papa?'

'The child does not inconvenience me, Kate, but you must remember that when you are occupied on other matters, daily tasks, preparing for the wedding, looking after him devolves upon the servants.'

'I know, but the wedding plans are well advanced, Lizzie is in her element arranging the wedding breakfast, and Joan is a great help to me here.'

But, though Joan did the cleaning and washing, she could not do anything for the child himself because, in the absence of his mother, he let it be known in bouts of temper that he would have no one but Kate to touch him. His hurt went deeper than his physical condition; he was deeply wounded inside and Kate knew only too well what that felt like.

'He needs a good smack,' Lady Morland said.

'No, he has had too much violence in his life already,

Grandmama,' Kate said, picking up the pieces of a smashed plate that Joe had thrown on the floor. 'We must be patient.'

'It is to be hoped that Dr Redfern can do something about him urgently or I dread to think what the Viscount will say. After getting rid of the children once, to have one of them back again will not please him.'

Kate would not let that influence her. Her relationship with Robert had changed. In the face of his blackmail, she was not going to be a biddable and malleable just-out-of-the-schoolroom bride, afraid of his displeasure. If she had to marry him, and it seemed she must, then she would assert herself, stamp her own personality on the marriage and that meant taking an interest in whatever charity she chose. 'I could not turn him away, could I?'

'I think your papa should write to Dr Redfern. We have seen neither hide nor hair of him for two days. It is as if he has left the child with you and washed his hands of him.'

'Oh, Grandmama, you know that is not true. Si—' She stopped suddenly, realising that she had been about to utter the doctor's Christian name aloud. 'Doctor Redfern would never do such a thing. I am sure he is trying his best to find a solution.'

Simon was in the office of the Hartingdon Home, facing Lady Eleanor. She had inspected the books, the children and the home and been satisfied with what she saw, except that he had done nothing about the over-crowding. 'You should never have let Mrs Meredith take those four,' she said. 'Now we've got them back and what we will do with them, I do not know.'

'I realise that. But Michael Sandford is leaving today and so is Sarah Thomsett. If we could only find more foster parents, we could let some of them go; very few of the women who make a living fostering young children are suitable, as you know. Mrs Meredith is ideal, but she is to be married soon and there is a little boy with her who must be placed. I thought if we could offer some financial help to the family and they were visited frequently, he could go home.'

'I assume you are speaking of Joseph Barber.'

'Yes.' He did not tell her he was already paying the rent of the Barbers' room in Maiden Lane. It was the only way they could be got out of Seven Dials and he was determined Joe would not go back to that degrading place.

'Giving money to that family would be pouring it down Mr Barber's throat.'

'Then what do you suggest?'

'Let them get on with it. Some people just do not want helping.'

He gave up and went to visit Mr and Mrs Barber to see if he could talk some sense into them.

Alf was not at home, but his wife was. She invited him in and asked eagerly after Joe. 'He is coming along nicely. The bandage will soon come off and he will be his old self.' He looked about him. What little furniture had been there before had been broken and there was nowhere to sit but on the bed. She plumped herself down on it while he stood looking down at her.

'When can he come home?'

'Mrs Barber, how can we know he will be safe? Your husband…'

'Oh, 'e's gorn agin and I don' want 'im back. I never oughta married 'im in the first place, but I was pregnant and I didn't 'ave any choice. My pa made me.'

'I agree that was not the best reason in the world to marry, but you must have been fond of your husband if you allowed him liberties in the first place. And Joe is his son.'

'Better off without 'im, I am.'

He was inclined to agree, but on the other hand she needed what little money her husband brought in. 'Let Mrs Meredith keep him for a little while longer. Without your husband, you need work.'

'I could work for you.'

'At the Hartingdon, you mean? I suppose I could find you a few hours each week cleaning at the Home.'

'No, I didn' mean that. I meant work for *you*.'

He smiled at the absurdity of the notion. 'I do not think so, Mrs Barber. I am a bachelor and do not keep a large household.'

'I wouldn't need payin'. You could look after me and I'll look after you.'

He was taken aback by the suggestion. 'No, Mrs Barber, that will not serve.'

'I'll clean myself up. I know how. You won't never need to complain.' She jumped up and seized his arm. 'Take me away from 'ere. You don' know what it's like with Alf, not knowing what 'e's goin' to do next. We could be so 'appy, you, me and Joey.'

It was at that point, while he was trying to free himself from Mrs Barber's grasp, her husband returned home.

Kate and her grandmother had returned from shopping and were taking some refreshment in the drawing room when the Reverend came to join them, bringing the newspaper he had been reading. He folded it and handed it to Kate, tapping it with his finger. 'Better read that.'

She skimmed it quickly and then, unable to believe what she was reading, went through it again. 'Fracas in Maiden Lane', the headline read. It went on to describe in lurid detail how Mr Alfred Barber, a dock worker, had come home to find his wife and Dr Redfern on the bed together. 'Mr Barber was naturally incensed that the doctor should abuse his position as physician to the family and a struggle ensued during which Dr Redfern was injured. Dr Redfern is heir to Lord Redfern of Grove Hall and is well known for his charitable work among the poorer children of the metropolis. It seems in this instance he has overstepped the bounds of decency.'

It went on to pontificate about a doctor using his position to fulfil his carnal desires and they could hardly blame the injured husband for taking the law into his own hands and giving the man the hiding he deserved. 'Mrs Barber has confirmed that the doctor forced himself upon her,' the report went on. 'He has naturally been suspended from all connection with The Society for the Welfare of Destitute Children and it is questionable whether he will ever be allowed to work as a physician again.'

Kate was appalled. She dropped the paper on to her lap and stared into space, trying to imagine what had really happened; she would not believe, for an instant, that the newspaper account was true. Simon would never do such a thing. How badly had he been injured? How could she find out? What could she do to help?

Lady Morland had picked up the paper and read it for herself. 'Good Lord!' she exclaimed. 'Whoever would have believed it?'

'Well, I certainly don't,' Kate said. 'And I shall tell him so.'

'No, my dear,' her father put in. 'You will stay out of it. Well out of it. You cannot be seen to have anything to do with that young man now.'

'But he is innocent!'

'So he may be, but mud sticks, just remember that, will you?'

She subsided and said no more, but she could not get Simon out of her head. How he must be suffering! The newspapers should not be allowed to publish such lies. Simon was good and true and… She stopped her errant thoughts before they became too tangled to unravel.

She was left wondering what was to happen to Joe, who was being amused by Joan in the garden. His welfare must come first, but Simon had said they were legally not allowed to keep him from his parents. Poor, poor child. Poor, poor Simon. Papa had said not to involve herself, but to do nothing would seem as though she was deserting him in his time of trouble.

She went out to the garden, whose borders were colourful with lupins and delphiniums, marigolds and phlox, interspersed with sweet-smelling roses. Joan and Joe were sitting on the lawn making a daisy chain. She sat down beside them. 'Has he been good, Joan?'

'Yes, though he still don't like that bandage.'

'I expect Dr Redfern—' She stopped. Who would look after little Joe's injuries now? 'I expect it will soon be taken off.'

Joe held up his necklace of interwoven daisies. 'I made this. For you.'

'Did you, sweetheart? Shall I put it on?' She bent towards him and helped him slip it over her head. 'There, that is lovely.' She kissed his pink cheek. 'Thank you, Joe.'

Susan came down the garden path to them. 'Mrs Meredith, you have a visitor.'

Kate scrambled to her feet, thinking it might be Simon. Surely her father would not refuse him admission? She brushed stray bits of grass from her muslin skirt and hurried into the house, washed her hands, tucked a stray curl out of the way and went into the drawing room, where she stopped. It was not Simon, but Lady Eleanor who sat with her father and grandmother.

'Lady Eleanor, how do you do?' She was suddenly aware of the rope of daisies round her neck and touched it, laughing. 'Little Joey made me a daisy chain.'

Eleanor managed a smile. 'I am come to discuss what is to be done about the boy. In view of Dr Redfern's suspension, I am taking over his work until he is replaced.'

'Oh, surely he will come back to you when all this nonsense blows over.'

'No, Katherine, we cannot be seen to condone what he has done.'

'But you surely do not believe it?'

'Perhaps I should have said alleged to have done, but, guilty or innocent, it makes no difference in the long run. We cannot allow the Society's name to be dragged through the mud. Our generous donors would never give us another groat, if they doubted my competence to keep out undesirables.'

Undesirables! 'Doctor Redfern is not undesirable. He is a caring and tireless worker for the good of the children. You surely know that. It is a scurrilous attack on an innocent man.' She was becoming heated and her grandmother was looking at her as if she had said something startling. Perhaps she had let her feelings get the better of her.

'Perhaps. The inquiry will decide.'

'What about Joe? We cannot keep him if his parents want him back, can we?'

'I had a long interview with them both,' Eleanor said. 'They have agreed to leave him with us until after the inquiry.'

'What has that to do with it?'

'They are to give evidence and it is best to get that over with before any decisions are made. And they ought to find somewhere else to live.'

'Why? It is infinitely better than that awful place in Seven Dials.'

'Good Heavens! Do not tell me you went there.'

'Yes, when Joe was lost and we were looking for his mother.'

'Is there no end to the doctor's indiscretions? You could have been attacked, robbed, caught something vile…'

'Dr Redfern is well known and well liked thereabouts. I was in no danger. I think it will be a dreadful shame if he cannot practise there again.'

'That is for the inquiry to decide. I think it is highly unlikely his name will be cleared, given the evidence.'

'They are lying.' Eleanor looked sharply at her and Kate found herself blushing. 'I mean, why on earth would Dr Redfern seduce Mrs Barber? It does not make sense. There is something or someone else behind their accusations, someone with a grudge perhaps, or they think they can get money out of him.'

'I have advised him that would be the best course, but he is determined on clearing his name.'

'Why should he not? If he paid them off, they would come back for more and it would not silence his critics.'

'No, especially if it ever got out that he has been paying the rent of the Barbers' room in Maiden Lane.'

Kate did not know that, but she pretended she did. 'It was done so that Mrs Barber could tidy herself up, get a job and have Joe home with her again.'

'That may be so, but we must not spend time speculating. The trustees will settle matters once and for all. In the meantime, we must do what we can for the boy. Until we have appointed a replacement for Dr Redfern, I have taken over his visits and require to see Joseph Barber. Would you fetch him, please.'

Joe was duly fetched from the garden where Joan had been amusing him. He clung to Kate and would not go and stand before Lady Eleanor as she asked him to. 'You are spoiling him,' she told Kate.

'After what he has been through, surely a little spoiling can do no harm,' Kate protested, hugging the little boy to her.

'We must think of the long term, Katherine. If you spoil him, he will expect the same when he goes home and you can be sure he will not be indulged there.'

'No, he will be beaten black and blue again. Can nothing be done?'

'We cannot remove him permanently from his home without his parents' full agreement and consent. As yet they have only agreed to a temporary arrangement for us to hold on to Joe. He's as settled here as he's likely to be anywhere. Are you able to keep him for a few days longer?'

'Of course.' Kate handed Joe back to Joan; though he went reluctantly he did not cry, for which she was grateful. She did not want Lady Eleanor to have further evidence of him being over-indulged.

Her ladyship took her leave and Kate went back to the schoolroom, where Joan was trying to amuse a little boy who did not want to be amused.

Robert, when he returned from Austria and called on her, was decidedly annoyed to find her chasing Joe down the hall. Both were laughing gleefully. 'I thought you had ended your association with that charity,' he said.

'No. Why should I? The welfare of poor children will always concern me.'

'I did not mean that. Of course one must support such charities, but I meant having the boy here. I understood he had left you.'

'He did, but he was in an accident and had to come back. He is only here for a little while until Lady Eleanor can make other arrangements for him.'

She took the opportunity while he was greeting her father and grandmother to scoop the newspaper up and hide it under a cushion. Her precaution was in vain because he came straight to the point.

'I have been reading about Dr Redfern in the newspaper, Katherine. It really is a scandalous situation. I hope you have severed all connection with him.'

'My lord, you should not believe everything you read in the papers. I am sure there has been some dreadful mistake.'

'I fail to see what. The newspaper seems to have taken a great delight in publishing all the disgraceful details.'

'Someone is lying,' she said, hotly.

'My dear, it does you credit that you feel you must defend him,' he said, through gritted teeth. 'But you will oblige me by refraining from voicing your opinion in public and, naturally, you will not speak to the man again.'

She was about to protest that he had no right to dictate to her, when she saw her grandmother slowly shaking her head at her. She changed the subject abruptly and they went on to talk about the wedding arrangements, then he rose to take his leave. 'We are to visit the opera tonight. You have not forgotten, have you?'

'No, I have not forgotten.'

'Then I will call for you at eight o'clock. I have booked a table for supper at Grillon's afterwards.'

The opera, though good, was not enough to take Kate's mind off Simon Redfern. She imagined him in his rooms alone, shunned by society, unable to do the work he loved, worrying about the children who had been in his care, worrying especially about Joe Barber. Would he dare to go out? Would he try to defend himself against such outrageous accusations? Would his friends rally round him? What had really happened in the Barbers' apartment? Simon would never have touched the woman. Mrs Barber must have lied. But why? What did she hope to gain?

'You are quiet, Katherine,' Robert said in the interval. 'Were you paying attention?'

'Of course. I was enjoying the singing. It is very fine, do you not agree?'

'I have heard worse, but on the other hand I have heard a great deal better. Austria is famed for its opera houses and its singers. We shall enjoy going to concerts when we are there. We shall be entertaining, too, but I am sure you will manage that. I have rented a fine house, but have yet to engage all the staff. No doubt you will help me with that.'

She murmured that she would do her best as the curtain went up again and she turned her attention to the stage. She was afraid she was going to have to defy everyone and speak to Simon. She could not bear not to know what had happened; once she did, she would know how to defend him. Mrs Barber was lying and she must be made to admit it.

Chapter Nine

Next day at noon, Kate was standing on the other side of the road, looking up at Simon's rooms, but there was no sign of life from any of the windows. It was certainly not considered proper for a lady to visit a bachelor in his rooms, but how else was she to find out what was going on except by standing outside, hoping he would see her and come down to her?

If she stood there much longer, she would begin to attract attention and would do better to walk boldly up to the door and ask for him. Looking around to ascertain there was no one about who might recognise her, she dodged the traffic and crossed the road. The apartments had been converted from a row of terraced houses. Each had a name etched in a brass plate on the front wall. She found Dr Redfern's name and climbed the stairs to the first floor, where she stood a moment to get her breath and calm herself before knocking.

The door was opened by a thin elderly man in

breeches, silk stockings and a blue silk coat. 'Is Dr Redfern at home?' she asked him.

'I will endeavour to ascertain. May I take your name?'

'Mrs Meredith.'

'Please come in and be seated,' he said, holding the door open for her. He gave no indication that he was surprised or shocked or even amused; his features remained immobile.

Kate could not bring herself to sit down on the only chair in the small hall, but paced the floor, three steps in one direction, three back again. A moment later, Simon emerged from one of the rooms. His face was covered in bruises. There was a cut above his eye, which he had endeavoured to hide by combing his hair forward over his forehead, and a swelling on his jaw, which was half-hidden behind the tallest collar he could find and a flamboyantly tied cravat.

'Oh, you poor thing!' she exclaimed, taking a step towards him and then stopping. He was not one of her children to be comforted when they were hurt and she was overstepping the boundary of acceptable behaviour, not that she had not already done so by coming to his lodgings in the first place.

'Kate, what are you doing here?'

'I came to see how you are and to find out—' She stopped as she saw the suffering in his grey eyes. 'I'm sorry. If you would rather I left…'

'No, of course I would not. You are like a breath of fresh air. Come in. Will you take refreshment? Tea, coffee…ratafia, perhaps.'

'Tea, please.'

He turned to the old retainer. 'Tea for the lady, Harvey.'

The man shuffled away and Simon conducted her into a small drawing room. It was neat and clean and adequately furnished, but there were no refinements at all, no pictures or ornaments, no flowers. 'Sit down, Kate, and tell me why you have been so foolhardy as to come here.'

She noted he was using her given name again. 'How else am I to see you?'

'I cannot think, for the life of me, why you would want to. I am quite beyond the pale and not fit for a lady's eyes. And if anyone saw you arrive...' He paused, his feelings of concern, of sorrow, of gladness, of love, were all mixed up together. 'Did anyone see you?'

'I do not think so.'

'Thank God for that.' He watched her seat herself on a sofa and then sat down beside her. The sofa, like everything else in the room, was not large and they were sitting so close together his knees were touching the folds of her dress, a blue silk, decorated with embroidered poppies. 'Kate,' he said seriously, resisting the temptation to take one of her hands, folded on her lap. 'Pleased as I am to see you, it was sheer folly of you to come. You are endangering your reputation.' He gave a harsh laugh. 'Mine, of course, has already gone beyond redemption.'

'I am very sorry for it.'

'You do not believe all the lies they printed about me, do you?'

'No, of course not. I would not be here if I did. I

came to offer my sympathy and to ask you if there is anything I can do to help.'

'You do not ask what happened. Do you not wish to know?'

'Only if you want to tell me.' She managed a smile, which twisted his gut into knots. 'But I am a little curious as to how you came by all those bruises. I surmise it was Mr Barber.'

'Yes. Mrs Barber seized my arm in an effort to persuade me to…' No, he could not tell her that, it was too humiliating. 'I was trying to free myself and make my exit when Mr Barber arrived. He has a temper on him, that man. I thought he meant to kill me. He might have succeeded but for a neighbour sending for the Watch. On the other hand, if she had not done so, I might have been able to leave and no one would be the wiser. As it was the man bundled me into a cab and took me to hospital. No doubt he hurried to the newspaper office the minute he left me. Now I am being accused of seduction and the abduction of the child.'

'But if what the papers printed is all lies,' Kate said, 'surely that is libel and you can bring an action against them?'

'I could try, but with Barber enjoying his role as the injured husband and his wife so afraid of him, she could only back him in what he said, I have small hope of succeeding.'

Harvey arrived with the tea tray and they stopped speaking as he set out everything on the table, poured them each a cup of tea and then retreated, shutting the door behind him.

'You could tell the papers your side of the story,' she suggested.

'No, I have decided a dignified silence would serve the Society best. Starting up a ding-dong battle in public would be too demeaning.'

'But, Simon,' she said in anguish, 'if you do nothing, you will be for ever damned and all your good work will count for nought. If you cannot do anything, then I must. Do you think I could persuade Mrs Barber to retract, to tell what really happened?'

'She will not do that, Kate. Barber will not let her. You must stay out of it. I thank you with all my heart, but there is nothing you can do.' He turned and seized both her hands in his own and was searching her face as if it was the last sight he would ever have of her and needed to remember it. 'I cannot let you become mixed up in a scandal.'

'Simon, I cannot abandon you. Everyone else is being so unkind…'

'You must. There is to be an enquiry by the Board of Trustees of the Society. I am lucky Barber has agreed to abide by its findings and I am not to be subjected, to full court proceedings for seduction which is what he had in mind. I do not know who put that idea into his head; I doubt he would have thought of it himself, but even so…'

She was reminded of Robert's threat to sue Simon for enticement and blacken his name. She thought she had prevented that, but it seemed he was still to be made to suffer. Surely Robert was not behind it? 'Then I shall give evidence on your behalf.'

He gave a cracked laugh. 'How can you? You were not there. Please, Kate, my dearest Kate, leave me to my fate.'

She stared at him, her heart pumping wildly. Had he really said those words? Had he called her dearest? What did that tell her? Was she dear to him? As dear as he was to her? It was better not to know. Seeing the shocked expression cross her sweet face, he gave her a wry smile. 'I have given myself away, have I not? Now you know how much I care for you. I love you.'

'But you can't...' She was confused, afraid. Not of him, never of him, but of herself, of where this conversation was leading. 'I am...'

'To wed another man, I know that. I also know perfectly well that such a declaration on my part is reprehensible and I should never have made it. Of late, I seem to be blundering from one indiscretion to another. Please forgive me.'

'There is nothing to forgive.' She stood up suddenly. 'I must go.' If she stayed any longer, she would find herself confessing what had been staring her in the face for weeks, that she loved Simon Redfern, loved him with all her heart, had done almost from the beginning. He was all in all to her. She loved him so much she would do anything for him, but she realized, almost in the same moment, that bringing it out into the open would not help.

'Yes, I suppose you must.' He stood beside her, so close she could feel his warm breath on her check. 'Kate, I wish you happy. With all my heart, I wish you happy. Forget me. I am not worth your tears.' He rang a bell on the table; when Harvey arrived, Simon instructed him to fetch a cab. While they waited for it, he paced the room, and she stood with her back to him and stared out of the window on to the busy street. Everyone was going about their business, walking, riding, driving carts and carriages, just as if nothing momentous had happened, just as if the world had not stopped turning and her life had not been turned upside down.

She saw the cab stop outside the door and Harvey emerge from it. She turned to Simon. 'It is here.' It was an effort not to sound as if she were about to cry.

He turned towards her, saw the bright tears on her lashes, and strode across the room to her, taking her shoulders in his hands. 'For the first and last time,' he murmured, and kissed her.

It was a gentle kiss, a sweet kiss, not openly passionate, and yet the passion was there, carefully restrained. It was a kiss that promised much and yet nothing at all.

She fled down the stairs and out to the cab, climbed in and was driven home through thick traffic, none of which she noticed, being almost blinded by tears. Not wanting anyone to see her in that state, she pulled herself together and dried her eyes; by the time the coach drew up in Holles Street, she was outwardly in command of herself. Inside was another matter entirely.

The rumours about Simon continued to fly about. Few questioned why a man of impeccable breeding, an educated man, dedicated to healing the sick, would want to make love to a woman so far beneath him. If it was a wife he wanted, he could have the pick of almost any débutante on the social scene, or he could have done before this dreadful scandal overtook him. And if it were anything else, why, there were ladies of easy virtue in plenty who could oblige him. Kate's heart ached for him—would, she told herself sternly, have ached for any man in his position.

She wondered what he was doing. Was he hiding away in his rooms, afraid to venture forth? Had he gone home to Grove Hall? What was his family making of it all? Surely his uncle and aunt would not turn their backs on him? She could not go to him again, could not even speak of him, for fear of giving herself away. She could not forget his kiss. It had put her emotions into such a turmoil, that she could hardly contain them, awakening something in her she had thought long dead. Desire. The desire for a man. After Edward's death, she had not expected to fall in love again, had been prepared to accept fondness as a substitute, but it was not enough.

Robert did not love her, he wanted a wife to satisfy his superiors in the Foreign Office and have a mother for his girls. Not that she was going to be allowed to do much mothering of them with Mrs Withersfield in charge. But she had to go through with the marriage, had to stand at the altar and vow to love, honour and obey and all the time her heart would be elsewhere, with the man she loved who did not deserve the ignominy being heaped upon him. She could not make it worse for him.

And there was Joe, still with her. Poor little boy. What was to become of him? Lady Eleanor had not visited again, so Kate did not know what fate lay in store for him.

Even Robert was staying away. He was busy, she knew that; there was so much to be done before he could take up his appointment in Austria, arrangements about the upkeep of his country estate and his London home to be made, which of the servants he would take with him, which should remain, which should be let go, financial matters to arrange, his investments to be gone through and any that might seem to be inappropriate sold off, his daughters' education decided on with his sister. All this he had explained to Kate. 'All that, besides shopping for clothes and supervising the packing,' he had told her the last time he called. 'I hope you have your own packing in hand. The chests and trunks will be fetched two days before the wedding. You need to take on board only what you need for the journey.'

She had assured him it was all in hand and Joan, who had been looking after Joe, had agreed to accompany her as her maid. He had been surprised that she had not taken on a trained lady's maid, but she had said she wanted someone she knew and who knew her, when she was starting a new life among strangers. She still had not told him about Annie attending her, nor that she had no idea when Joe would be leaving her. Simon had been forbidden to do his work, so who would look after the little boy? Oh, it was all such a dreadful, heart-breaking muddle and her head was spinning.

Simon knew nothing could be done until the inquiry had either condemned or exonerated him and he was left kicking his heels, unable to do the work he loved.

He knew he was the subject of the most salacious scandal; his aunt kept him informed through her cousin Emmeline, who was also known to Captain Feltwell. And no doubt it had been passed on to Viscount Cranford too.

The latest *on dit* was that he had taken the child away from his family in order to have his way with Mrs Barber, who was young and inexperienced in the ways of the world. Alf Barber was known to be a violent man, but he had never harmed his son, whom he loved; even the accident, which had set off the train of events that led to Dr Redfern taking the child away, was only because he got in the way when Mr Barber was chastising his wife. And there was no law to say a man could not beat his wife if he chose.

Simon admitted to himself and to Lady Eleanor he should not have stayed with Janet when he realised Alf was not at home, nor should he have taken the boy back to Mrs Meredith, though strangely the newspapers seemed not to be interested in the child's present whereabouts. How long before they began asking questions about that? His biggest worry was what effect the gossip would have on Kate and her future prospects. Kate, whom he loved to distraction. How could he avoid her becoming involved? He had loved her enough to let her go before all this happened; it was doubly important he should do so now.

He paced about, unable to sit still. He had to be on the move; thinking of Kate as he constantly did reminded him that he had promised to try to find her diamond necklace. That was something he could do while he waited.

He dressed himself in the shabbiest garments he could find, crammed a round hat on his head, put a small pistol into the pocket of his baggy coat, together with a bag of sovereigns, and left his rooms on foot. He had not shaved for several days and had a fine growth of beard, which helped to disguise him. His footsteps took him to the rookeries of London, the haunt of thieves and footpads and receivers of stolen goods.

He strolled down the streets, keeping a sharp look about him, conscious of the money he had in his pocket. Men had been knifed to death for less than he carried. But he needed it because he would undoubtedly have to pay for information, and probably the necklace when and if he found it. He needed help and it came to him in the shape of Harry Tomkins, a ne'er-do-well, who had once been a good soldier, but now made his living in any way he could, both honest and dishonest. Harry recognised him from his army days and hailed him. 'If it isn't the old sawbones from the 53rd, I'll eat my hat,' he said. 'You come down in the world, Doc?'

Simon grinned. 'How did you recognise me?'

'Last time I saw you, you was in the medical tent after the battle of Vimiero, dressing my wounds and looking just as you do now, worn out with taking the world's ills on your own shoulders.'

'I hadn't shaved then, either. Come and have a quart of ale with me. I need your help.'

He guided the man to the nearest tavern and, over a tankard of ale, explained about the missing necklace.

'Don't seem like your or'nary mill ken to me,' Harry said. 'A professional housebreaker would have took the lot. I reckon you should be looking closer to home, servants, perhaps, other people in the household, someone with a grudge…'

'The servants have been declared innocent, though there were foster children in the house at the time, a boy of four, a girl of seven, another of ten and a young cub of twelve. We questioned him and I'll stake my oath he did not take it.'

'What about the others?'

'The girls?'

'Why not? Girls make good thieves too, you know.'

'Yes, I know, but they would have had no opportunity to dispose of the necklace. I took Sarah back to the Hartingdon Home and you can be sure her belongings would have been gone over thoroughly when they were unpacked. As for Annie, she came from a good honest home and her parents would surely have found it and handed it back.'

'Sometimes temptation is 'ard to resist. If I was you, I'd look in that direction.'

Simon was loath to do that, but then he remembered something Kate had said about Annie commenting on the necklace. It was worth pursuing. He thanked Tomkins for his advice, gave him two guineas and left him.

Once home he washed, shaved and changed into the plain but respectable clothes he usually wore for visits to his charges and set off for Annie's home, knowing he was disobeying his instructions not to go anywhere near any children the charity had placed. He was banking on the fact that Mr and Mrs Smith would not have heard rumours that circulated only in the *ton*, and did not read newspapers.

He interviewed the child in their presence. It was a ticklish situation; he knew if the child was innocent and they made a public fuss, he would be in even worse trouble. 'Annie,' he said gently, 'Mrs Kate is very worried that she is going to be in trouble with Viscount Cranford. You know who he is, don't you? He is the man Mrs Kate is going to marry. You are to be one of her attendants. You are looking forward to that, are you not?'

'Yes. But I don't like him. I told her she oughta marry you instead.'

He laughed and looked at her parents, who stood beside her chair looking bewildered. It was not amusing, not amusing at all. He returned his attention to the child. 'Did you do anything you should not have done while you were staying at Mrs Kate's, Annie?'

'Don't know what you mean.' It was said sullenly and he felt she knew only too well what he meant.

'Look here,' Mr Smith said, 'What are you accusing Annie of?'

Simon ignored him. 'Annie, did you take Mrs Kate's necklace?'

'Now, I ain't havin' any o' this,' her father put in. 'Annie's not a thief. You can search the house if you like. I'll swear she brought nothing home she shouldn't have.'

Annie began to sob. Simon squatted down beside

her. 'Tell me what happened, Annie. If you tell the truth and give it back, you won't be in trouble.'

'Can't give it back. Ain't got it.'

'What did you do with it?'

'Hid it, then Mrs Kate wouldn't have to wear it and then she wouldn't marry the nasty man.' It was said with several sniffs, deep breaths and the knuckling of her eyes.

He sat back on his heels and laughed aloud. 'Oh, Annie, that's priceless. But where did you hide it?'

'Under a rock at the bottom of the garden. In the corner under the tree with the purple flowers.'

He ruffled her hair. 'Thank you, Annie. Now we know where to look, nothing more need be said.'

'Are you going to tell Mrs Kate it was me?'

'I am afraid I will have to, but I am sure she will not be angry when she has her property back safe and sound, so you just pray no one else has found it first, eh?'

He reassured Mr and Mrs Smith and left them. Kate would be relieved to know her jewels had not been stolen, but how was he to tell her when he could not even see her? For one very short moment, he was tempted to let the matter lie, to see what Cranford would do about it, but swiftly banished the thought because it would be Kate who suffered. He went back to his lodgings and wrote to the Reverend Morland.

'It's here,' Kate said to her father, as she knelt under the lilac tree in front of a large stone she had just removed. Underneath it, lightly buried, was the box the necklace had been kept in. She picked it up, dusted off the soil and opened it and there it lay, sparkling in its icy hardness.

'Thank goodness,' the Reverend commented.

'And thank Dr Redfern,' she added. 'We would never have found it otherwise.' She scrambled to her feet. 'I am so pleased it was never stolen. Now Robert need know nothing of its disappearance.'

She was amazed that, in the middle of all his troubles, Simon should remember about the necklace and his promise to help find it, especially when she had all but forgotten it herself, or at least pushed it to the back of her mind. She had had so much else to think of: Robert and her feelings for him, or, to be more accurate, her lack of feeling, the wedding and the prospect of years and years of being married to him, knowing he was the wrong man for her.

'I must go and see Annie,' she told her father after they had returned to the house and the necklace, along with all her valuables, had been locked in a secure cupboard in the library where he kept his own jewellery and important papers. 'May I use the carriage this afternoon?'

He gave his permission and she went to see Annie where she heard the tale exactly as it had been told to Simon. Having scolded the girl and then hugged her, she left and directed Daniels to take her to Lady Woodham's House in Duke Street.

'You will have to go abroad,' Lady Redfern told Simon. The house in Duke Street was one of the few to which he was still admitted, though he did not go when Lady Woodham was holding one of her interminable gatherings because he would undoubtedly come across someone who knew him and he did not want to embarrass her. 'Live quietly in France until all the fuss has died down.'

'I cannot do that. There is to be an inquiry. It would be dishonourable and an admission of guilt if I absent myself from that. I have done no wrong and will not hang my head in shame. Go back to Grove Hall, Aunt, then you do not need to listen to the tattle. Take Isobel with you.'

'Perhaps I will, for wherever I go, I feel the whispers behind my back, though no one dare say anything to my face. I do not believe them, of course, but mud sticks.'

'That is why I think you should go home. You will not hear them there.'

When she left town, he would be entirely alone, without friends of any sort. Except Kate. But Kate's friendship was denied to him, not by her, but by those around her. He wondered if she had found her necklace. Almost as if to answer his silent question, Kate was announced.

She came into the room, rehearsing what she wanted to say, curtsied to both ladies, then stopped suddenly when she saw Simon there, standing with his back to the window. His bruises had faded, but he looked exhausted and his grey eyes, dark-rimmed with sleeplessness, had lost their sparkle. One blond curl flopped over his forehead, as if he had been running his fingers through his hair. Even so he smiled at the sight of her and hurried forward to greet her and make her known to his aunt and Lady Woodham.

'Aunt Matilda, Lady Woodham, may I present Mrs Meredith. You remember, I spoke of her.'

They inclined their heads and Kate, recovering a little, curtsied again. 'I am sorry to disturb you, ladies. I could not think of what else to do...' She faltered because Simon's expression was unnerving her. If ever a man was conveying love in a look, he was doing it. His grey eyes, his mouth, his brow, his firm chin, all silently repeated, 'I love you.' She took a deep breath and made herself go on. 'I owe Dr Redfern a great debt for retrieving my lost property and I wanted to thank him. I hoped you might convey my gratitude to him. I had no idea he would be here...' Her voice tailed off, her racing heartbeat loud in her own ears.

'You owe me nothing,' he said gently. 'The shoe is quite on the other foot.' He turned to his aunt. 'Apart from yourself and Cousin Emmeline, Mrs Meredith is the only person in this great metropolis who believes in my innocence.'

'I am sure I am not the only one and the truth will soon be out and you will be exonerated and everything will go on as before,' Kate said.

'Not quite as before,' he murmured. 'Nothing will ever be the same again.'

She knew that was true. Even if he was found innocent, he would not be trusted with children again, which was a terrible pity, when he was so good with them. No child, high or low, rich or poor, would ever be at risk with him. He would make a wonderful papa, so very different from the usual aristocratic father, who saw his children hardly at all in their first few years and then they were sent away to school to be seen infrequently during the holidays. If they were boys, he might teach them to ride and hunt, but it was more likely that task would devolve upon one of the grooms. If they were girls, he might allow them into the drawing room to show them off occasionally until the time came to marry them off. Simon, she knew, would not be like that; he would become closely involved with the upbringing of his children. She could just picture him, on all fours on the floor, playing with them as he had played with the charity children staying with her. His wife would be lucky indeed. The thought made her insides ache so much she felt the tears welling in her eyes and it was an effort of will to contain them.

'I have suggested my nephew should live abroad for a time,' Lady Redfern said.

Kate turned to him. 'Will you?'

'It depends on the outcome of the inquiry. If I am found guilty...'

'God forbid!' his aunt exclaimed. 'We should never live it down.'

'When is the inquiry to be?' Kate asked.

'Next Monday at the Hartingdon Home. Three of the charity's Trustees will sit in judgement on me.'

'I shall be thinking of you.'

He bowed. 'Thank you.'

There was nothing else that could usefully be said and Kate took her leave. Daniels was standing beside the coach, waiting to open the door for her. She had hardly settled herself when Simon dashed from the house and leaned into the vehicle. 'I could not let you go without thanking you for your faith in me. It will sustain me in my ordeal.'

'I intend to be there in the flesh as well as in spirit.'

'Not a good idea, Kate, not a good idea at all.' He clambered into the coach and sat beside her. Daniels took this as a signal that he was being taken up and shut the door. 'You will not be allowed to speak and the last thing I want is for any of the mud to stick to you.'

'Nevertheless, I shall be there.' The carriage gave a jolt as they began to move off. She forced a laugh. 'It seems I am abducting you.'

'I can think of no sweeter abduction.'

'Don't, please don't.' There was anguish in her voice. 'I am to be married…'

'And I wish you were not. It is my fate that I met you too late. Do you think you will be happy?'

How could she answer that truthfully? 'We cannot see into the future,' she said slowly. 'But I know Robert will be a good husband and I shall want for nothing.'

'That does not answer my question.'

'And why is it so important to have an answer? It will not change anything.'

'No, you are right. But will you remember one thing? If you ever need me, I will come to you, no matter how far, nor how long the time that has intervened.'

'Simon, you are being fantastical. You will marry and have a brood of children and be a wonderful husband and father, and in the fullness of time will become Lord Redfern. This time in London will become a distant memory. The gossip will be forgotten. I certainly hope so.' Oh, the effort it took to say all that!

'Bless you, but one cannot order one's memory, or one's heart.' He took her hand and raised it to his lips, making her shiver with tension. It would not take much on his part to make her throw herself into his arms to relieve it.

'Not on my account, Simon, please.'

'I wish you happy, Kate. It is all I wish.' He rapped on the roof, to let Daniels know he wanted to alight. The coach drew to a stop. He had no idea where they were, nor did he care that he would have a long walk back. Those last few minutes with her were precious and would remain with him along with other memories: Kate rescuing Joe from the Serpentine, Kate playing with the children, Kate laughing, Kate with Joe on her lap, kissing the top of his head, Kate playing hoopla at the Hampstead fair, Kate dancing a waltz in the school-room, a lifetime of memories crammed into a few short weeks. He kissed her cheek and was gone.

She leaned forwards but she could only see his blurred form striding away because of her tears. She pulled the door shut. 'Home, Daniels,' she said, then leaned back and gave way to her misery as the coach moved off again.

Reluctant to go home, Simon walked the streets until he was exhausted, but it did not help—he could not stop thinking about Kate. Had he felt as bad as this when Isobel had jilted him for his cousin? He did not think so. There was no comparison between the two women, nor his feelings for them. The one was an immature infatuation, the other something so deep, so lasting, it could never be erased. Kate was part of him, part of his mind and body, his very essence. There was nothing he could do to ease the pain, however much he wished otherwise, but he could try to clear his name and begin all over again.

But not with The Society for the Welfare of Destitute Children—that avenue was closed to him now, Lady Eleanor had made that abundantly clear. It would have to be something new. He could follow his aunt's suggestion and live abroad; there were destitute children all over the world. He would never have any of his own now. Reluctantly, he turned his steps towards Piccadilly and home.

The panel, making up the inquiry into Simon's conduct, consisted of three of the Society's Trustees: Earl Hardingham, Sir Abraham Lyons, a wealthy industrialist, and Lady Somerton, a widow and old school friend of Lady Eleanor. They were sitting at a table on which were scattered bundles of papers. Lady Eleanor sat to one side, a few feet from Simon, who had been brought in and asked to sit in a chair facing the panel.

Kate, dressed in her grey cambric dress, a light shawl and a plain bonnet with a big brim, was sitting in the body of the hall along with a crowd of interested spectators and several newspapermen. How they had heard about it, she did not know. Her father and grandmother had tried to persuade her not to come, that she ought to distance herself from the doctor, but how could she stay away when the man she loved was fighting for his reputation and his right to administer to the destitute of the city?

Sitting where she was, she could only see his profile: his long straight nose, firm chin and jaw. He appeared calm, but she could tell by the way he held his head that he was tense. Every now and again his jaw twitched and occasionally he ran his hand through his fair hair. She did not think he had seen her, but that did not matter, she was there, every fibre of her reaching out to him, silently giving him her support. If he had allowed it, she would have spoken in his defence, but he had been adamant she was to stay silent.

The first witness to be called was Alf Barber, who was sober, shaved and had made an effort to smarten himself up. He was deferential, toadying to the panel as he told of returning home from a hard day's work to find his wife and Dr Redfern locked in each other's arms. He had seen red. 'Who wouldn't?' he demanded. 'I pulled 'im off her and 'it him. Can you blame me?'

He was asked if he had any idea before that, that the doctor had designs on his wife.

'No, your honours, but he did call at the house a lot, said it was to check on Joey. Didn' need to do that, did 'e? Joey were all right.'

'But you did hurt your son—wasn't he taken from your house because he was in danger?'

'That were an accident. I knocked his cot over and he fell out.'

'How did that happen?'

Alf looked across the room at the spectators as if seeking guidance. Kate, curious as to who might be coaching him, turned and saw Captain Feltwell and Mrs Withersfield sitting together. The Captain gave him an almost imperceptible nod. What in heaven's name had they got against Simon? For a second time she wondered if it was Robert's doing. He had said he would blacken Simon's name, but that was before she had agreed to marry him after all. Protecting Simon had been the only reason she had retracted her rejection. She sat there fuming on his behalf, only half-listening to the evidence.

'Jan and me were having an argument and it got a bit rumbustious. It were somethin' and nothin', no reason to take our son from us. We want 'im back.'

'All in good time,' Sir Abraham told him. 'What did Dr Redfern do when you hit him? Did he defend himself? Did he hit you?'

'Didn' give 'im the chance. Laid 'im out I did.' There was a titter at this which was quickly silenced. 'Then the watchman arrived and took him away.'

They let him go and his wife was sent for. Kate gasped when she saw her. Someone had helped to make her look her best. She was shining with cleanliness, her fair hair had been washed and brushed and was held back with a dainty ribbon. Her dress was a striped gingham in pale lemon and cream, fastened under the bust with a wide yellow band. He feet were encased in cream stockings and tan leather shoes, every item of which looked brand new. Kate was more than ever convinced someone was behind this farce of an enquiry and she did not have to look far to discover who that might be. Why? Why persecute a good man?

She forced herself to pay attention, to hear Janet saying, in a voice that had also been carefully schooled to eliminate the dropped consonants and tortured vowels, that Dr Redfern forced his attentions on her and she did not know how she would have escaped if her husband had not returned at that moment to rescue her. It took all Kate's self-control not to cry out that the woman was lying.

At last Simon was allowed to tell his side of the story. He spoke firmly, explaining how he came to have his arms round Mrs Barber, answered the panel's numerous questions without hesitation, even when they asked the same ones over and over again until his head was spinning. He had not retaliated when struck because he did not want to make a bad situation worse and he had expected Mrs Barber to explain exactly what had happened after he left. No one could have been more surprised than he was when he found himself accused.

Lady Eleanor was asked about his character and his work for the charity. She agreed that perhaps he had a tendency to become too involved with the families in his care. She had warned him about it on several occasions. Simon wished she would come down firmly on his side instead of maintaining that cool impartial attitude. It was damning with faint praise and did more harm than good. Kate, bless her, had offered to give evidence on his behalf, but he could not allow that. It would do her reputation no good, Cranford would be disagreeable about it and the panel would cross-examine her and somehow his feelings for her would be exposed.

At last the questions came to an end, but the ordeal was not over because Earl Hartingdon announced that the panel needed to deliberate and would pronounce their verdict in a week's time. In the meantime, Dr Redfern was not to go anywhere near Mrs Barber or her child. There was a murmur among the audience who had expected to be able to relay the doctor's disgrace to all their friends who could not get into the room, and were now deprived of the juiciest bit of gossip. Not that an innocent verdict would help very much; he was already condemned in the eyes of the *haut monde*.

Simon turned to go and suddenly saw Kate, who was standing up with the rest of the crowd. His eyes lit up and a faint smile hovered about his lips, though there was nothing to smile at, nothing at all. She was pushing her way through the crowd, not making for the door as everyone else was doing, but straight for him. 'Kate, I told you not to come.'

'I could not stay away. They were dreadful, weren't they? All those personal questions. You were so calm, I would have been angry and shouting. I wanted to tell everyone you were innocent.'

'I was far from calm. And inside I was shouting to the heavens, but they were only doing their job and it could have been worse. Now, I am going home and you must too…' He looked up. 'What the devil are they doing here?'

She turned in the direction he was looking. Two

pairs of eyes were watching them. 'Oh, the Captain is only here to gossip, you know what he is like.'

'Yes, I do,' he said. 'Good day to you, Mrs Meredith.' He bowed formally and hurried away, leaving her standing alone and puzzled.

He hated himself for doing that to her, but those two boded ill. They would make the most of her association with him and the fact that Joe was staying with her. He had to disassociate himself from her as quickly and firmly as he could for her sake.

Kate managed to incline her head in a coolly polite greeting as she passed them and hurried away. Mrs Withersfield would undoubtedly tell Robert she had seen her, even if the Captain did not. She would be in for another jobation. She wondered if it would be enough to make Robert refuse to marry her, but decided it would not. His pride was at stake.

There were cabs to be had, but she felt like a walk after sitting in the stuffy room for so long and she wanted to think. Mrs Barber had lied, she was convinced of it. Someone had put her up to it, given her new clothes, probably money, too, to besmirch Simon's name. Could she be persuaded to retract her evidence and tell the truth? How? Kate did not have the resources to buy her off.

Deep in thought, she hardly noticed a coach pull up beside her until she heard her name. It was Lady Eleanor. 'Katherine, get in, do, you should not be walking unaccompanied. The tattlemongers have enough to talk about without you adding to it.'

Kate climbed in and took her seat next to her ladyship. A companion occupied the facing seat.

'I was surprised to see you at the inquiry, Katherine,' her ladyship said as the coach moved off.

'Someone had to support Dr Redfern. All his so-called friends seem to have deserted him.'

'You could do nothing to help him and you have jeopardised your own reputation. For someone who aspires to be a Viscountess, you have a strange notion of propriety.'

'Why did you not defend him? You know as well as I do that there is nothing in Mr Barber's allegation. And did you ever before see Mrs Barber dressed like that? Someone is determined to ruin the doctor. What I want to know is why?'

'Could it be because he is seeing too much of you?'

'Me? Whatever gave you that idea?'

'The rumours are not all about Dr Redfern and the Barbers, you know.'

'Oh, you are referring to Captain Feltwell and his vicious gossip. I take no note of that and nor would anyone else with a grain of sense. I am not a silly chit of a girl, I am a mature widow and may go out and about with whom I please. And if Dr Redfern is so kind as to take me up in his gig and save me a long walk, then why should I not accept?'

'Because it simply is not done. And you have resurrected all the old rumours about Dr Redfern that we had thought he had lived down.'

'What old rumours are you referring to?'

'He was once engaged to Lady Isobel Stewart-Smith and jilted her two weeks before the wedding. He could not face the thought of being leg-shackled and ran off to the Continent. The poor girl was heartbroken.'

'She was not heartbroken for long,' Kate said. 'She married his cousin.'

'So she did. I gather he was a great comfort to her.'

'I do not think we should be having this conversation, my lady. It is not fair to talk about people behind their backs.'

'I only mentioned it to warn you. Now let us not go over the past and talk of the future. I was coming to see you in any case. About Joseph Barber.'

'What about him? Do you think I am not looking after him properly?'

To some extent, looking after him had taken Kate's mind of her other problem, but it had not gone away and would not go away. She loved Simon Redfern with every fibre of her being, nothing could alter that, but in less than a week she was due to pledge her love and her life to Viscount Robert Cranford. Could she still go through with it? But if she did not, the consequences would be dire. She would be shunned by polite society, unmarriageable to anyone who valued their reputation and Robert would surely see to it that Dr Redfern's name would be dragged through the mud all over again.

'Oh, I am sure you are. But Mrs Barber would like to visit her son.'

'She can do that at any time. I am not keeping her from him. It is Mr Barber I worry about. Joe's bruises are fading and his arm is healing, but he still cries at the sound of raised voices and flinches whenever a door bangs.'

'Does he?' Eleanor sounded surprised. 'But you are right. I am not inclined to let him go home until we can be sure his father will not harm him, but perhaps Mrs Barber can come and visit him at Holles Street.'

'Of course. I have no objection.' It occurred to Kate that she might question the girl and get to the bottom of her perfidy.

'Then will it be convenient to bring Mrs Barber to Holles Street tomorrow afternoon?'

'Yes, of course. We will expect you.'

The coach was drawing up at Hartingdon House. It was only a short step to Holles Street and Kate said she could easily walk the rest of the way. Surprisingly Eleanor did not argue.

Chapter Ten

Lady Eleanor and Mrs Barber arrived the next afternoon in the old coach with the Hartingdon Home name on it; Kate suspected Eleanor would not have the girl in her own carriage. Susan showed them into the drawing room where Lady Morland, full of curiosity, waited with Kate. Lady Eleanor greeted her great-aunt and took the seat she was offered, leaving Mrs Barber standing uncertainly.

Kate presented Janet to her grandmother and then hurried to fetch Joe. She carried him down from the nursery and stood him on his feet at the door of the drawing room, expecting him to run to his mother, but he hid behind her skirts, sucking his thumb. Gently she plucked him out. 'Look, Joe, there is your mama come to see you. Go and give her a kiss.'

He hesitated and Kate took his hand and led him forwards. Janet, too scared to move from the square foot of carpet on which she stood, waited for them to approach, then squatted down and held out her arms. 'Joey, love, come to your ma.'

He ran to her and Kate breathed a sigh of relief. 'I thought we might have a picnic in the park,' she said, having guessed that Janet would feel uncomfortable and overawed in the Holles Street drawing room, especially if her grandmother started to quiz her. 'Would you like to join us, Lady Eleanor?'

'No, I haven't the time. I will call back later to take Mrs Barber home.'

'I can do that,' Kate said. If, in taking the girl, she were to run into Simon, she could find out how he was, talk to him, reassure him of her continued support. Her hunger for him was such that even a sight of him might assuage a little of it. Oh, she knew she was being foolish, more than that, utterly mad, but she could not help it. Her body ached for him, her mouth craved his. One kiss to last a life time; it was not enough.

Lady Eleanor was on her feet ready to go, when Susan announced the arrival of Robert. As soon as he entered the room, Kate felt the atmosphere change. It became charged with tension and Kate supposed it was because he knew she had been to the inquiry and knew she would have to appease him. And yet, she did not see why she should.

'I must be leaving,' Lady Eleanor said and took her leave.

Full of self-confidence, Robert smiled, greeting Lady Morland with a bow and Kate with a hand raised to his lips. He did not turn her insides to jelly when he took her hand, as Simon did; he did not make her want to fling herself into his arms. She smiled inwardly at the thought. If she did that, he would be shocked and would push her away and tell her not to be so foolish.

'I have brought Roberta and Charlotte to see you,' he said, either not seeing or ignoring Janet and her son, sitting quietly in a corner. 'They are waiting in the carriage. I thought we might go for a drive.'

Kate was nonplussed. 'Oh, my lord, I wish I had known you were coming. I promised Joe a picnic.'

His brow darkened. 'Joe? Oh, you mean that bantling you are fostering. You can take him on a picnic another day, surely?'

'No, my lord. Mrs Barber has come today especially to see him and I cannot turn her away.'

He was not pleased, Kate could see that. Always used to having his every whim satisfied at a moment's notice, it had not occurred to him that she would not find it convenient. 'Why not join us? I am sure the girls would enjoy it. I really would like to spend some time with them and being out in the open air and having a picnic will be a good way of getting to know them.'

'Fetch them in, my lord,' Lady Morland said. 'I should like to meet them.'

Her ladyship could not be gainsaid and he left to do her bidding.

'Oh, dear,' Kate said. 'He would have to come this afternoon. Why could he not have given us a little notice like any other visitor?'

'But he is not any other visitor, is he, Kate?' Lady Morland reminded her.

'Shall I go away?' a timid voice queried from the corner.

'No, certainly not. I promised Joe a picnic and a picnic he shall have.' Kate didn't seem to care any more about upsetting Robert's plans. She could not spend a lifetime bending her will to his, subjugating herself, becoming no more than his shadow.

He returned with his daughters and presented them to Lady Morland. They curtsied to her. 'You remember Mrs Meredith, do you not?' he prompted them and they turned to Kate.

'Yes,' they said together and curtsied. Kate grabbed their hands to pull them to their feet, and drew them towards her to hug them. They looked startled for a moment, then Charlotte giggled.

'Roberta, Charlotte, this is Mrs Barber and her little boy,' Kate said, indicating Janet. 'He is called Joe.'

They turned and would have curtsied to Janet, but their father touched their shoulders and shook his head. It incensed Kate. 'We are going on a picnic,' she told them. 'Shall you like to come?' She smiled at them as she spoke and received a tentative smile from Charlotte. Roberta, older and, to some extent, able to understand about having a stepmother, looked impassive.

'No, Katherine,' Robert said, glancing at Janet with distaste, though the girl was wearing her new clothes and looked respectable enough. 'I do not think such an outing is appropriate under the circumstances. I wish you to postpone your picnic and come with us.'

'I cannot do that, my lord. Mrs Barber is only on a short visit and I have promised Joe a picnic. Promises to children should not be broken. Surely you understand that.'

'You should never have made such a promise.'

'My lord, if I had been expecting you, I would not have done. If you had sent word…'

'Must I make an appointment to see my own wife?' he demanded.

'My lord, I am not yet your wife. When that happens, then, of course, I shall be yours to command.' It was said sweetly, but she could see the cold anger in his eyes. Viscount Robert Cranford did not like being crossed, but she was nothing if not stubborn and it was becoming a test of wills.

'This is neither the time nor the place for this conversation,' he said. 'I will take my leave. I assume you are able to leave your duties to accompany me to the concert tonight.'

With everything else that had been happening she had forgotten all about that. She never felt less like going, but to refuse to do so would compound her failings in his eyes. 'Of course. I am looking forward to it.'

'Then I shall call for you at half past seven.' He bowed to Lady Morland who had been sitting silently listening. 'My lady, your obedient. Come, girls.'

They looked bewildered, but obediently followed him. Kate, as usual, accompanied him to the door. 'I really am sorry, my lord,' she said, picking up his hat from the hall table to hand to him. 'I would not for the world disappoint you or the girls. Perhaps we can all go for a ride tomorrow.'

'Perhaps,' he said, taking his hat and clamping it on his head. 'We will arrange it this evening.'

She watched him stride off to his carriage, followed by his daughters, then she went back to the drawing room. 'Now,' she said briskly to Janet, who was sitting, dumbstruck and nervous, with Joe on her lap. 'Let us go and have our picnic.'

Once in the park, Kate walked away from the usual paths and carriage ways to find a spot where they could spread out their picnic and where Joe could run about and play with a ball while she talked to Janet. She was determined to find out who and what was behind Alf Barber's accusations.

Joe was more interested in the contents of the basket than in playing and stood beside Kate while she unpacked chicken legs, cold meat pie, bread and butter, fruit tartlets and lemonade. She sat him down and gave him some food on a plate, then turned to offer some to Janet, who ate hungrily. The girl seemed little more than a child herself, though Kate knew the reality was very different. Janet Barber had endured poverty and hardship and she knew how to lie and manipulate.

'You are looking very attractive today,' Kate said by way of a beginning, after Joe had eaten all he wanted and been given his ball and told to run about and play. 'That is a pretty gown.'

'Yes, prettier than I ever had before.' She was trying her best to articulate in the way she had been taught.

'Did someone buy it for you?'

Janet looked at her questioner sharply, knowing what was coming. 'I bought it with me...my wages.'

'I see. So you have work that pays you well, then?'

'It's not bad.' She shut her mouth firmly on disclosing anything else.

'Janet, why did you lie about Dr Redfern? He has always tried to help you and did not deserve what you have done to him.'

'Ain't done nothin'.' Her careful speech slipped.

'Oh, but you have. Even if the inquiry exonerates him, the gossip and scandal will mean he cannot work for the Society again.'

'I didn't lie. It's what happened. Not my fault Alf came home when he did.'

'Are you afraid of your husband?'

Janet gave a grunt of a laugh. 'Have you seen my old man?'

'Yes.'

'Then you know the answer. I want to get away from him. Doctor Redfern said he'd take me and Joe away.'

'Are you sure you did not misunderstand the doctor?'

'Course not.'

Joe had been throwing his ball further and further from them and now it had rolled under a seat where a man was sitting with his coat collar turned up and his hat pulled down over his eyes. He seemed to be watching them and Kate hurried to rescue the boy and his ball. She approached the bench and only when she bent to retrieve the ball did she recognise Simon. Her outstretched hand dropped to her side and she sank on to her knees, looking up at him in shock. He was unshaven and gaunt-looking, his eyes dark-rimmed, as if he had not slept or eaten for a week.

He managed a weary smile. 'Kate.'

'What are you doing here?'

'Taking the air.'

'Have you been following us?'

'Not exactly. I am forbidden to come to Holles Street while Joe is with you, and I needed to see you.'

She felt the breath being squeezed out of her body. She was still on the ground and could not have stood up if she tried. 'Oh, Simon, don't do this to me. Every time I see you, a little bit of me gets broken off and carried away. There will soon be nothing left of Kate Meredith but an empty shell.'

'I am sorry, Kate, truly sorry. I should never have involved you in the work of the Society, nor brought Joe back to you when he was hurt. I am more sorry than I can tell you that I made you the subject of gossip and sorry that I let you see how I feel about you. That was wicked and selfish of me. And sorry that I turned my back on you at the inquiry. After you had come to support me, it must have seemed ungrateful.'

'I knew why you did it and you don't have to apologise for that. Nor for anything else.' She turned to look behind her. Janet had not recognised him, but it would not be long before her curiosity overcame her and she would stop eating and come across to see what was going on. 'We cannot talk here. Mrs Barber—'

'Damn Mrs Barber!'

'And Mr Barber and Captain Feltwell and Mrs Withersfield and—'

'Robert Cranford,' he added. 'Him most of all.'

Joe had picked up his ball and offered it to Simon.

He laughed and threw it for him. It was that laugh that alerted Janet to who he was. She scrambled to her feet and ran over to them. 'Doctor Redfern. It is you.'

'Yes, Mrs Barber, it is.' He stood up. 'I must go.'

'Oh, no!' Janet grabbed his arm. 'Don't go. Come and have some of our picnic. There's lots left over and we can talk.'

'We have nothing to talk about,' he said coldly, disengaging her hand from his sleeve.

'You are cross with me.'

'Do you blame me?'

'I am sorry for that, indeed, I am, but it was Alf. He was so angry…'

'Don't I know it. I still have the bruises.'

'He made me say what I did. He said Captain Feltwell told him he could get hundreds of pounds in damages if he sued.'

Simon gave a rough laugh. 'And no doubt the good captain told him and you exactly what to say.'

Janet hung her head, but did not reply.

'I cannot stay here,' he said. 'I am forbidden to speak to you or Joe. Good day to you.'

Kate watched his stiff back receding and wanted to cry, to run after him, to tell him to stay with her, that she would happily forgo her society wedding and her good name to be with him. It took several deep breaths before she could turn towards Janet.

The girl was looking sullen. 'You've driv him away,' she accused Kate. 'He was goin' to take me away and be a father to Joe.'

'Janet, you already have a husband and Joe already

has a father.' Kate went back to the picnic site and began packing the basket ready to return home.

'Oh, he's disappeared again. I've had enough of 'im, not knowing when he's coming home or if he'll be drunk or sober. We will be safe with Dr Redfern, me and Joe.'

Kate did not answer. Janet Barber was deluded and nothing she could say would alter that. She took Joe's hand and led the way across the grass to the Cumberland gate and out on to Oxford Street.

They stood a moment, waiting for the traffic to clear before they could cross. As they stood there, a closed carriage drew to a stop for a man to alight. Alf Barber got out, grabbed Joe, clambered back in and was driven off before anyone could do a thing to stop him.

Janet screamed and ran out into the road, waving her arms while Kate gazed at the back of the disappearing vehicle, shocked into immobility. It was only the shout of a phaeton driver that alerted her to Janet's danger and she hauled her back to safety.

'What's he goin' to do with him? Where's he took him?' Janet's hysterical screams were drawing a large crowd. 'Go after him, someone.'

'How can we?' Kate asked. 'He is out of sight already. Do you think he has taken him home?'

'Dunno.' She stopped crying and sniffed. 'Why would he?'

'I expect he wants Joe home as much as you do. Shall we go and see? I must go and tell my father and grandmother what has happened, then we will take our carriage. I was going to take you home in it in any case.' It took a great deal of effort to remain calm, but being as hysterical as Janet was not going to find Joe. The poor child would be frightened and upset, especially as he had firsthand experience of his father's violence. The sooner they found them the better.

The Reverend and Lady Morland were told what had happened while Daniels harnessed up the horses and brought the coach to the door. Kate and Janet climbed in and were taken at a cracking pace to the tenement in Maiden Lane. There was no one there, no Alf, no Joe. Kate looked up and down the street. It was busy, but no one she asked had seen the man or the boy. She went to find a watchman, but he was decidedly unhelpful. 'If the boy ha' bin took by his own pa, there's nothing I can do. There ain't no law ag'in it.'

'Have you any idea where Alf might have taken Joe?' she asked Janet. 'Somewhere he likes to go.'

'No. There's the tavern. He spends a lot o' his time there.'

Kate was reluctant to enter a tavern but, deciding there was nothing for it, she gritted her teeth and went in. It was dingy, smoky and reeked of stale ale. And it was a waste of time. No one had seen Alf since the day before when he'd been boasting how he was going to be rich on account of suing a so-called toff for enticing his wife away from him. He had been very drunk and then maudlin, talking about his boy and how he was not allowed to see him. No, they had no idea where he would go to ground if he wanted to hide.

Kate realised they had no hope of finding Joe

without help and the most influential person she knew was Lady Eleanor. They returned to the carriage and set off for Hanover Square.

Her ladyship was not pleased to see the two rather bedraggled and distraught women on her doorstep, nor was she sympathetic. If the boy's father had him, then there was nothing she or the law could do. 'Go back home, Mrs Barber,' she said. 'Your husband will bring the boy back sooner or later.'

'I am afraid he might harm him,' Kate told her.

'Why should he do that? His quarrels were always with his wife, not the boy. Go home, Katherine. I warned you not to involve yourself too deeply and now you know why. Go home, for goodness' sake, and practise a little decorum. You are becoming quite, quite eccentric.' She looked Kate up and down as she spoke, taking in her dishevelled appearance, not hiding her distaste.

Kate grabbed Janet's hand and dragged her away.

'Where do we go now?' Janet asked.

'I am taking you home. You need to be there in case your husband comes back with Joe. I shall go on searching.'

'I don't want to be there on my own. Let's go and tell Dr Redfern.'

'No, you have caused him enough trouble already. And he won't know where your husband has gone, will he?'

They returned to Maiden Lane. As soon as Kate had seen Janet safely indoors, she told Daniels to take her to the Bear in Piccadilly. It was a very busy coaching inn and she hoped that with so many people coming and going no one would notice her. 'Wait here for me,' she instructed him, when he drew up in the inn yard. And then she walked to Simon's lodgings.

'Kate! What, in heaven's name, are you doing here?' Simon had just arrived himself, having walked and walked until he could walk no more and had decided there was nothing for it but to come home. He would not be welcome at his club, nor in any of the drawing rooms of the *ton*. A lonely evening lay ahead. He had not bargained for finding Kate on his doorstep. He took her arm, pulled her inside and shut the door on them. 'Are you mad?' he demanded and then he gathered her into his arms and kissed her.

She did not object. His arms were warm and protective; his mouth, moving over hers, sent ripples of sensuous desire all over her body, from the tips of her ears, down her arms and torso to her groin, and then her thighs and feet. Every inch of her trembled with it. There was no denying it. She clung to him, kissing him back, running her hands through his thick hair and down his back, pulling him closer, so close she felt she was melting into him, boneless, only kept upright by his arms about her.

At last, breathless, she leaned away from him. 'In answer to your question,' she said, 'yes, I do believe I am a little mad.'

'That makes two of us.' He took her hand and ushered her upstairs and into his drawing room where he led her to the sofa and pulled her down beside him. She turned towards him, her mouth swollen and her eyes clouded with love.

'Is there a cure?' she asked.

'I do not know of one.' He was searching her face, knowing she loved him as he loved her and wondering how he could get them both out of the coil they were in.

'What are we to do?' she asked in a strangled whisper.

'You say. I will do whatever you suggest.'

'I don't know. I cannot think…'

'Then why did you come, if it wasn't to—?' He stopped suddenly. She would not throw up her reputation to run away with him. He was even madder than he thought.

'It's Joe,' she said miserably.

'Oh.' He deflated like one of those great gas balloons that sometimes took off from the park. They rose on the air, drifted about aimlessly for a while and then the gas was let out and they came back to earth with a jolt. 'What has happened?'

She told him, not making a great deal of sense because her wits were still reeling from his kisses. 'Janet wanted to come and tell you, but I wouldn't let her. I told her to wait at home, that Alf might bring the boy back.'

'He might.'

'Maybe, but judging by the look of determination on his face when he grabbed Joe, I do not think so. He came in a carriage and he doesn't own one. I thought perhaps we could ask the people who hire out such vehicles. He would have to return it, wouldn't he?'

'He might. On the other hand, he might simply

abandon it.' He was not really paying attention—his mind was on other things, mainly his fractured heart.

'If he did and we could find it abandoned, we might know where to start looking.'

'I will see what I can discover. It would help if we knew Alf Barber's haunts.'

'I went to the tavern Janet said he frequented, but they knew nothing.'

'Kate!' he exclaimed. 'Have you no thought for your own safety? Anything could have happened to you. Will you please not do anything like that again? Promise me, sweetheart.'

'I promise.'

'Does Lady Eleanor know anything of this?'

'Yes, we told her first, but she was disinclined to help.'

'I am not surprised. Joe is with his father and Alf has committed no crime that we know of. It is no one else's business. And Lady Eleanor always said we should not have taken Joe on.'

'You mean you think we should not do anything, just let him go?'

'No, I will do what I can.' He stood up. 'How did you come?'

'In our carriage. I left it with Daniels at the Bear.'

'Wait here while I change, then I will escort you back to it.'

He went out and she heard him going along the hall and into another room. What had happened was a dream, something that she should never have allowed to happen. She should have stopped him kissing her like that. If it were only her reputation she needed to consider, she would have had no hesitation in telling him she would stay with him and be damned to the gossip. But there was more to it than that. There was Simon's good name; she hoped fervently that the inquiry would exonerate him and he would be allowed to continue his work. The slightest whiff of scandal would jeopardise that. And there was her father to consider. He was a man of the cloth, a good man who had brought her up to know right from wrong. His standing among his peers would be wiped away, the book he had spent so many years writing, pronounced worthless. Grandmother, Earl Hartingdon and Lady Eleanor—all would be tainted by her wickedness. She did not consider Robert. His recent behaviour had swept away sympathy for him.

She stood up, went to the door and looked along the hall. There was no sign of Simon. She crept downstairs and let herself out of the front door and then hurried as fast as she could down the street to the Bear and climbed into her carriage. 'Home,' she told Daniels.

Her father and grandmother were waiting for her in the drawing room. 'Kate, where have you been?' Lady Morland demanded. 'We thought something must have happened to you too. Are you ill? You look strange.'

'I am perfectly well.' She was all too conscious of the fact that Simon's embrace had not been too careful of her hair and clothes. 'Tired, though.'

'Did you discover anything?' her father asked. 'Was the boy at home?'

'No.' She went on to give them a carefully edited account of what had happened. When it came to telling them she had met Simon, she implied they had come across him in Maiden Lane on his way home from the Hartingdon, forgetting he had been forbidden to go there. She wondered if they could tell what had really happened; she felt as if it were emblazoned on her brow, that they could not fail to notice she could not say Simon's name without stumbling over it. 'He is going to see if he can find them. Lady Eleanor would not help. She said there was nothing she or the law could do—' She stopped as Susan came in and announced Viscount Cranford.

He came in, dressed immaculately in evening wear, carrying a posy of flowers and a small box. He bowed to everyone, then turned towards Kate, who had risen from her chair in a panic, only then remembering she was supposed to be going out with him that evening. 'Katherine, you are not ready. We shall be late.'

'I am not coming. I can't.'

'Why not? Are you unwell?'

'No, but Joe is lost and we are all very worried about him. His father snatched him.'

'Joe?' he queried. 'Oh, you mean that slum child. But if his father has him, what are you worrying about? People like that can look after themselves. Hurry and get ready. If we spring the horses, we should be there in time.'

'No. I am sorry, my lord. I should be very poor company in any case. Go without me. Say I am not well, say anything you like.'

His face became like granite, his eyes especially

were hard, his mouth unyielding. But she did not intend to yield either. It was not only that she was worried about Joe, it was as much to do with the time she had spent with Simon that afternoon. The memory of it still hung about her, still filled every sense: the sight of him looking at her with eyes full of love, the sound of his murmuring voice, the feel of him as he enfolded her in his arms, the taste of his lips, even the masculine smell of him. How could she possibly spend an evening with Robert after that?

'Then I bid you goodnight. Lady Morland. Reverend. Katherine.' He bowed to each in turn and strode out without waiting for anyone to ring for Susan. Kate followed him into the hall, but he hardly noticed her. She turned and went up to her room, sat on her bed, put her head into her hands and wept.

Her grandmother found her there half an hour later. 'I have told Cook you will be at home for supper after all…' she began, then stopped as Kate lifted red-rimmed eyes to her. She rushed to sit on the bed beside her and put her arms about her. 'Kate, whatever is the matter? Are you upset because you quarrelled with Robert?'

'He is so insensitive. He does not seem to understand how I feel about Joe.'

'How do you feel?'

'I don't know. Responsible, I suppose.'

'Oh, Kate, we warned you when you brought those children into the house not to become too fond of them. You made that foolish promise to Annie, you took Joe back without a moment's hesitation and now you have put that child before the wishes of the man you are going to marry. No wonder he is displeased.'

'You cannot stop yourself loving someone. It just happens.'

Lady Morland put her hand under Kate's chin and turned her face towards her. 'You aren't talking about the children now, are you?' And when Kate did not answer, she looked closely at her granddaughter. 'It's Dr Redfern, isn't it?'

Kate was about to deny it, but found she could not. 'I love him, Grandmama.'

'Good heavens! Does Viscount Cranford know?'

'He guessed. He threatened to sue Simon for enticing me away if I broke off the engagement. He said he would ruin him.'

'Oh, my dear child, I wish you had told me. When you said you had changed your mind, I thought… Oh, how you must have suffered! I had no idea.'

'It would have made no difference and I did not want you or Papa to be drawn into it.'

'Never mind us. Call the wedding off, child. You will be condemning yourself to a life of misery, if you do not. I am quite out of countenance with Viscount Cranford.'

Kate gave her a wan smile. 'There will be no end of gossip.'

'Yes, but you can no longer protect Dr Redfern from scandal, not after what happened with Mrs Barber.'

'Nothing did happen. Mrs Barber was paid to lie and so was her husband.'

'Goodness, who did that?'

'Captain Feltwell, but I think he did it at the behest of the Viscount.'

'Oh, I see.'

'That is more than I do. I agreed to marry him, after all.'

'It is my guess he wanted to make sure you could never see or speak to Dr Redfern again, but he is too lofty and too careful of his career to subject himself to gossip. Mr Barber attacking the doctor presented him with a golden opportunity for ruining him through a third person.'

'I did not think anyone could be so wicked.'

The old lady smiled and stroked Kate's wet cheek. 'That is half your trouble, child, you believe the best of everyone.'

'But the truth will come out. It has to and then Simon will be vindicated. I must do nothing to jeopardise that. I must not see him again; I do not want to give the Viscount more ammunition.' It was said with a heavy heart.

Her grandmother pulled her into her arms and said nothing.

Kate had not seen Robert since she sent him away. It began to look as if he would not appear again before the ceremony. He was doing it on purpose, confident she would not dare leave him standing at the altar. Dare she? That would make the gossip a hundred time worse. She sat down and wrote him a letter. She was polite and apologetic, but made herself quite clear: she would not be at the church. Once it was sealed and given to the garden boy to deliver, she felt as if a great cloud had been lifted from her shoulders.

Wandering round the house, with nothing to do but wait for a reply, was jangling her nerves to breaking point. She needed to go out and took herself off to Hanover Square to ask Eleanor if she had discovered anything about Joe's disappearance, but Eleanor was not at home. She left a message and turned to go home again.

She was approaching Oxford Street, head down, her footsteps dragging when she became aware of someone walking beside her. 'Deep in thought, Kate?'

Startled, she looked up at Simon. He was studying her face, as if memorising its features. He often did that and at first it had disconcerted her, but she was used to it now. It would be so easy to tell him of her decision not to marry Robert, to tell him she was his if he wanted her, but she stopped herself. He would be tainted by it unless she could distance herself from him. 'I was thinking about Joe. Do you have any news?'

'None, I am afraid. Alf Barber did hire the carriage and horses and was supposed to have brought them back yesterday evening, but he did not arrive. The hirer is after his blood.'

'Does he have any idea where Mr Barber was going?'

'No.'

'He could have left town. We'll never find them now.'

'There is hope,' he said, and he wasn't only talking

about Joe. 'Remember Pandora. She had a mysterious box she was not supposed to open, but she did and all the ills of the world flew out to torment people, except hope.'

Kate gave him a wan smile. 'Do you want me to cling to that?'

'If it helps.'

'I don't know if it does. Time is not on our side, is it?'

He knew she was not only thinking of Joe when she said that. 'I will keep looking.'

'Do that, please.'

'Why did you rush out without waiting for me yesterday? I came back to the drawing room and you had gone.'

'It was for the best. I knew I should not have come.'

'I am glad you did.'

'No. Simon. No more. I cannot bear it. We must say goodbye now.' He would never know the effort it took to say that.

'Then I wish you happy.' He sounded hurt and she longed to tell him she did not mean it. 'With all my heart I wish you happy.' Then he strode away through the bustling crowd.

She crossed the road into Holles Street, walking like an automaton. He had taken the last little bit of her away with him and there was nothing left but the pain of amputation.

'Mrs Meredith!' The voice was so loud it forced her to lift her head. Alf Barber was leaning out of the hired carriage that had come to a stop beside her.

'Mr Barber.' She stepped up to the carriage, trying to peer past him. 'Is Joe there?'

'Come and see.' He opened the door. She moved closer. He grabbed her arm and dragged her into the vehicle. She might have struggled more if she had not thought Joe was with him. But he was not; by the time she realised that the horses were galloping, hauling the old coach through the traffic, its driver yelling at anything that got in the way. Strangely she was more angry than frightened. 'Where are you taking me?' she demanded, rubbing her arm where his fingers had bruised her. 'What do you want with me?'

'I ain't agoin' to 'urt you,' Alf said as they took a complete circle round Cavendish Square, back past her home and turned down Oxford Street. She was tempted to try and jump out, but at the speed they were going it would have been suicidal. 'I want to talk to you.'

'The only thing I want to know from you is what you have done with Joe.'

'He is safe enough, but 'e's nothing if not a handful. He won't talk, won't eat and he cries all the time.'

'Is it any wonder? You have taken him from his mother, and from me and a home where he was looked after and loved, and no doubt frightened him to death. Where is he?'

'He is safe enough,' he said. 'But I can't manage him. Then I thought of you.'

'Why not his mother?'

'She's not a lot o' good, too busy mooning after that doctor. It was a bad day when she met him. Filled her head with nonsense, he did, making her idle and dreamy. Not that she weren't idle and dreamy afore that. Now she's got ideas above her station. Mind you,' he added, 'you ain't blameless in that respect neither.'

Kate had given up all idea of trying to escape. If he was taking her to Joe, so much the better. 'I am sure I did not mean to make her discontented,' she said. 'But don't you think there is something to be said for trying to better oneself? You have to admit she looked very fetching in that new gown she had for the day of the enquiry.'

'Mrs Withersfield bought it for her, said she couldn't give evidence looking like a trollop; no one would believe what she said. I'd ha' knocked the daylights outa her, talkin' like that about my Jan, if'n the captain hadn' promised me he'd make me rich.'

What he said bore out what Janet had told her, but getting either of them to admit it publicly was another matter. She also realised Alf was protective of Janet, even if he did beat her. He was a complex and confused young man. 'Where are you taking me?' she asked as she noticed they had left the crowded streets and buildings of the metropolis behind and were on the open road.

'To Joe.'

'Yes, but where exactly?'

'You'll see.'

She wished she could think of a way of leaving a trail that could be followed, but decided that would not work. No one knew she had been forced into the same carriage that had carried Joe off. If only Simon had stayed with her a little longer, if only he had not gone striding off just as she was crossing the road, he might have witnessed her being taken. Simon. The love of her life. How soon before he heard about her disappearance? What would he think? One thing she was sure of:

she would not go through with that wedding whatever Robert did. Surely he would have read her letter stating her intention by now? Her father and grandmother knew of her decision—had they cancelled the arrangements? Everyone would think she had had cold feet at the last minute and jilted Robert, which in truth was exactly what she had done. Simon was supposed to have jilted Lady Isobel, but that was difficult to believe; he was no more a coward than she was and would not have run away. Why was she sitting there, wondering about the past and the future neither of which had any relevance in her present situation; all that mattered was what was happening now. Concentrate on Joe, she told herself. Watch where you are being taken, because if the time comes for you to escape with the boy, you will need to have your wits about you.

Chapter Eleven

Simon had eaten a lonely supper and now sat in his drawing room sprawled on the sofa, the sofa on which he and Kate had kissed so ardently, with a bottle of brandy and a glass on the table at his elbow. He was less than thirty years old and yet he felt his life was over.

He ought to go to Grove Hall, which, in spite of his unhappy childhood experiences, was still the only home he had known. And there were some happy memories: the lovely old house with its nooks and crannies where he had played hide and seek; the verdant fields; solid farmhouses; the river in which he fished and swam and on which he rowed; the wild deer grazing in the park; the rabbits and foxes he would never dream of hunting to their deaths. His uncle, who had always been a great hunter, had derided him for that, called him soft as a girl. That had hurt, but he never let it show. He simply refused to ride on the days of the hunt.

His cousin had died, thrown from his horse under the

hooves of another while hunting, and he ought to go back to take up his responsibilities. One of those was to marry. But he wasn't ready for that, wasn't sure he ever would be, not while Kate, his beloved Kate, was shackled to Viscount Cranford. He tried not to, but he found himself imagining the ceremony, hearing her voice, steady and unhesitatingly promising to love, honour and obey the man at her side. It was purgatory and he stood up and paced the room, imagining another scenario when he rushed into the church and carried her off before anyone could stop him.

He turned as Harvey entered the room, glanced at the nearly empty brandy bottle and intoned that the Reverend Morland wished to have a private word with him. Then he scooped up the bottle and glass and hid both under the tail of his coat as he made his exit, passing the Reverend on his way in.

'Doctor, forgive the intrusion,' he said. He sounded breathless as if he had run all the way from Holles Street. 'Have you seen Kate?'

Simon was unsure how to answer that, but there was obviously a degree of panic in the cleric's voice and it behoved him to speak the truth. 'I saw her this afternoon, leaving Hanover Square. I assumed she had been to see Lady Eleanor. We had a few words together and parted on the corner of Oxford Street.' He did not add 'for ever', though it was in his mind.

'She went there, but did not stop to speak to her ladyship. After that, nothing.'

'You mean she did not reach home?'

'No. Besides going to Hartingdon House, I have

been to Morland House, to the Hartingdon Home, to the Barbers' place in Maiden Lane, Kate's friends, everywhere I can think of. No one has seen her. What can have become of her? I am in fear of her life, especially after that brute Barber grabbed the boy. Do you suppose she discovered something about that and set off after them?'

Simon tried to stay calm but a cold fear was wrapping itself about his heart. 'Surely she would not do that without telling you first?'

'No, that is what worries me.'

'Does Viscount Cranford know she is missing?'

'No. I went to his London house, but I was told he was not at home. The butler told me he had taken Mrs Withersfield and his daughters back to Cranford Manor.'

'You do not suppose Kate has gone with them, do you?'

'That is unlikely. She has told the man she will not marry him.'

Simon stared at him in astonishment. 'She has? Why did she not tell me?'

'According to my mother, she was trying to protect you from calumny.'

'Good heavens!' Some of the strange things Kate had said and done suddenly became clear. Oh, foolish, foolish girl! He would have something to say to her when he found her. *When* he found her. 'I will go out and search for her.' He picked up his coat and shrugged himself into it as he spoke.

'Do you know where to look?'

'No. I shall scour the streets, go to the coaching inns and the cab drivers, ask anyone who will listen.'

'Thank you. My carriage is outside. Just in case the Viscount does know where she is, I will go to Cranford Manor. His lordship ought to be informed in any case.'

Simon was halfway to the door. 'How long will it take you?'

'An hour, perhaps a little longer in each direction, a few minutes to ascertain if Kate is there. Three hours, perhaps four, considering it will be dark for the return journey.'

Simon looked at his fob watch. 'It is eight o'clock. I will call on you at Holles Street at midnight, always supposing I have not found her by then.' He paused to bang the front door shut behind them. 'Or would you rather I waited until morning?'

'No, I would not sleep in any case. Come, no matter what time it is.' He gave instructions to Daniels and clambered into his coach. 'God go with you, my boy. I know how hard this is for you.' And then he shut the door and rapped on the roof with his cane.

Simon set off at a run for Oxford Street, musing on what the older man had meant. Had he made his feelings for Kate so obvious? Had others noticed? Was that the reason for that farce of an inquiry—to get him out of the way? He wasn't going, not yet, not until Kate was found at any rate. Supposing she had been injured in a road accident and taken off to an infirmary, no one knowing who she was? If she had, it must have happened almost immediately after they parted, which was only two minutes from her own front door.

He knocked on every door on her route, demanding to know if there had been an incident, anything out of the ordinary in the street outside that afternoon about three o'clock. Some, realising the urgency of his enquiry, answered civilly; others were distinctly rude that he had interrupted their dinner and sent him on his way. He went home, was about to saddle his horse, then decided if he found Kate he would need a conveyance to take her home, so he hitched up his gig instead and visited every infirmary, every workhouse, every coffee shop within a two-mile radius. Against the explicit instructions of the Hartingdon Trustees, he roused the families of every child who had been in the Hartingdon Home in the last three months. None had seen Mrs Meredith. Then he went to the coaching inns, rushing from one to the next, all in vain. The man who had hired the coach out to Barber was still waiting for him to return it.

It was nearing midnight and he had still not been everywhere, but he had a feeling he was wasting his time. He made his way to Holles Street, hoping and praying the Kate had returned safe and sound.

The Reverend Morland, looking old and exhausted, was waiting up for him. 'She wasn't at Cranford Manor,' he said. 'Neither was the Viscount. Mrs Withersfield told me he had taken her and the girls home and left again. I must have passed him on the road. What did you discover?'

'Nothing. You would think someone had seen her, wouldn't you? She was less than five minutes from home when I spoke to her. How I wish I had insisted on escorting her the rest of the way. If I had…' He stopped, reliving for the hundredth time that painful parting.

'Do not blame yourself. Whatever happened, I am sure Kate was not a party to it. She would never distress us unnecessarily. Something dreadful has happened to her. My mother is distraught and has been given a strong tisane to help her to sleep. I am fagged out, but reluctant to go to bed.'

'You cannot do anything more tonight,' Simon told him. 'We'll start again at first light.'

'Yes. Goodnight, Doctor.'

Simon left him and returned to pounding the streets. He peered down alleys, under archways, down cellar steps, in the gardens of the elegant squares. He even went in search of Harry Tomkins and enlisted his help; Harry knew the darker side of London, the mean streets, the low taverns, the ruffians who made their money in a thousand nefarious ways, including kidnapping wealthy young ladies for ransom. Harry was initially put out at being woken from his bed, but when Simon explained what he wanted, he promised to keep his ear to the ground.

It was almost dawn and a rosy glow outlined the chimney pots and spires to the east when Simon decided that neither he nor his horse could stay on their feet any longer. He went home and sprawled on the sofa, too exhausted to undress and go to bed.

Kate woke to the gentle rocking of the boat, wondering for a moment where she was. Apart from the sound of lapping water and a gull calling somewhere, there was no sound. Beside her, little Joe slept. She lay there, still fully dressed, covered by a far-from-clean blanket and went over the events of the previous day.

From the position of the sun while there was daylight left, she knew they had travelled in a north-easterly direction the day before, rattling through small towns and villages. They had stopped for a change of horses four times; calculating that was done every twelve miles at the pace they were doing, they were about forty-eight miles from London. That is, if they had gone in a straight line; she could not even be sure of that. She had been allowed to alight when they stopped, when Barber bought her drink and food and allowed her to use the inn's conveniences on her promise not to run away while his back was turned. She would not have done that in any case, knowing he was taking her to Joe. What he intended after that, she had no idea. She did wonder how he could afford to hire the coach, change the horses and buy refreshment, but then remembered Captain Feltwell had paid him for his evidence at the inquiry.

It had been fully dark when they stopped and Alf jumped out and held the door for her. She remembered stepping out onto muddy grass. By the light of a fitful moon, she had seen the glint of water, but no buildings and no trees except a few drooping willows. He had dismissed the coachman and led her to a rickety wooden landing stage where a small boat was moored. In the dark it had been difficult to see what kind of boat it was, but she calculated it was about the length of her father's drawing room. 'Get on board,' he had commanded, giving her a none-too-gentle push in the back.

It was difficult because she could not see where to put her feet and the gap between the landing stage and the boat seemed to grow wider as she tried to step over it. Alf pushed past her, jumped on board and grabbed her hand. 'Come on, I've got you.'

She jumped, half-expecting to be thrown down into the water and crushed, but found herself on the deck. He went towards what looked like the outline of a hut, opened a door and clattered down some steps. She hesitated, wondering whether to follow him. She heard him strike a flint and then the steps were illuminated by a lantern. Gingerly she made her way down them.

The first thing she noticed was the smell, and almost at the same moment Joey asleep on a bunk, tied by his wrists to its supports. The smell was coming from him.

'Good god, man!' she exclaimed, rushing to untie the child. 'Have you left him here like that all day?'

'Had to. He's all right. You clean him up while I get us some food.'

Joe had woken and turned a tear-streaked face towards her. 'It's all right, sweetheart,' she said soothingly because he seemed not to know where he was. 'It's Mrs Kate, I've come to look after you.'

He silently held out his arms and she pulled him to her, kissing his tear-stained cheeks and his poor, chafed wrists.

She took off his filthy clothes, dressed him in some fresh clothes Alf had brought for him and nursed him until he went to sleep again. She would not put him down and ate the food Alf produced from the galley with one hand, and afterwards lay down beside the little boy. Where Alf went she had no idea.

And now the morning had come and somehow she had to persuade Barber to take them back to London. Papa and Grandmama must be worried to death about her disappearance. Would they have started searching? Would anyone believe that she had not gone of her own accord? Would she be labelled notorious as well as eccentric? Had Simon been alerted? Oh, Simon, I seem to be in an even bigger coil than I was before, she thought.

Joey stirred and started to whimper, so she thrust her own concerns aside and gathered him into her arms to soothe him. He did not speak, had not uttered a word since she arrived.

The boat had rocked on its moorings all night, but now she realised with a start that the rhythm of it had changed and the river bank was gliding past the little port hole. They were on the move. 'Where are we going?' she shouted, not knowing where Alf was.

He came in bearing a plate of bacon, eggs and bread and set it on the table in the middle of the tiny cabin. Then he fetched cutlery from a drawer and put it beside the plate. 'Breakfast,' he said.

It looked greasy, but she realised she was hungry and refusing to eat would not help. She offered some to Joe, who shook his head and shut his mouth firmly against any attempt to persuade him to eat. 'Come, sweetheart, just a little bit,' she coaxed. 'I am going to have some. It looks delicious.' She put a forkful into her own mouth and pierced another tiny piece of bacon and offered it to him. He opened his mouth a fraction and she popped it in. By dint of alternating her own forkfuls with a little for him, she managed to get a good breakfast into him, which was washed down with weak tea. She did not trust the water, fearing it came from the river.

'It's the first 'e's eaten since I fetched 'im,' Alf said, looking up through the companionway to see the horse he had hitched to the tow rope plodding stoically along the towpath.

'Poor little fellow,' Kate said. 'How frightened he must have been all that time alone. It was cruel of you. What if something had happened to the boat and it sank? He would have drowned.'

'Didn't hev no choice.'

'You could have taken him back to his mother.'

'She don't want 'im, too wrapped up in that doctor cove.'

'I am sure that is not true. Poor little chap. Have you any idea what it's like to be small and afraid and insecure?'

'Oh, yes, I know what tha's like, all right. I knew what it were like afore I were his age.'

'Tell me.'

'Why?'

'I want to understand.'

He looked at her for a moment, apparently considering this, before speaking. 'I don't remember my father,' he said. 'I don't reckon my mother knew who he were either. She were a whore, you see.'

'Oh.' Kate stifled her feeling of revulsion. 'What happened to her?'

'She died in the gutter. I were looked after for a time

by older street boys, but one day I were caught with a gold watch that weren't mine and into chokey I went. When I came out I were sent to a charity school and when I were a bit older, I was sent as an apprentice to a printer. Then I met Janet. She were a pretty little thing, daughter of an innkeeper and way above me, but we 'it it off. When she got with child, her pa hustled us to church. Weren't sure I were ready for that…' He gave a grunt of a laugh. 'Then he washed 'is 'ands of 'er. You know the rest.'

'But you did love each other?'

He shrugged, as if love was something alien to him. They would have been happy enough, he told her, if he could have found work, but the only accommodation they could afford was that dreadful place in Seven Dials. Maiden Lane was better, but he resented the fact that it was Dr Redfern who provided that. It was up to him to provide for his family, not some toff.

'I am sorry,' Kate said, feeling the first stirrings of pity for him. 'I am trying to understand how you feel, but surely you must want Joe to have a better life than you had.'

'Course I do. I didn't 'ave a pa, but 'e's got one and I mean to mek sure he keeps 'im.'

'He won't if you are sent to prison again.'

'What for? I ain't done nothin' wrong. I c'n tek my boy for a little 'oliday, if I choose.'

'Yes, but you kidnapped me. That's a different thing altogether.'

'I needed you. See, Joey is 'appy now you're here.'

'But I can't stay, Mr Barber, you must see that. We

have to go back. If you take us back now, today, I will say I came with you of my own accord.' She paused, considering the implications of that, but decided it was too late to worry about her reputation. 'Everyone will be searching for me and the longer you keep me, the worse it will be for you.' She asked herself if she could bear to leave Joey alone with him, even if he let her go, and realised she could not. She might as well say goodbye to the shreds of her reputation; even when she did return, she would be labelled a… No, she could not put a name to it.

'They won't find you. I want you here until Joey settles down.'

She tried arguing with him, but that only made him angry and he said if she didn't shut up, he'd tie her up and gag her. 'And who will look after Joe if you do that?' she asked evenly. If she wanted to escape she would have to swim for it because they were out in the middle of the river and she would not even try because of Joe. She had no idea where they were.

The vessel was a houseboat intended to pull a string of barges. It had a galley with a fire where the cooking was done and two cabins, one of which also did duty as a living room—not, he told her, that the men who worked the barges had time to sit about. Normally when working the rivers and canals a whole string of barges was pulled behind the houseboat by a horse on the towpath, but sometimes when the weather was suitable they used sails.

After another hour or so—she had no idea of the time—they came to a wide expanse of water, where he punted them into the bank, unhitched the horse, tied it to a stake and then set a brown sail. As it filled he pulled the tiller over and they moved out into the middle of a large lake. She could barely see the far bank. It was going to be a long, long day.

She set about tidying the cabin, sorting through the clothes Alf had brought on board for Joe, and finding out what provisions he had, wondering, as she did so, if he might be forced to find civilisation in order to buy food. If they did, she might find a way of making her predicament known to someone.

Simon woke when dawn dispersed the shadows in his drawing room and he was able to make out the shape of the furniture and realised he was still on the sofa. He got up stiffly, raked his fingers through his hair, and went to his room where he rang for Harvey and ordered hot water for a wash and shave, and some toast and coffee for his breakfast. Half an hour later, dressed in a brown frock-coat, beige pantaloons and calf-length boots, he left his lodgings to go to Holles Street, hoping for good news.

But there was none. Kate was still missing and Lady Morland was prostrate with despair and had not left her room since the previous afternoon. Simon and the Reverend spoke for a minute or two about what could be done to further the search, but neither could think of anything.

'We cannot give up,' Simon said, guessing that the older man knew the truth of his feelings for Kate and wondered how many other people had noticed. 'She must be found, please God, alive and well.'

Simon left him to start his search all over again, but he knew they needed a miracle. And then one came.

He had gone home for a bite to eat and a change of clothes when he heard Harvey arguing with someone at the front door. He went out in his shirt sleeves to find out what the commotion was about, discovered Janet Barber on his step with a plump woman dressed in a wide black skirt and a huge shawl. She had heavy boots on her feet and a battered bonnet on her iron-grey hair.

'Let us in,' Janet was saying, trying to push past Harvey who blocked the entrance. 'We must see the doctor.'

'Mrs Barber, you know you should not come here,' Simon said.

'But I know where Alf have took Joe. This here's Mrs Bedson and she come to tell me.'

'I am sorry, Mrs Barber, but I have other things occupying me at the moment. Mrs Meredith has disappeared too.'

'I reckon she's with him,' Mrs Bedson said. 'He told me he were goin' to get someone to look after the boy. I couldn' do a thing with 'im meself. Cried and screamed, he did, flung 'is food all over the place and the crockery with it. Bit me too. I'd do anythin' for Alf, but I weren't 'avin' me home wrecked, so I told 'im to tek the boy somewhere else.'

'And?' Simon, having sent Harvey for his coat, was shrugging himself into it. 'Do you know where he went?'

'I told 'im he could use my boat. 'Tis moored on the Stour.'

'And you think Mrs Meredith is with them?'

'Don't know the lady's name, but he said he knew someone who'd looked after Joey afore and the boy trusted her.'

That was enough for Simon. 'Come on, you can tell me the details on the way. He ran to the mews, followed by the two women. He harnessed the gig, all three squeezed into it and he set off for Holles Street. The Reverend was told the news and Simon asked if he might borrow his carriage and Daniels to drive it, a request that was unhesitatingly complied with. While it was being got ready, the Reverend told Simon that he had not been able to see the Viscount. On the eve of his wedding he seemed to have disappeared too. Simon was too absorbed with worrying about Kate to bother his head with that.

Kate knew she was drowning; the water was full of weeds that tangled themselves about her legs and her clothes were dragging her down. Something wet and slimy brushed across her face. She struggled to swim, but the current was swift and she could make no headway, especially as she was holding Joe in one arm, trying to keep his head above water. She could hear voices—the voices of her father and Simon. They were calling to her. 'Kate, where are you?' she heard Simon shouting. She tried to answer, but no sound came from her throat. She was being pulled down and down; just as she could stay afloat no longer, she woke.

The nightmare had been so real, it was a moment or two before she realised she was lying on the bunk in the cabin with Joe lying across her, his head in her neck, so that she could hardly breathe and the blanket was tangled about her legs. She gently moved him, kicked off the blanket and sat up. The boat was rocking in a strengthening breeze. It was daylight, but the sky was overcast. Were they in for some rough weather? Would it make any difference to what Alf did?

She rubbed the back of her neck and stretched her cramped limbs, trying not to wake the still-sleeping Joe. Today, she realised, would have been her wedding day. Robert had not answered her letter and she wondered what he would do. It was out of her hands now and suddenly she felt almost light-headed. But she did wonder what was happening at home. Was there any chance she would be found or must she do something to free herself. But how? The nightmare had brought home to her that trying to swim with Joe would result in them both drowning.

They had spent the whole of the previous day rocking at anchor in the middle of the lake. She had concentrated on Joe, soothing him, trying to make him eat and talk because Alf had said he would let her go when Joe was happy to stay with him. Not that she would leave the boy. Her plan was to persuade Alf that he should go back to his wife, but he was adamant and became angry when she persisted. Afraid of his violence, she had decided the direct approach would not do.

They had talked on and off all the previous day and she had learned more of his dreadful childhood and how the only person who had any time for him at all was a woman called Martha Bedson who had worked as a cleaner at the charity school. 'She used to talk to me,' he said. 'Brought me little treats and took me out for the day sometimes, more mother to me than me own ma ever was. If'n I were in trouble, she'd always help. But she couldn't do a thing with Joe. He screamed and beat 'er when she tried to pick him up and he threw 'is food at her and broke her plates. We couldn't stay there. This 'ere's 'er boat. Her husband were a waterman afore he died and she kept it. She used to tek me out on it when I was a little 'un. I always enjoyed that. I thought Joe would too.'

'Perhaps he would under other circumstances. You have frightened him. Take us back, Mr Barber. We can't stay out here forever. We will run out of food and water.'

He was silent for a long time, then he put up the sail and weighed anchor. She held her breath and the boat slowly turned and they fairly skimmed over the water towards the bank. There were many more craft on the river than there had been the day before and Alf, no waterman, found it difficult to steer between them. He was trying to make for a waterside inn that Kate had not noticed when they arrived in the dark two nights before. It was obviously a place where boat people bought their provisions and filled their water containers. Kate began to hope.

A sudden scream from Joe and a whooshing sound made her turn and dash down the companionway. Flames were shooting out of the galley and into the cabin. Kate's first thought was for Joe. She dashed into the flames and hauled him out of the galley. His hair was singed and his shirt smouldering. She rolled him in the blanket and put out the flames and then ran up on deck with the boy in her arms.

'The galley's on fire,' she gasped when Alf turned to her.

He let go the tiller and dashed down to look, but was soon back, his face a picture of horror and disbelief. 'It's an inferno down there. There's burning wood all over the floor and it's set the deck alight. Can you swim?'

Kate's dream came back to her in all its horror as she nodded an affirmative.

'Then over the side with you. I'll hand the boy down to you. Make for the inn.' She turned to look. They were already sailing dangerously close to the other boats anchored at the staithe.

This was no time for false modesty. She flung off her gown, kicked off her shoes and slipped over the side, hanging on to a rope with one hand while he bent over to put Joe into her arms. Then she took a deep breath and struck out. This was no dream—it was reality. She turned over on her back to hold Joe on her front. She saw the boat move away from her and thought it was simply because she was swimming away from it, but then she saw Alf at the tiller, surrounded by flames, taking the boat back out into open water, away from the other craft and the people on their decks who were watching in helpless horror. 'Leave it!' she shouted. 'Jump, Alf, jump!'

He appeared not to hear her and then, with a sudden whoosh, the whole boat was engulfed in flames and sank in less than a minute. All that was left was floating debris. Kate choked back her sobs and started to swim.

It was further than she thought and, though she had dispensed with her gown, her petticoat was weighing her down. Her nightmare was very real as she struggled against a current with weeds in a green curtain swirling about her, slapping over her face and making Joe cough.

'Hold on, Kate. Hold on, sweetheart.' It could not be Simon's voice; it was all part of the nightmare.

The next minute someone took Joe from her. 'I've got the boy. You take the young lady.' Surely that was Daniels's voice?

Someone put his arms under her shoulders and kicked out. 'You are safe now, my lovely brave Kate. I've got you.' It really was Simon. 'Kick, sweetheart,' he murmured in her ear. 'Help us along. We will soon have you warm and dry.'

A few minutes later, they reached the staithe and he rose out of the water with her in his arms, carried her up the steps and into the inn to the accompaniment of the cheers and applause of the watchers.

The landlady ran out of the inn with a blanket which she wrapped round Kate. Simon smiled as he thanked her. Kate's flimsy petticoat and chemise were sticking to her skin, outlining every inch of her lovely curves. 'A room, please,' he said. 'Hot water, a bath, a warm drink.'

'At once, sir.'

'Joe…' Kate began. She felt she could have walked, but it was so comforting to be in Simon's arms and she clung to him, her arms about his neck.

'He is with his mother. Don't worry about him any more.'

'Alf… He died saving the other boats.'

'I know.' He was carrying her upstairs behind the landlady as he spoke and now she threw open a door and he took Kate inside and gently put her on the bed. 'Go and get the hot water,' he instructed the woman who hesitated in the doorway. 'And do not worry about leaving her with me. The lady is about to become my wife.'

'Simon!' Kate protested as soon as she had left.

'It is true. You are going to marry me, aren't you?'

'But…'

He wrapped his arms about her and silenced her with a kiss, rousing a passion in her she never knew she could experience. It filled her to the exclusion of everything else. She forgot the dreadful ordeal she had just been through, forgot that there were still unsolved problems keeping them apart and let herself go. 'Oh, Simon.'

'Are there any more buts?' he queried with a quirky smile.

Her answering smile was a little wobbly. 'No, but we are going to have to live down a prodigious amount of scandalous gossip.'

'I am used to it,' he said with a wry smile, kissing the tip of her nose and then her forehead and each cheek. 'And as for you, you will be the idol of the *ton* for saving little Joe.'

'How did you find me?' She was shivering, though whether from her immersion or her emotions, she was not sure.

'It is a long story and all down to a lady called Mrs Bedson. I will tell you all about it later.' He got off the bed as the landlady returned, followed by two men with a bath and two maids with jugs of hot water. 'They found the boy's pa,' she said, as the men put the bath down and left. 'He's badly burned, but 'e's alive. They've sent for a doctor. His wife's with him. And the little boy.'

'Thank God for that,' Kate murmured.

'You'd best go and get dry yourself,' the landlady said, giving Simon a disapproving look. 'I'll see to the young lady.'

Kate watched him go. Simon was with her and he would not let her go again. How he had found her she did not know, but it was a miracle and must surely mean that God was on their side. She allowed the maids to help her bath and dress in a rough skirt and blouse belonging to the landlady. It was much too big, but she pulled it in with a belt and went downstairs to the parlour, where she was enthusiastically applauded by all the boat people who had crowded into the room. Simon, dressed in the innkeeper's clothes, came forwards to take her hand. 'You look very fetching in that, my love.' He could not stop grinning. 'Are you hungry?'

'A little, but I want to see Mr and Mrs Barber and little Joe.'

He understood. Children would always come before her own comfort. 'Come, I will take you.'

Alf was lying in bed in another room. His hands and face were swathed in bandages and he was barely conscious. Janet was on one side of the bed, nursing Joe, one of whose hands was also bandaged. On the other side was a plump woman who was introduced to Kate as Mrs Bedson. 'Mr Barber spoke very lovingly of you,' Kate said. 'How is he?'

'He'll be better bye and bye,' Janet said, reaching out to touch his arm. 'He were a brave man to risk his life to save everyone else. I thank God he was thrown into the water. It saved his life.'

'And Joe?'

'He is fine and for that I thank you.'

'And do you think you could all be happy together now?'

'Yes, oh, yes, thanks to you and Dr Redfern.'

They did not want her gratitude and quickly took their leave. 'I want to go home,' Kate said as they went downstairs.

'Of course. But have a bite to eat first and then we will be on our way. Your father's carriage is in the inn yard.'

'What about the others?'

'They will stay until Alf is well enough to be moved. I have left them enough money to tide them over. We do not need to worry about them any more.'

'I am glad, but we should not forget they brought us together.'

'I am not likely to forget and for that reason I shall try to find work for Alf that will keep him out of mischief. Now let us eat, I am as hungry as a hunter.'

An hour later they were in the Morland carriage, being driven at a sedate pace back to London by

Daniels, who had also been fêted as a hero. Kate was sitting snugly against Simon, her head on his shoulder and his arm about her. If it were not for her concern for her father and grandmother, she would have liked the journey to last forever.

'Simon,' she murmured, as he kissed her for the hundredth time, 'tell me what happened after I disappeared.'

So he told her about the search and the unexpected arrival of Mrs Bedson. 'She was incensed by Alf's tale of his treatment at the hands of his wife and as soon as he left her house, she hurried to Mrs Barber, intending to tell her exactly what she thought of her, but when she realised what was really going on, she decided she had to do something to reunite them, so they came to me. I borrowed the coach and away we came. It was late when we started and dark as pitch when we arrived at the place the boat was usually moored and it had gone.' He stopped speaking to kiss her. 'We had to wait for daylight to go looking for it. We were standing at the staithe debating whether to hire a boat to come looking for you, when we saw you coming back. And on fire at that. You can imagine how I felt. I dived in and Daniels with me.'

'Thank God for it,' she said fervently.

'How did the fire start?'

'It was my fault. I left Joe on the bunk in the day cabin while I went up to try to persuade Mr Barber to take us home. I think he wandered into the galley and poked the fire. When I rushed down to him, there was burning wood on the floor and it had set the deck alight. We could all have gone up in flames.' She shuddered at the memory.

He stroked her wet hair from her face. 'All's well that ends well.'

'But it hasn't ended, has it? We shall have to live through a deal of gossip.'

'Shall you mind?'

'Not for myself.' She tilted up her head to be kissed again and it was some time before the conversation was resumed. 'I am worried Viscount Cranford will sue you for enticing me away from him. He said he would.'

He was thoughtful. Now he understood why Kate was so determined to go through with the wedding. 'Why did you not tell me?'

'You had enough problems without me adding to them, what with Mr Barber's accusations and the inquiry…'

Now he understood what the business of Janet Barber was all about. If Barber sued, then Cranford would be saved the humiliation of doing so himself. 'I think, my love, Viscount Cranford is too proud to admit anything like that could happen.'

'But why was Captain Feltwell so obnoxious?'

'Besides being the Viscount's friend, he is Mrs Withersfield's cousin by marriage. She was living in luxury at Cranford Manor, acting the lady of the manor, pretending it was all hers, and your arrival did not please her. You stood between her and the comfortable life she had been enjoying at the Viscount's expense. She saw herself being sent to live in a cottage with a tiny pension and no power at all, and the prospect did not please her, or Feltwell, who had been sponging off her ever since he left the army. By spreading gossip about you and me, they hoped the Viscount would change his mind about marrying you. Unfortunately that did not work. Cranford could not afford any scandal to touch either him or the lady he planned to marry. He was not interested in his sister's motives, only his own reputation. That little fracas with Barber gave him the opportunity he was waiting for. Feltwell had to do as he asked and get Barber's co-operation and that was not difficult with a little bribe.'

'So everyone was using everyone else for their own ends?'

'It looks like it.'

'How can people be so wicked?'

'I do not know, but they could not have done it if I had not been so foolish as to visit Mrs Barber. I had no idea what was in her mind. Thank God, I was able to convince her while we were travelling that her future lay with her husband. Mine is with you.'

They jogged along, stopping to change the horses and to eat at wayside inns and Kate slept a little with her head on his shoulder, secure and content.

'What about the Hartingdon Home?' she asked, as they neared the metropolis. 'Will it continue?'

'I imagine so, though whether I will be allowed to be part of it is another matter.'

'Of course you will. Mr and Mrs Barber will retract their accusations and you will be exonerated. And even if you do not go back to the Hartingdon, there are other children, all over the country, all over the world, who need you.'

He laughed. 'Oh, darling, I am beginning to understand how Cranford felt, having to play second fiddle to a mob of children.'

'You think I should forget them?'

'Certainly not. It is what I love about you. Your tender heart. We will do something for the children, I promise you, but I sincerely hope we shall have children of our own in the not-too-distant future.'

'Oh, so do I. It is my dearest wish.' She stopped herself suddenly, realising where that wish had taken her before and added, 'Only second to my wish to be married to you, of course.'

'Mine, too.' He laughed and gave her a last kiss as they turned into Holles Street and drew up at her door, which flew open almost before the wheels had stopped turning and Lady Morland ran out, arms outstretched.

Kate jumped out and ran into them and was hugged so tightly the breath was almost squeezed from her body. 'Oh, Kate, thank God you are safe.' She stood back and looked at her granddaughter. 'How did you come to be dressed like that?'

Kate laughed and reached behind her for Simon's hand as Daniels took the coach away. 'It is a long story, Grandmama.'

'Come indoors, you can tell it to me while you have some refreshment. You, too, Doctor.'

Her father was waiting for her. He looked suddenly old and drawn and Kate felt a pang that she had been instrumental in worrying him. But he beamed with joy at seeing her and hugged her tightly. 'Thank God, you are safe,' he said, repeating his mother's words.

While food and drink were fetched, Kate, sitting beside Simon on a sofa with her hand in his, explained what had happened to her and Simon gave his side of the story, which so astonished them, they were full of questions and the tale had to be repeated over and over again.

At last Kate was able to ask her own questions. 'Did you cancel the wedding?'

'I did,' her grandmother said. 'But some of the guests arrived. They would not go home when I told them what had happened, but must wait for you to be brought back. And as the food was prepared...' She shrugged. 'It seemed a pity to waste it.'

Simon laughed. 'It is the first time I have heard of having a wedding breakfast without a wedding.'

'The Viscount?' Kate queried.

'Oh, he did not come. But you will never guess what has happened. Lady Redfern came to tell us. He has gone off with Lady Isobel.'

Simon burst into laughter. 'Oh, that is rich. A Viscount is a far better prospect than the heir to a baron. I wish them well.'

'Kate, I am persuaded you are not heartbroken,' her father said.

'Not at all. She will make a much better diplomat's wife that I ever would and I have found my match.' And she turned and smiled up at Simon.

At last they were satisfied and Kate was ushered off to change her clothes, which operation was achieved in record time and then, dressed in the blue evening gown she had worn to the Hartingdon charity ball, she went downstairs again where Simon had returned after dashing home to change into evening wear himself. Then all four went to Morland House, where the story of Kate's bravery and Simon's rescue had preceded them. It was here they realised the gossip would not be anything like as bad as they had feared. Far from castigating them for what had happened, they applauded them and the fact that the Viscount had so quickly found someone else proved Kate had been right to turn him down.

The tale of little Joe was told over and over again, but once everyone's curiosity had been satisfied and they had been invited to another wedding, everyone went home. After a little conversation with Lizzie and James, the Morland coach was called up and Kate, Simon, the Reverend and Lady Morland went back to Holles Street.

As soon as they arrived, the Reverend suddenly discovered he had work to do in his study, which he had not been able to set his mind to in the last two days, and Lady Morland pronounced herself fagged to death and took herself off to bed. Kate and Simon were alone at last. They sat together on the sofa, his arm about her shoulders and her head nestling in the curve of his neck, and made plans for a wedding.

'Let it be soon,' he said, kissing the top of her head. 'No fuss, just a quiet ceremony to make you my wife.'

'That is exactly what I was thinking.' She turned her head up to look at him. Her eyes were shining and her lips were temptingly parted. He bent his head to kiss them, setting up such a delicious quake all through her it was some time before she could add, 'With Annie as my attendant.'

'Of course. We must not forget Annie, must we?'

'Guess what she said to me on the night of the Embassy ball?'

'I am sure you are about to tell me.'

'She said she did not like the Viscount and that I ought to marry you.'

'How perceptive of her! In that case we must certainly invite her to our wedding.'

'I can't wait.'

'Neither can I,' he said, kissing her again and again, each time more passionately. 'And if I do not take myself off home this minute, I shall disgrace myself.'

He stood up and pulled her to her feet. 'Goodnight, my darling girl, sleep well, and before you know it, it will be morning and I shall be on your doorstep again.'

The wedding took place three weeks later and this time Kate had no doubts, no doubts at all. She was going to spend the rest of her life with the man she adored. Simon had been cleared of all wrongdoing and reinstated at the Hartingdon Home, which had benefited from all the publicity over their adventures, which, according to the newspaper reports, now favourable, came from their dedication to the cause of the deprived children. After a short holiday in the West Country, they returned to live in the villa Simon had leased for them, where Alf and Janet, now part of their domestic staff, waited to welcome them home.

* * *

A year later, they and their newborn son, were guests of honour at the opening of the new Hartingdon Home, built away from the slums in the clean air of Paddington. It was light and spacious and able to accommodate two hundred children in small family units. Simon looked down at Kate, who was nursing little Thomas, surrounded by the children from the home, and his heart swelled with love and pride. He bent and whispered in her ear. 'I love you, Mrs Redfern.'

She looked up at him and smiled, her answer in her bright eyes.

MILLS & BOON
Historical

On sale 6th November 2009

Regency

DEVILISH LORD, MYSTERIOUS MISS
by Annie Burrows

Lord Matthison has the reputation of the devil, but secretly still yearns for the true love he lost seven years ago. When he encounters a fragile-looking woman, the image of his betrothed, Matthison is convinced Cora Montague still lives – and he's determined to claim her…

Regency

TO KISS A COUNT
by Amanda McCabe

Leaving her feelings for Count di Fabrizzi behind her in Sicily, Thalia Chase returns to England – where she's shocked to encounter him with a suspected thief! The Count's dangerous mission doesn't leave room for beautiful Thalia. But what is a gentleman to do when a lady is so insistent on adventure, and so *very* passionate…?

2 FREE BOOKS
AND A SURPRISE GIFT

We would like to take this opportunity to thank you for reading this Mills & Boon® book by offering you the chance to take TWO more specially selected books from the Historical series absolutely FREE! We're also making this offer to introduce you to the benefits of the Mills & Boon® Book Club™—

- **FREE home delivery**
- **FREE gifts and competitions**
- **FREE monthly Newsletter**
- **Exclusive Mills & Boon Book Club offers**
- **Books available before they're in the shops**

Accepting these FREE books and gift places you under no obligation to buy, you may cancel at any time, even after receiving your free books. Simply complete your details below and return the entire page to the address below. You don't even need a stamp!

YES Please send me 2 free Historical books and a surprise gift. I understand that unless you hear from me, I will receive 4 superb new books every month for just £3.79 each, postage and packing free. I am under no obligation to purchase any books and may cancel my subscription at any time. The free books and gift will be mine to keep in any case.

Ms/Mrs/Miss/Mr_____ Initials _____

_____

Surname _____

Address _____

_____

_____ Postcode _____

Send this whole page to: Mills & Boon Book Club, Free Book Offer, FREEPOST NAT 10298, Richmond, TW9 1BR